ADMISSIONS

Jennifer Sowle

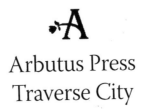

Arbutus Press
Traverse City

This book is a work of fiction. Names, characters, businesses, organizations, places, events, and incidents either are the product of the author's imagination or used fictitiously. Any resemblance to actual persons, living or dead, or actual events is entirely coincidental.

All rights reserved. Published in the United States by Arbutus Press, Traverse City, Michigan. www.arbutuspress.com

ISBN 978-1-933926-24-7

Library of Congress Cataloging-in-Publication Data

Sowle, Jennifer J.
Admissions / Jennifer J. Sowle. -- 1st ed.
    p. cm.
ISBN 978-1-933926-24-7 (alk. paper)
1. Psychiatric hospital patients--Fiction. 2. Depression--Fiction. 3. Loss (Psychology)--Fiction. 4. Psychiatric hospitals--Fiction. 5. Mentally ill--Rehabilitation--Fiction. 6. Michigan--Fiction. 7. Psychological fiction. I. Title.
PS3619.O98A67 2010
813'.6--dc22
                                        2010018026

Printed in the United States of America

GRATEFUL APPRECIATION GOES TO

My supportive family who are all fabulous story-tellers in their own right.

Doreen, especially, who accepted endless hours of my nose against the computer screen with grace and encouragement.

My writing group. Especially Trudy Carpenter and Marilyn Zimmerman who endured the earliest drafts of this novel and helped mold it into a novel. David Marshall and KC Thompson who came late, but left their mark. And, of course, our mentor Steve Lewis, who guided the process with candor and good humor.

Finally, to Susan Bays, editor and Gail Schneider of Arbutus Press.

for my two sons

Trevor Michael
Damon Harold

Chapter 1

Traverse State Hospital is stark, the glossy linoleum tiles yellow from years of waxing. I expect Jeff to follow the attendant to the tiny room, but I'm alone. Did he ask to come with me and they turned him down? I close my eyes as I wait for the doctor. My chest compresses like an accordion; reminds me of the time I was twelve and tried water skiing—the time I almost drowned in Coldwater Lake. My brother-in-law took off his shirt and stood on the diving platform when I surfaced, no doubt contemplating if I was worth a rescue. Ready to explode, I gulped air like a perch flapping in the bottom of a boat. I want that relief now, but no matter how many deep breaths I take, my lungs feel flattened. My mind a beehive, thoughts buzz, circle, but never come in for a landing.

I try to take hold, pluck a string of reason and unravel the tangle inside my head. Monitors blipping and bleeping in my ear. Jeff crying into the edge of the mattress. Mom helping me to the window, the frosty city tiny and far away, as if I were looking through the wrong end of binoculars. What happened? The medication pulls down a curtain. The questions terrify me. Over and over, I ask Jeff what happened.

My breathing becomes so shallow, I think I might suffocate right here in this plastic chair. Another hospital. My face twitches. Visions of Alexander riding his red tricycle back and forth in front of the house, the back wheels tipping up over the broken sidewalk. Alexander waves, smiles at us. Our hands fly up as if connected by an invisible string. I wiggle my fingers, Jeff waves his hand. Alexander cranks his tiny legs on the pedals, his head turns toward us until Jeff says, "Howdy little buddy" at each passing.

Something familiar clicks inside my head. Stepping into a mental file room, I scan rows of cabinets reaching out to forever. I inch slowly down the aisle; my mind's eye scans the silver label windows on the drawers.

Then I see it. A file drawer labeled *Alexander*.

I finger the folder in my hand that says *Alexander riding his bike*. I open the drawer and slide it in among the others, watch the drawer roll shut, ending in a crisp snap.

My breathing begins to slow. Turning back, I balance on a tightrope. I feel my jaw loosen, my throat opens. In my mind, I see a door marked *Exit*, the maze of file cabinets falls behind me with each careful step. The door swings open at my approach, closes as I pass through. I feel calm, open my eyes.

"Mrs. Kilpi? I'm Dr. Nielsen." A round man in a white medical jacket extends his pudgy hand. He slides out a chair and sits down. As he crosses his legs, his pants strain across his thighs, pull at the inseams. A tiny foot in a black oxford dangles from the end of his brown knit pant leg.

"Where's my husband?"

"Filling out forms. You won't have visitors for a while," he says.

"I want to talk to him, say goodbye."

"I have some questions." He moves quickly through the forms as I fill in my history and symptoms—like reading a script. He closes the file, leans back, and taps his pen on the desk. "Now, why are you here?"

I feel as if I should make something up to make the doctor happy. I smile at him, get no response. "I don't really remember what happened."

"Oh?" He pauses, looks directly into my eyes. "You are admitting yourself to the hospital voluntarily?"

I really don't know why I'm here, I can't remember back to I'm not sure when. "Yes, I'm here voluntarily."

He points to the form and hands me a pen. "Please sign here. And here." He stands up and shakes his leg to release his pant leg. "The attendant will be right in." As the door clicks shut, I feel like I just signed a confession to a horrible crime. All I have to do now is wait for execution.

The door opens. "I'll be showing you to your room. Will you come with me, please?"

I blink. "Daddy?" His clear blue eyes crinkle at the corners; his white hair is carefully swept back from his ruddy forehead.

I clear my throat, find my voice. "I need to say goodbye to Jeff. Dad, do you know where Jeff is?"

He smiles, his eyes connect with mine as if we share a secret. "I'm assigned to get you settled in, ma'am. You can ask the nurse in *Receiving* about that. I know there's no visitation on Mondays."

"This is Monday?" I press the heels of my hands against my forehead, try to squeeze out a memory.

"My name is Carl. I'll help you get checked in."

My mind feels numb, broken … "No, you're not. At least, I don't think…"

"Okay. Right this way, ma'am."

He reaches down for me, holds me by the arm as he leads me from the room. He smells familiar. Old Spice after shave and the faint scent of cherry blend pipe tobacco. He holds my arm firmly as he guides me down the hallway, stops at a door. *Exit. Receiving. Staff Only.* I lean into his shoulder. "Thanks for being here." My hip jangles a large key ring hung from a fob attached to his belt loop. Wide as his hand, it holds a bunch of dark metal skeleton keys, some regulars, and two metal discs. He wears his work uniform. But the key chain is new. He hadn't worn a key chain. It swings and jingles when he walks.

The skeleton key turns in the lock as he leans his weight against the thick metal door to the outside. A white van idles in the driveway. He helps me into the rear, slides in beside the driver, then glances back through the iron mesh. "It's just a short ride, Mrs. Kilpi." He sounds so formal.

"Are you mad at me?"

He turns. "What's that?" His voice sounds strange. "Mrs. Kilpi? Okay back there?"

I stare at the back of his head. He stares straight ahead as the van turns onto *Red Drive*. The street signs are painted the color of the name, goofy looking, like they belong in a cartoon. We drive down *Gray Drive*. Maybe if I squint I can bring something into focus. Trees soar high, naked branches like horny fingers. The dim silhouette of the State Hospital, towers and spires looming high above the trees.

"Oh my god." I know my lips move, but I can barely hear my voice. It sounds like my words are coming from somebody else. Somebody far away.

We pull up in front of a small courtyard surrounded by an ornate fence. He opens the van door. Gingerbread trim,small peaked attic windows, wooden balusters and railings, like the large summer homes on Grand Traverse Bay. Quaint visions of women sitting pleasantly on porches enjoying a summer afternoon are marred by the thick yellow iron mesh wrapped around each porch, looking like giant two-story cages hung on the back of the building. Saliva dries to a sticky paste inside my mouth.

"Right this way, ma'am." The attendant touches my hand. As I turn toward him, I feel the panic rise in my chest, my vision collapses in, like the lens of a camera. At the end of a dark tunnel, I see him pull up his key ring, struggle with the padlock on the gate. The key hits home, the lock swings free.

He tugs gently on my arm as he unlocks the front door. It opens into a large foyer, polished wooden floors, potted ferns. A nurse, starched hat perched on her sprayed hair, sits behind a desk, *Mrs. Cassidy, RN.*

I sit next to him to wait. My thoughts skip across my mind like a stone over water.

"Mrs. Kilpi?" The nurse doesn't wait for an answer. "Come with me." The attendant hands her my file.

```
Patient Name: Luanne S. Kilpi DOB:
1/19/1944  Age: 24
Date of Admission: 11/18/1968
Diagnosis: Depression with psychotic
features.
Date: 11/18/68
Notes: Attempted suicide on 11/16.
Psychogenic Amnesia. Pt. on Valium
20m qid. Rule out acute grief
reaction. Rule out Schizophrenia.
Rule out Psychosis: unclassified.
Rule out Depersonalization
Disorder. Evaluate for medication.
```

Chapter 2

THE OBSERVER   *November 18, 1968*

Page 12
Admissions:
Angeline Dowd, Alpena, Michigan
Randal Kilbourn, Clare, Michigan
Luanne Kilpi, Saginaw, Michigan
Marilyn Street, St. Johns, Michigan
Blanche Foley, Ludington, Michigan
Bernard Peltier, Reese, Michigan

I'm Mrs. Cassidy. I'll be getting you settled in. Please follow me." She turns the lock. I follow her down a long hallway of red and cream linoleum squares. "All of our admissions go to the infirmary for a day or two. We like to make sure you're healthy."

"I'd like to see my husband."

"He's gone home. You can see him when you're ready for visitors." She takes me to a small room, pulls a sheet from a cabinet, and spreads it out on the floor. "Remove your clothes and put them right here on this sheet."

"I have to take my clothes off?"

"We need to label them."

"Is there a robe?"

"No. That isn't necessary. It's a short walk to the showers."

I take off my desert boots, set them aside; pull my sweater over my head, toss it onto the sheet. I unzip my jeans. They drop straight to the floor. Standing in my underwear, I look at the nurse.

"Everything off," she says.

A shade pulls down inside my mind. I see myself toss my bra, panties, socks on the heap. The nurse grabs the corners of the sheet, ties it, and makes a hobo bag around my clothes. She pins a piece of paper to the knot— *Luanne Kilpi 11-18-1968.*

"Follow me."

"Like this?"

"This is a hospital. We see naked women all the time."

I step out into the cold hallway, glance around and bring my arm across my chest to cover my breasts, tuck my right hand under my armpit. I spread my left hand over my pubic hair. An attendant approaches.

"Hello, Bruce." The nurse nods.

"Afternoon."

I look up and see him run his eyes over my body. I follow the nurse into a large bathroom with a dozen or so sinks along one wall, no mirrors. Toilets, like porcelain toadstools, sit out in the room in rows. Two have wooden partitions between them, but no doors. She steers me through a doorway marked *Showers*, a firm hand on my back.

"Soap's in there."

The dark yellow cake lying on the shower floor has jelled. Along the way, it picked up hairs of all shades and textures. I stoop to retrieve the bar and pick at it. But the hair is melted into the cake and won't budge.

I look down at my hands. I feel them gliding over fake brocade. I imagine snipping them off at the wrists, stacking them on the soap dish, blood streaking down the wall, swirling into the drain. I tip my head back, close my eyes, open my mouth. Turkeys drown this way.

"Hurry up. You have to get situated before second shift." The nurse's voice echoes off the tile walls.

The tepid shower smells of iron. The water pressure is waning. My hands drag on my arms—heavy, too heavy. I step out of the shower and blink to clear my vision. A weak attempt to rinse my hair leaves it in a spongy wad plastered on top of my head. I face a stranger—the new nurse wears a white uniform, a blue starched cap, and a name badge: *Miss Lobsinger, LPN, Nurse Attendant*.

"About time. What do you think this is, the Ritz Carlton? Come on. I got better things to do." She gives me a shapeless denim smock that hangs almost to the floor, my brown desert boots, no socks.

"Where are my clothes?" I need my clothes...to feel human.

"Don't worry about it. You'll get them when they're ready. Come on."

At the end of the hall, the sign says *Infirmary. No Admission Without Written Orders.* The nurse unlocks the door, steps back. My hands fly to my face, cover my nose and mouth. But it's too late to keep the sickening smell from coating my throat.

"Keep moving." The nurse pokes my back, nudges me to an empty bed among a sea of white metal hospital beds. Moans and snores from dozens of sleeping patients, a loud shout, "Let me out of here!" from a bed by the nurses' station.

"What's wrong with her?" I ask.

"We have to restrain her, she's violent." The nurse takes my elbow, half pushes, half swings me toward the bed. I soften my fall by catching the edge with my hand. The nurse turns up my palm, drops two pills into it, a small round orange one and one that looks like a green bubble.

I try to sit up, so I won't choke. The pills stick to my tongue until I take the one gulp of water from a tiny fluted paper cup. I crane my neck like a baby bird, swallow several times ...my eyes water with panic. Finally, the pills squeeze down my throat and break free into my stomach.

Nurse Lobsinger takes a small package from the cabinet and pulls a stand forward. "Everybody gets an enema. That's the rule. After, if you need to go, there's the bedpan. You're not allowed out of bed, period."

I close my eyes as the nurse fills the bag. The pills explode in my brain, swirling, pulling me down, pushing me into sleep.

Chapter 3

No pills this morning, toots…your lucky day…Hall 5…meet your buddies…take a drink." The voice pulls me from a drugged stupor. The nurse tunnels her arm under my back, holds a small cup of water in front of me. My tongue is stuck to the roof of my mouth. The skin on my lips cracks, I try to talk.

"Luanne, drink this water." It feels like my throat is stuck shut all the way down to my chest. She touches my lips with a wet cloth, and they come unglued. I take a small sip. I feel like a newborn, my head rolling to the side, flopping back on the stiff pillow. I hear the nurse's footsteps grow faint.

"Wake up, Luanne. Let's get going." The nurse is back. She tugs at my sheet. "Augh, you stink." She pulls me upright by my wrists, my bones rub together and it hurts. My legs are like rubber, they slip sideways, dangle over the edge of the bed. My knees buckle as my toes hit the cold linoleum.

The nurse cinches me roughly around the waist. "Walk now. I'm not going to carry you. Walk!"

I try to tighten my body into an upright position as she drags me out the infirmary door and down to the bathroom. Several women sit on toilets. Two aides stand in front of them, talking.

"Betty, help over here," Nurse Lobsinger shouts.

"I'm busy."

"Betty, you lazy bitch. I swear to god. Get over here and take her arm." Grabbing my elbows, they pull me through the doorway into the shower room. Nurse Lobsinger reaches into the stall, turns the handles. The shower nozzle sputters to life, a fat spurt of water becomes an intermittent spray.

"Hold her up. I gotta get this stinken' nightgown off." Betty does as she is told, holding me around the waist as Nurse Lobsinger raises the gown over my head.

"I'm not gettin' wet holdin' on to her," Betty says.

"Nope. She's on her own." Nurse Lobsinger grabs my shoulders. "Take her arm. Steer her in under the spray."

They walk me a few steps. As soon as I enter the shower stall, they let go. I stagger, reach for the wall, but my hand slips. I fall back against the hot and cold handles. My heels skid through the soap scum. My arms are too weak to break the fall and my tailbone thumps against the tile floor. Pain runs up my back as the cool water splats onto my head.

"While you're down there, scrub between your legs," Betty says.

"Yeah. Try to get the dried shit off your ass," Nurse Lobsinger laughs.

Their voices sound muffled. My hand moves in slow motion, chasing the gooey soap, trapping it in the corner, lifting it onto my thigh, making circles across my leg. I feel the corners of my lips pull, then crack, as my mouth flies open. It starts with a barely perceptible thin cry, like the distant call of a soaring bird, grows in depth and volume as it fills my chest, rumbles up through my throat until my anguish erupts in heaving sobs.

My hands take over, running the soap up and down my legs and arms, gliding it over my breasts, across my stomach. And I *do* scrub between my legs, all the way back to my throbbing tailbone. The cool water, the pain in my spine, coax me back.

I can hear the two women chatting outside the shower stall. Then Nurse Lobsinger reaches in and shuts off the water, pulls me up and out. Betty brings out a hospital gown. I raise my arms to receive it. They set my brown boots in front of me, hold me upright as I slide my sticky feet into them. As frail as I am, I can wobble along with the nurse holding my elbow.

As the medication wears off, the terror creeps back. Each step I take feels dangerous. Like descending into the cave of a sleeping giant.

The giant could wake.

I feel the blood rush through my heart, feel it quiver in my chest. "Mommy." I look around—the voice is mine. I clasp my hands in front of me to keep them from flying off.

The nurse unlocks the door to Hall 5. The hallway is wide enough for chairs on both sides. There sit the women, rocking, no distractions, no clutter. As I pass, I notice a small strip of tape stuck between the shoulder blades of each woman, her name written in black ink. "Margaret, sit down," the attendant says. "Sit quietly now."

More women pop up, then sit back down on command like targets on a shooting range.

Dim white lamps, like giant mushrooms, hang on long chains from the high ceiling. The creaking and thumping of the steam radiators under the windows, low murmurings of patients create the backbeat for my welcome. I hug myself against the cold. I hug myself to keep from breaking apart, spraying across the walls.

The nurse fingers her keys, picks one, and turns it in the keyhole of Room 12. She pushes me across the threshold of a tall thick door. I lean against it to keep from falling, my hand resting on the deadbolt. I look around the room, my eyes stick on the large window covered by a heavy metal screen.

In the tiny room, two scarred iron beds are stripped down to stained mattresses, the once white stripes of their ticking yellow. No box springs—the two-inch thick mattresses sit directly on iron mesh anchored to the beds with large bolts. Sheets and pillowcase, a gray rubber pad, and a thin black blanket lie folded at the foot of one of the narrow beds. A white metal nightstand is bolted to the floor, a dented granite bedpan sits on its lower shelf. That's all.

"Lie down and relax." The nurse hands me a green bubble pill.

"What?"

"Just relax." She watches me swallow the pill and hustles to the door, crepe soles squeaking against the tile. The heavy door bangs shut, the click of the lock. The clank of the deadbolt echoes, footfalls fade down the hall.

I quickly pull a case over the flat pillow, peel open the stiff sheets and spread them on the bed. I'm not sure how much time I have before the pill kicks in, so I leave my boots on. I lie on my side, bring the thin blanket up around my shoulders. No explosion in my head this time, just the shade coming down. Muffled screams fade to black.

Chapter 4

THE OBSERVER   *November 25, 1968*

Page 4
Notice: Patients are strictly forbidden to borrow
money, cigarettes, gum, playing cards, games,
stamps, magazines, and other personal items from
other patients. Fights have broken out because of
misunderstandings in this regard. Do not approach
fellow patients for favors.

L adies, ladies."
   I stretch out of a dreamless sleep to start another day.
   The Nurse Supervisor on the disturbed ward of Building 50 chants as she sways the hand bell up and down the hall. "Breakfast, ladies." The bell rings at six a.m. Keys begin to turn in locks.
   I strain to clear my head. A dream? Waking from medicated sleep is like emerging from a dark cave, the blackness gives way to a gray haze. Where am I? I squint, my eyelids flutter against the harshness of the overhead light, like gazing into the sun. Click! The realization races through my body like an electrical current, shocking me awake. I drum my fingers on my chest. One, two, three, four...this is my seventh day, five days in the infirmary, two days on the hall.
   Every day starts the same: The attendant rings patients awake, prods us out into the hallway in our coarse white nightgowns, herds us down to the women's dining hall. I hear the attendant say, *twenty-three*, feel the tap, as I pass through the double doors of Hall 5.
   Cold, I'm always cold.
   Patients creep along, their chins jutted out, eyes focused intensely under furrowed brows, on a mission.
   "Hi, Lulu." It's the patient I met in the dayroom yesterday.

"Hi, Betsy." Still loopy from the medication, I try to sound cheerful.

"Hurry, ladies. The dining hall will open in three minutes."

All forty of us from Hall 5 stand waiting in front of the doors. The key turns in the lock at six-thirty a.m. Attendants stand on each side of the doorway to tap and count as we pass into the dining hall. Attendants sit at tables on an elevated platform along the east wall, supposedly a vantage point for them to observe, keep order. I notice them laughing and talking, oblivious to the chaos. I know I have to keep an eye on patients wandering through the dining hall, snatching food, eating it with their hands. Yesterday, I lost my applesauce, today I'm prepared. I hunch over my bowl, my mouth inches away from the steaming glob of oatmeal. I clutch my milk carton.

After breakfast, I skirt the med line in front of the nurses' station and sneak down the hall to the dayroom. Before long, my night medication wears off and a hollowness settles down on me full length. I back against the wall to avoid a woman twirling across the floor. Others are dancing or marching around the room. The hall smells of smoke, urine, and lye soap. Like the new kid at recess, standing on the outskirts of the playground, I'm alone. Only this is scarier. I begin to shake.

I try to remember how I landed in the hospital—flashes of a castle in a snowstorm, Alexander's face, a cardboard casket. A vague feeling of time passing while I dream. My legs are weak, my back hurts. I remember the little cubicle, the fat doctor. Jeff fidgeting in the chair in the waiting room, pretending to read a magazine. Where is he? Finally, I take a deep breath, push off the wall toward a woman sitting by herself under the wall television.

I walk up, draw close, look directly into the woman's face— nothing. "Hello." If eyes are windows to the soul, these women have moved out, boarded up. I'm not like them. I'm in the wrong place. Somebody has made a terrible mistake. I need a mirror. I need to see if it's really me. But there are no mirrors. I stare down at my hands. The small diamond chip wedding ring looks familiar, the one Jeff claims he got from a Cracker Jack box. I must be me.

"Hi." I try a thin patient rocking on a straight chair. The woman jumps to her feet, raises her hands above her head, starts cawing like a crow. I freeze as the caws grow louder and louder. The attendant jabs my shoulder. "Move on."

I retreat to the wall and watch. Jesus, Mary and Joseph, a crow?

The attendant pushes the crow woman back down on her seat. "Quiet, now. You don't want to lose your cigarettes, do you?" I reach into the pocket of my state-issue and pull out a crumpled pack of cigarettes. I catch the attendant's eye.

I drag deeply as the attendant lights my smoke. "Thanks." I let out a long stream. Maybe I can puff up a smoke screen, become invisible until I feel safe, materialize only when somebody holds the door open, lets me go free, like steam from a teapot.

I made a mistake skipping the med line. I can't remember anything, now I long for the oblivion of the pills, the blessed journey somewhere else. I can't do anything about it now, they'd lock me up. From across the room, a toothless crone smiles at me. One more try. I hesitate briefly, then make my way over, lean down next to her chair.

"Hello. I'm Luanne." I stick out my hand.

The shriveled woman ducks her head as if she's in a bomb raid. "Luanne, Luanne, Luanne..." She chuckles softly, starts to rock.

Jesus. I feel the hair on my arms spring up. I walk away, resume my position against the wall. I take one final drag down to the filter, flick the butt into the metal ashtray, look up.

A large woman strides across the room toward me. I press my back against the wall, chew my nails. Friend or foe, friend or foe? I nod toward the attendant, and bend my head in the direction of the patient heading my way. Is she safe? I size up my options for escape. Adrenaline pumping, I tense my legs, ready to make a run for it.

The patient smiles broadly, rolls her eyes. "You're barking up the wrong tree there. The chronics—not home, if you know what I mean." She thrusts her hand toward me. "I'm Isabel."

```
Patient   Name:   Isabel   P.   Jackson
DOB:  6/2/1913   Age:  55
Date  of  Admission:  8/13/1968
Diagnosis:  Alcohol  Abuse:  Chronic,
Severe,  Recurrent.
Date:  11/19/68
Notes:  Thorazine  increased  to  150m.
No  observed  aggressive  behavior.
```

I squeeze the tips of the woman's fingers and give a quick shake. "Hello. I'm Luanne."

"They're doomed. Botched lobotomies or too much electro or too crazy to get better. Thorazine zombies. Hall 5, it's for the real lunatics. Now, us—we aren't that crazy. That's us, over there." She stabs her thumb toward the west side where tall windows let in a good amount of natural light. Several women stare over at us.

"Come on." As Isabel leads me across the dayroom, a naked patient whirls up to her, takes her by the arm. "Bitch," the woman says, spinning away. Isabel doesn't blink or break stride. She stops in front of the smoking women, waits for me to catch up, and grabs my arm.

"Girls, this is Luanne." Four women look up. Isabel extends her arm and motions toward each woman in turn. "Luanne, this is Autumn, Heidi, Beth, and Estee." They each smile, nod, or say hi.

Heidi runs her hand through her greasy hair, rests it at the back of her neck. "Got any cigs?"

"Sure." I pull out my red and white Tareyton pack, draw out two cigarettes and hand them to her. Heidi looks like a punk, a kid from a girl gang or something. I don't care. I'd give the girl the whole pack if she'd just talk to me. Heidi's hand shakes as she reaches out, small chips of tangerine polish scatter across her stubby nails.

"Thanks." She turns the cigarettes in her hand, wrinkles her forehead as if trying to figure out what they are. "Thanks a whole lot. I ain't had one for almost an hour and a half. I should be gettin' one from the attendant. These'll hold me over just fine. Thanks." She waves toward the nurses' station. An attendant arrives with a lighter. Heidi looks up after a flash of fire crackles her cigarette tip. She exhales slowly.

"I'm broke, so I have to wait for state cigarettes. They'll only give you one every two hours. So, what you in for?"

"Depressed." I pull up a chair. What else can I say? I have no idea what's wrong with me.

"Depressed? That don't sound too serious." Her eyes dart around the group. "I'm in for drugs. My mom's a bitch. She turned me in." She sounds hostile, but has tears in her eyes. I stare at her face as she talks, something is different. She has an angry case of acne on her cheeks, neck and chest, but that's not it.

"Yeah, she didn't pay attention to me since I was really little, then she goes and calls the cops on me. I had to go to court and all. My dad said he'd help me, but he never showed up. The judge said I needed treatment. Shit. This place ain't treatment." She glances over at Isabel.

Isabel looks directly at me. "I'm a drunk. This is my third time here. You'd think it was Las Vegas or somethin' the way I keep comin' back." She smiles, looks down. There's a short silence.

"What do you think of the Lobster?"

"The lobster?" Did I miss a lobster dinner?

"Nurse Lobsinger. The Lobster, we call her."

I feel a small smile cross my lips, the first one in weeks. "I didn't know."

"Well, I wouldn't say it to her face if I were you." Isabel laughs.

It didn't take me long to figure out that Doris Lobsinger, the nurse attendant on the afternoon shift, runs roughshod over Hall 5 from two fifteen until the nine o'clock evening bell.

About eight p.m. Monday night, my first day out of the infirmary, stomach cramps hit, a reaction to being scared to death, medication, and hospital food. Nurse Lobsinger escorts me down to the bathroom and stands in front of me while I sit on the toilet. I feel hot and prickly, my stomach churns.

"Jesus Christ. Hurry up." Nurse Lobsinger holds her nose. "What crawled up your ass and died? Hurry up. I don't get paid to stand around watching while you take a crap that lasts a week and stinks to high heaven. That's it. Mary, she's all yours." Thank God she walks out and leaves me under the supervision of the bathroom aide. Women come and go, using the toilets next to me. Each time somebody comes in, they ask the aide for toilet paper. She doles out two squares at a time. The aide informs me I have reached my limit.

When the night bell rings at nine p.m., I'm still in the bathroom. "I'm going to have to get my supervisor." The aide walks to the door and calls for her.

Nurse Lobsinger stomps through the door and rests her hands on her hips. "You still in here?"

I double over in pain, but ask as politely as I can. "Sorry. I'm sick. Can I please stay?"

"Nope. You're in bed for the night, Missy. You should have thought about that earlier when you had bathroom privileges."

"But I wasn't sick then."

She grabs my arm and pulls me up. "Nope. Get up. You've got a date with the sandman." I try to hold my gown closed as she drags me through the door. Staff, who just finished night check, stand in the hall as I waddle by, my legs soiled and sticky.

The Lobster—I like the sound of that.

Chapter 5

THE OBSERVER   *December 5, 1968*

Page 5
Hall 5 had a Popcorn Party Saturday Night,
sponsored by the Knights of Columbus Women's
Auxiliary. They had popcorn and Kool Aid, and the
nurses let the patients help pop the corn! A fun
time was had by all.

I motion for a light. *The Price is Right* blares from the black and white TV mounted on the wall above reach. Chronics sit silently in front of the screen, their necks craned back.

"How long have you been here this time?" I ask Isabel.

"'Bout three months." Isabel screws her lips to the side, lets out a puff of smoke.

"I been here fourteen weeks," Heidi butts in. "Withdrawal is a bummer." She scratches her arms. "They doped me up. I think I slept for a good three weeks solid." She brings her knees up, wraps her arms around them. "If I knew how crappy it was being awake, I'd have asked for more of those pills." She rubs her hand along the side of her face and across her forehead.

I can't help but stare at Heidi's face. That's it. Her eyebrows are missing. "I shouldn't be in 5," Heidi continues. "I was doin' pretty good in 9, but I started savin' my meds. Just stuck 'em up between my teeth and top lip. Really pretty easy." She shrugs. "I wasn't gonna o.d. or nothin'." They found 'em and—Bam! Here I am on Hall 5." Her voice lowers, she looks toward the nurses' station. "They stripped me and put me in a protection room. Nothin' but a mattress on the floor." She takes a long drag.

"Well, hell. I shouldn't be here either." Isabel folds her arms behind her head, tips back her chair, balancing it on two legs.

"The Doc says I can go back to 9 as soon as they're sure I'm not violent."

"Violent?" My chair squeaks as I shift in it.

"Nah, I'm gentle as a puppy. The Lobster had one of the little retarded girls crying. Told her nobody likes her, that her mom wouldn't ever come to see her, on and on. I couldn't take it anymore, so I told her to shut up." She leans toward me. "She got right in my face so close she spit on me. I pushed her back, and that was it. She called for backup; they put me in a jacket and brought me to 5."

"I've always been in 5. The whole time. Probably a homicidal maniac." We all turn toward Autumn.

```
Patient Name: Autumn A. Bauer  DOB:
3/23/1936 Age: 32
Date of Admission: 4/5/1967
Diagnosis:Manic-Depressive
Disorder.
Disorder: Severe, with Psychotic
Features. Borderline Personality
Disorder.
Date: 11/24/68
Notes:  Patient   continues    in
observation     for      aggressive
behavior. Controlled by medication
at   this   time.  Thorazine   600m,
Chloral Hydrate 50m.
```

Autumn shakes her long hair and pulls it back, using her hand as a clasp in the center of her head. She winds the ponytail around with her other hand. She has an exotic beauty, dark hair and eyes and luminescent caramel skin. But her face charts the course of her life.

Isabel raises her eyebrows. "Autumn had a bad marriage."

"Ladies, Ladies." The bell summons us to the dining hall. I sit with my new friends at a round table. We wait silently for our food. No sense trying to talk with the chronics babbling and yelling.

Patients on kitchen detail place trays in front of us, a small bowl of vegetable soup with crackers, a half peanut butter sandwich, a cheese slice, milk. I take a bite of cheese and look over at Beth cutting her sandwich into small pieces with the side of her spoon and moving them around her plate. Beth puts down her spoon. She stares at her soup bowl. She picks up her spoon, dips it in the soup and takes a small sip. She lays down her spoon, crosses her hands in her lap. She waits. She picks up her spoon again, repeats.

```
Patient Name: Elizabeth A. Shaffer
DOB: 8/12/1950
Age: 19
Date of Admission: 8/14/1967
Diagnosis: Anorexia Nervosa.
Date: 11/24/1968
Notes:  Pt.  refuses  to  maintain
normal body weight. Body Dysmorphia,
Anxiety. 5' 6", 73 lbs.
```

I figure Beth is almost an adult. But without makeup, she could be sitting in the cafeteria of any junior high. Her thick bangs crowd across her thin face, large pale blue eyes sink into sallow skin, a full mouth, even teeth. The neck of her state-issue clearly shows her collarbones and every bone of her upper spine.

One by one, our group finishes lunch and heads to the exit doors to wait for the attendant with the key.

I turn back and watch as the dining room supervisor approaches Beth. The supervisor stops across the table, splays her hands on the tabletop, leans so that her face looms over Beth's tray. "If you don't eat something, we will have to force feed you again." Beth stares down at her food. I have a brief thought about saving her. Save her how? "You cannot stay in here past one o'clock. Go line up. We'll give Dr. Cho an update on your lunch." The supervisor yanks away the tray.

I'm learning the routine. Every day, patients go to the dayroom after lunch for soap operas. Today, I sit next to Beth in our little circle near the windows.

Before I have a chance to duck, the attendants are on Beth, their elbows jabbing everywhere. One on each side, they boost her up out of her chair. She screams, digs in her heels, but she's no match for them. Her tennis shoes squeal across the floor as they drag her from the room. In a matter of two minutes, the dayroom returns to quiet. The chronics, not realizing anything has happened, stare up at the television.

"Beth came to Hall 5 two days before you did." Estee turns toward me. "The Lobster told her if she didn't eat, she'd never leave this hall. They're probably putting a tube down her nose right now."

"What do you mean?"

"She won't eat, she's losing weight. She told me yesterday she weighs seventy-two pounds."

```
Patient Name: Estee R. Weisman
DOB: 2/27/1945
Age: 23
Date of Admission: 9/29/68
Diagnosis: Schizophrenia:
Undifferentiated Type. In partial
remission.Date: 11/24/08
Notes: Continues to respond to
treatment. Thorazine 700m. Postpone
ECT.
```

"I don't know how many times she's been to the infirmary to be force fed," Isabel says quietly. "She told me what happens. They hold her down, stick this brown rubber tube through her nose, into her stomach. Then they pour some kind of nutritional crap down the tube. They keep her there until they're pretty sure she won't puke it up."

"Man."

"When she comes back, her hair is all matted, face all blotchy and red like she's been bobbing for French fries. They expect her to eat when her throat is so raw she can't talk. Hell, I'm no doctor, but there must be another way to get the kid to eat." She reaches into her pocket, takes out four cigarettes, passes them to Heidi, Autumn, Estee and me. We sit smoking, staring at the TV set. But nobody watches the Soap.

I look down at my hands. They are becoming my mother's hands, fingers boney, crepe paper skin crinkling across the faint blue patterns beneath. I'm fading, just like Beth. Fading away to nothing. My breasts ache for Alexander. When I sit back and run my fingers over my tummy, I think about my pregnancy. For the first time, I felt like a woman. When I close my eyes, I feel Jeff's hands gently caress my belly. His voice cooing his admiration. He said I never looked so beautiful and, for the first time, I believed him. I felt full then, expectant. Now I'm empty.

We sit around the dayroom after dinner watching TV when Beth comes in. She wobbles slowly across the floor, hands out in front of her to fend off spinning patients.

She sits down next to Isabel.

"Hi, kid." Isabel puts her arm around the back of Beth's chair. "How you doin'?"

"Okay." Her voice is raspy—obviously not okay. Her face is so pale, I can see the veins running under her skin, branching out as they disappear into her hairline. Her thinning hair hangs in greasy strings along the sides of her face, and the back is snarled up in a giant rat's nest. Beth clears her throat and swallows, her eyes on the TV. "Is that *The Brady Bunch?*"

"Yeah. Marcia's running for class president," Autumn says. "Welcome back."

"It's Popcorn Party night," Isabel says. "*Marcus Welby* at eight."

Chapter 6

"You met with the shrink yet?" Heidi drills up her nostril with the tip of a Kleenex.

"Dr. Cho talked to me yesterday," I answer. I like the calm nature of Dr. Cho, who took my hand as he asked how I was feeling. When I complained about drowsiness, how I dozed in my chair, my head bobbing onto my chest without warning, he ordered my Thorazine decreased.

"Not Cho. He's the pill guy. Murray," Heidi says. "Dr. Murray's the one you talk to."

"She's really nice," Beth says.

"It's a gal? The psychologist?"

I step back as the attendant raps on Dr. Murray's door. "Patient Kilpi, Doctor."

"Come in."

The attendant takes me by the arm and brings me into the office.

"Please sit down, Luanne. We'll get acquainted today. I'm Dr. Murray." She extends her hand, and I shake it. Girls don't shake hands where I come from. The Naugahyde chair squeaks as the doctor lowers into the seat. She crosses her ankles, smoothes her long skirt.

Dr. Murray reminds me of my aunt, hair pulled back in a chignon. Silver streaks like lightning bolts shoot through her hair. Aunt Faith would never wear those earrings though, dangly beaded ones, like hippies wear.

"How are you feeling?" Dr. Murray smiles, the chair squawking again as she sits back in it.

I feel like I'm holding on to a high ledge by my fingernails. "Okay, I guess." Doctor or not, Murray can't make me talk, force me to say the wrong thing.

"Can you tell me how you came to be admitted to the hospital?"

"No money."

"Oh?"

"We were broke, and I tried to kill myself, so we didn't have many options."

"I see."

"I don't belong here."

"Why do you feel you don't belong here, Luanne? You tried to take your life."

"I...I guess that's kind of crazy..." I look down at the thin smock bunched up between my legs. Holy Mother of God, I'm a bona fide lunatic. "Maybe it's Hall 5. I don't belong in Hall 5...I haven't seen the rest of the hospital." I squirm in my seat. Jeez, that was dumb. What did that mean? The rest of the hospital might be like a resort in the Poconos?

"The entire far northern wing holds the seriously disturbed and high-risk patients. You will be transferred out as soon as we evaluate you and find you are ready."

"I'm ready now."

"Do you mean you no longer want to kill yourself?"

"That's right." I lie. Dr. Murray seems okay, but can she be trusted?

"I'm happy to hear that. Now we just have to follow the hospital rules. Minimum of two weeks in Hall 5, and if you continue to do well, we'll transfer you to Hall 9."

Two weeks might as well be two years. My medication has been reduced, now every day ticks by one second at a time. "Okay." I whisper. What else can I say?

Dr. Murray flips back a sheet of paper from a file on her lap. "Nurse's notes indicate you've made some friends in Hall 5?" She looks up and smiles at me. "It sometimes can be difficult to make friends in here."

"Five other girls don't belong in Hall 5 either."

"Do you mind me asking who?"

"Estee ...Isabel, Heidi and ...Beth ...and Autumn."

"I see."

"I'm just getting to know them." Maybe I shouldn't mention names. It's hard to read the doctor, her voice barely changes. Neither does her face. Heidi is a smart-ass, could have made Dr. Murray mad. Beth is as skinny as a beanpole and that probably doesn't sit well either. Damn, how can I play the game when I don't know the rules?

"What happened, Luanne?"

"I…my…" I'd been taught to answer to authority, a good Catholic girl. But now a lump sticks in my throat, blocks my words. I feel my eyes fill with tears.

"Kleenex is right there on the table."

"Can we talk about something else?" The doctor bushwhacked me. I blow my nose, hiding behind the tissue.

"Tell me about yourself. You're from Saginaw, it says." Dr. Murray flips another page.

"I've been married for five years, to Jeff. I met him when I was a freshman in high school; he's two years older than me." I take a deep breath, sit back in my chair.

"How's your marriage?"

"Good…I thought so…I guess it's good. We've been together since I was fifteen."

"You two grew up together."

"I've always been his best friend. He relies on me."

"And you rely on him?"

"Well …yeah, I guess so."

"You don't sound sure."

"I usually handle our problems, try to keep on top of things. I guess it never mattered…until now."

"How's that?"

"I just wish I could lean on him. That he'd be here for me. It's not his fault, he's just not strong."

"You need him now."

"I don't know how I feel about him tossing me in here."

"You feel tossed away?"

"Sort of." I wipe my eyes with a balled up tissue. "I feel lost …like I'm in a bad dream…nothing seems real to me."

"I know, it's very scary."

"What if this is a nightmare?"

"You think this might not be real? You ending up here?"

I can't think. I rub my forehead trying to mold my thoughts into something that makes sense. "No, I know it's real …maybe it's just me…I'm not real, not the same. I can't seem to find myself …I can't explain it."

"It's okay. We'll figure it out together."

Why did I say that part about the nightmare? Is that a delusion? It sounds crazy. The medication clouds my head. "Do you think I'm crazy?"

"Well, Luanne, a suicide attempt is a serious matter. Suicide is a permanent solution to what is undoubtedly for you, a temporary problem."

Temporary problem. The doctor said it—temporary. "You mean … you think I'll get better? Some of these women …" At this point, I just shake my head.

"Yes. You will get better. How fast is up to you, Luanne. I'm going to put you in my therapy group. And we'll also continue to work together one-on-one. With medication and other services, you will get a comprehensive psychiatric treatment program here at the hospital. Pretty soon you will start to feel better."

"So, I'll get out of here? Go back home?"

Chapter 7

THE OBSERVER   *December 21, 1968*
Page 2
CHRISTMAS PROGRAM HUGE SUCCESS
*The annual Christmas Program, held at the
auditorium, was attended by over 750 patients
and staff. A nativity play, Christmas carols, and
a visit from Santa Claus highlighted the evening
festivities. Patients loved their gift baskets of fruit
and candy.*

I lean against the wall in front of the nurses' station waiting for the others. Heidi is the first to arrive. "Snowmen and Santa Clauses and them damn paper snowflakes on the windows don't make it Christmas," Heidi says. "Oh hell, what's the difference, I never liked Christmas anyway."

"The tree smells good." I try to keep it positive. Heidi can go on and on about how bad things are.

"Yeah, we can smell it, but the barricade around it kinda' ruins the mood."

"A patient pulled the tree down Tuesday."

"That's what I hear."

"I don't think anybody's going home for the holidays."

"Nope. Never any leaves from 5. Violent hall."

"I'm not violent," I say.

"Violent, psychotic, suicidal. It's all the same to them," Heidi says.

"Maybe the others don't have family close by. You know, too far to go home for Christmas."

"Those gals ain't goin' nowhere. They can't keep their clothes on let alone go for a family Christmas."

Autumn and Estee walk up together. We stand silently, waiting for the nurse.

"My god, I can't take this. I miss my kids." Autumn rubs her hands up and down her folded arms.

Beth walks quickly toward us, eyes toward the nurses' station, whispers to Autumn. "Don't get upset, they may hold you back from group."

"Ladies, ready?" The attendant unlocks the door.

"Hold up, I'm coming." I turn to see Isabel trotting down the hall. The attendant escorts us down a long corridor to Hall 9.

The nurse greets us. "Right this way, ladies. Same room."

"Nurse Judy, have you heard about any transfers for us?" Heidi asks.

"No, honey. Not yet."

This is my first group meeting. I sit between Isabel and Heidi in the circle of wooden chairs. Dr. Murray hurries in, her cheeks flushed. Wispy strands have escaped from her thick braid, hundreds of tiny freckles spatter across her face, earrings sway. She takes the empty chair in the circle.

"Whew, I'm glad I didn't have to go outside today. It's sixteen degrees and windy. They say the wind chill is five below zero. The tunnels are a godsend in this weather." She pulls a pad of paper and a pen from her briefcase and settles back in her chair. Dr. Murray's smile presses her skin into crow's feet. "Now, who would like to start today?"

I will someone other than me to meet the doctor's eyes, a silent whistle to get the ball in play. Autumn crosses her legs, shifts in her seat. Obviously, nobody wants to be first, standing blind at the end of a diving board without knowing if there is water in the pool.

Isabel always has something to say, but not today. I keep my head bowed, pick at my cuticles, glance around from the top of my eyes. Beth looks down, Heidi, too.

I know five of the girls and Dr. Murray, but still I'm shaking inside at the thought of talking in group. But I made a promise to myself. I will say something, anything, at least one time each group session, ease into the water, wade carefully to the deep end.

"I've been feeling pretty down lately. I miss my kids," Autumn starts. "Damn." She reaches for a tissue. Beth picks up the box, hands it to her.

"Go ahead," Dr. Murray says.

"Sometimes when I think about how I ruined their lives, it just hurts so bad." Autumn dabs at her eyes with Kleenex.

"*You* ruined their lives?" Dr. Murray asks.

"Yeah...well, yeah. They have no parents." She sniffs. "Thank God for my mom."

"He was a bastard," Isabel says.

"I know he was, but the kids loved him."

"Love shouldn't hurt," Dr. Murray says. "You did the wrong thing, Autumn. But you were driven by desperation, years of abuse. Something happens to women who are in marriages like yours, a kind of brainwashing. Sometimes they just snap. That's why you're here and not in prison."

"If only I could believe that," Autumn says under her breath. "Jim and my dad, two peas in a pod." Autumn sits straighter in her chair. "All the times my dad beat my mother, called me a wetback whore. I'm nine years old and he's yelling at my mom, saying she's screwing the pickle pickers on the farm next door. Ornery old drunk."

"Your dad called you a whore?" Beth asks.

"I can still see him looking at me, wrinkling his nose like I smelled bad. He got it in his head I was a Mexican bastard, never let me forget it."

"What did your mom say?" I ask.

"Mom was totally useless. She put up with it. Thank God she's found a little backbone now, taking care of my kids. Now that he's dead."

"He died?"

"Drank himself to death." Pulling at the tissue, Autumn tears it into thin strips. "I hate that old man." She wipes away tears. "And then I go and marry somebody just like him." She shakes her head. "Jim drank right from the start. He even hit me before we got married, and I married him anyway. Can you believe it?"

"Why'd you do it?" Isabel asks. "I don't get it."

"I don't know...stupid, I guess."

"Have you thought about why you married an abusive alcoholic, Autumn?" Dr. Murray asks.

"Of course! Of course I've thought about it. For god's sake."

"And…"

"I know this sounds really dumb, but Jim had blond hair and blue eyes."

"Go ahead. "

"I wanted to have kids with fair features …so …so I could prove to my dad I was okay. Unbelievable …I deserve what I got."

"All of us have unconscious directives. We can't change something we don't know about," Dr. Murray says. "When you learn why you do things, then you can change them."

"I guess. And …this sounds crazy, too. Jim being like my dad was comfortable. I knew what to expect, and I thought I could control it. It was my normal."

"Yes. I understand what you're saying," Dr. Murray nods.

"Sounds weird to me." The words are off my tongue before I know it.

"Thanks a lot, Luanne."

"No, not you, Autumn. I'm sorry. I never thought about how we can do things and not really know why."

"Yeah, like the time I put a dead cat under somebody's windshield wipers," Isabel says. "Hey, Doc, can I smoke?" Dr. Murray pulls a lighter from her pocket, sends it around the group. Everybody but Autumn lights up, drags on their cigarettes as if they connect to oxygen tanks.

"You're a bitch." Heidi's voice is so soft I think I'm hearing things.

"What?" Autumn says.

Heads swiveled toward Heidi.

"So worried about being called a whore. Big deal. I *am* a whore."

"What do you mean?"

"I'm a whore. What's so hard to understand? I screwed men for money and drugs. Just shut up. Shut up about whores." Heidi puts her Kleenex to her face, leans over her lap, cries. Nobody speaks. Dr. Murray reaches over and touches Heidi's arm. "Heidi, do you want to talk about this?"

Heidi talks into her knees. "Hell no. I'm done, done."

The clock ticks off the long moments of silence.

I think about trying to say something about myself, but my heart starts to go haywire, blub,blub-blub,blub. The silence is maddening, the pressure to speak. I put my hand on my chest. Stop. "My dad died when I was in the eleventh grade. The nuns excused me from final exams. " I inch out on that diving board.

"That's pretty young to lose your dad, Luanne," Dr. Murray says.

"I really miss him. I miss…"

"Go ahead, Luanne. Take your time."

I feel an overwhelming sense of doom. I've been through this kind of pain before, pain so great I'm certain I will fly wildly around the room like a balloon losing air, deflate, end up a useless flat blob under a chair somewhere.

"Are you okay, Luanne?" Dr. Murray asks.

"Yeah. I'll be fine." My stomach knots, forms a lump in my throat, sending shocks of pain into my jaw; my face goes numb. I'll be fine. I'll be fine …

The others sit back, smoking. I know nothing more will happen in group today. It's as if we silently agree to switch to small talk, complaints about conditions in the Hall, until the hour ends.

Dr. Murray looks at her watch. "Anything else?"

Everybody shakes their heads as they fidget and eye the door, like caged animals ready to escape.

Dr. Murray puts her notebook in her briefcase. "Just to remind you, I'm going to Chicago for the holidays to visit my son and grandchildren. I'll be back the day after New Year's which happens to be our group day, so I'll see you then. Merry Christmas and Happy New Year to all of you." She zips her briefcase and walks to the door.

The attendant waits to clear the room. Isabel puts her arm around Heidi as they walk down the hall. The rest of us follow silently. I look forward to getting lost among the crazies in the dayroom.

Chapters 8

L adies for a walk, ladies for a walk."
I know where to go. Once or twice a day, wards are cleared and everybody, except the most unmanageable, goes outside. I head for the large walk-in closet. It's just after a fresh snow. We all need boots, coats over our state-issues, along with hats and mittens. Patients shove their way into the room, jump on the tables piled high with outerwear, grab at the clothing. Hats and coats tumble through the air as if they're in an invisible dryer.

The Lobster shouts over the clamor. "Ladies, ladies. Settle down. Pick out one coat, a hat, and mittens. An attendant will help you with your boots." Slap fights break out among the chronics. Over the weeks, I've learned that unless they really hurt each other, the attendants let it go. After about twenty minutes, the scuffling and yelling die down, the Lobster checks for readiness. Two attendants lead the line, with patients in pairs behind them. Two more attendants bring up the rear.

I cross the threshold, *seventeen*, I feel the attendant's fingers thump my shoulder through my coat. I trail onto the sidewalk in formation, straight out from the building, stop. Patients stand there for ten minutes, arms flapping, feet shuffling for warmth.

I hear Alexander's laugh riding the wind. I can see him, his rosy cheeks squeezed into plumpness by his cap, arms rigid in his snowsuit.

"No, no," he protests when I tell him it's time to go in. His nose red with cold. "Snowman, snowman." It's so cold that day the snow won't stick. Jeff wants to try it anyway — he hates to disappoint his little boy. I'm the voice of reason. "Let's make a snow angel and then go have some hot chocolate." Alexander holds out his stiff arms as I lower him into the snow. He laughs as I pull him up. We all admire his angel. Then Jeff suddenly falls backward and waves his arms and legs. Alexander's laughter …I can hear it.

"Okay, ladies, turn around and head back in," the attendant shouts. We do an about-face, trudge back in our own footprints. I'm behind Raven, the nickname I gave the woman who caws. About five feet from the entrance, I poke her in the back.

"Hey, Raven, how's the weather for flying?"

She launches into her routine, loud caws growing in intensity until they echo off the brick walls.

An attendant takes her by the shoulders. "Jean, quiet down now." But the chain reaction starts. It slithers down the line. Obscenities cut the crisp winter air, gibberish, screams.

"Shut up, asshole."

"Bitch …bitch …bitch."

"Bastard."

Somebody sings *Winter Wonderland* off-key. A round woman in a pink fuzzy coat breaks from line, slips in the snow, lands on her back, arms and legs kicking like an overturned turtle.

"Ladies, ladies. Please. If you don't settle down, you will *all* be put in a protection room." The buzzing gradually stops, the line begins to move. A few of the women cry. I have no idea why I poked at Raven, like laughing during Mass. The pressure to conform sometimes blows out sideways. Or, maybe I just need to have control over *something*.

When I come into the dayroom, I notice the gang huddled in the circle under the windows, talking in loud whispers. It takes a good twenty minutes for the patients to get their gear off. I stand by the door as the chronics, still agitated, run in circles, punching at each other as they pass.

"Groovy." Heidi leans toward me as I join the group. "You had 'em comin' and goin'."

I feel like a movie star in front of an adoring fan. "It just kind of happened. I don't know. Ridiculous to get all dressed up to stand out in the snow for ten minutes." I fumble in my pocket for a cigarette. All hands raise for a light.

"You don't seem very sick," Estee says. "I can't figure out why you're on Hall 5."

"I tried to kill myself." I figure I might as well come clean. We're all in the same boat.

"How?" Heidi asks.

"Tried to drown myself."

"How do you do that, drown yourself?" Estee asks.

"Not very well, I guess …They found me floating down the Saginaw River late one night. I don't know how I got there …"

"I've thought about killing myself a lot," Autumn says. "But once I had my kids, I just couldn't do it, couldn't leave them with that bastard. I guess I ended up leaving them anyway. At least they're not with Jim."

"I thought about it, too," Heidi says.

The sounds of smoke exhaling, like long gentle sighs, leads to silence. My ears buzz. Life on the outside seemed so predictable. Now nothing seems real. It's like going to a costume party, trying to figure out who people are behind their masks. I look at Autumn, so gentle, fragile really. How does a person so nice end up here? And Beth—she's rich. What's she doing here? There must be private hospitals for eating problems. Estee seems completely normal. So, Isabel's a drunk. Big deal. I know lots of drunks.

"I don't really want to die, but I think I could," Beth whispers.

"Luanne, come with me please." Startled, we look up to see the Lobster.

"Why?" I'm panicked.

"Come with me, Luanne."

"Why?"

"You know why, dear." The Lobster smiles.

"No, I don't. Tell me!" I flick my cigarette in the can, hold on to the arms of the chair with all my strength. I plant my feet squarely on the floor and tense my leg muscles. Several attendants stand poised by the nurses' station. They are not regulars.

"Assistance with a patient, please." The Lobster shouts her command. The attendants are at my side before I have time to think. They drag me out of the room.

I scream, "I didn't do anything," over and over. I try to think how I can explain myself, escape what's coming.

The Lobster runs down the hall to keep up. "You acted inappropriately today on the outside. You created a riot among the patients."

When they open the door to the protection room, the stench is overpowering. The attendants try to hide their disgust, but noses wrinkle as they push me out at arm's length. They shove me in, pull the door closed. The only light comes through the transom. I blink to adjust to the dark. There is nothing in the room but a thin mattress on the floor, a black blanket, a bedpan. The walls and floor are rough concrete. They look clean. The pee and diarrhea must have seeped into the cement.

Chapter 9

I figure I've been in protection for eight days. The five-foot-square room is my dining room, bathroom, and bedroom. The food absorbs the stench as soon as they place the tray on the floor.

Yesterday, they took me out for a ten minute shower. "Just hand her the gown. Holy crap, what are we, the maids?" The Lobster pushes me, sends me staggering against the cement wall. "Get dressed. You're lucky you're gettin' clothes. Most of you troublemakers don't get nothin'."

I slip the flimsy state-issue over my head and lie on the mattress. I crave a cigarette so badly, I gnaw on my fingernails, rip my cuticles. The blood and ooze leave smatterings on my gown, like brown chicken scratches. If I finagle the thin blanket by holding on to the edge with my toes, I'm able to carefully pull it up around my shoulders. In a fetal position with the blanket barely covering my body, I try not to move. Even my bones are cold. The first day in protection, I wonder if I can survive.

Whether I want to.

When the attendant arrives late with my pills, I float to the surface, begin to think. It's no wonder I think about blankets.

Like a lot of kids, Alexander started carrying his blanket around with him as soon as he could walk. He stuck his index and middle finger into his mouth while he held the satin binding to the side of his nose. His blanket fell against his cheek and onto his lap, or it swung back and forth as he toddled along with it.

My brother Harry teased Alexander just like he had our little sister, Molly. I didn't let on to Jeff, but at first it got to me—I worried Alexander might become too attached. Look what happened to Molly. Despite years of teasing, she wasn't able to kick the habit.

Over the years, Molly's soft white crib blanket had deteriorated into three grimy little threadbare squares. It got to the point where she puckered her lips, set the square under her nose, and carried on with life. As a teenager, she walked around, did her homework, drove the family car, practiced cheerleading routines, changed the record on the hi-fi, did the twist ...she could even talk in a strange muffled voice with the blanket square nestled under her nose. I expected her to take it on dates, but even Molly had her limits. She was down to one gray square when I left home to marry Jeff.

It seems like a lifetime ago.

I wake up when I hear something buzz. I don't know how long I've been out—I never do. But it must have been awhile. My face is pressed against the bare cement and when I lift my head, my neck and cheek hurt. My state-issue is stuck to my body with sweat. The place is almost quiet, so I guess it's night time. The fly lands on my shoulder and walks around, down my back. I'm shivering so hard, I don't dare move for fear of losing my blanket.

Then I remember.

My body freezes. Now I'm afraid to move, afraid a monster will get me.

"I don't recommend an open casket," Mr. Morris said. "Perhaps you can make a collage of family photos."

Alexander's grandmother splurged on a new outfit for him to wear to Thanksgiving dinner and I was determined he would wear it. What difference did it make if it was too big? We brought the outfit to the funeral home along with underwear, navy blue knee socks, tennis shoes, and his blanket. Mr. Morris greeted us in the foyer, took my arm as he led us back into the showroom.

The caskets were lined up with little cards at the foot of each one listing the options, like a car. Only one model child's casket made of a composite material with a brocade finish, like fancy cardboard was available in four colors: gold, white, blue and pink.

"Where are the mahogany caskets, like we had for my dad?" I asked Mr. Morris.

"Oh, Mrs. Kilpi, children are *never* buried in wood. It's just not done." He wrung his manicured hands, flashed a weak smile.

We didn't ask questions, we ordered the white one. But I couldn't help wondering if it was a matter of supply and demand, or was a real casket just too big an investment for such a short life?

The second day after the funeral, I wandered to the kitchen, found myself snatching the tin-foil covered dishes from the refrigerator. I flung the food into the garbage, splattering the spaghetti, macaroni and cheese, potato salad, baked beans, and Jell-O salads until they ran together like a giant bug smashed on the bottom of the can.

The sticky dishes bumped around in the scalding water as I scrubbed them, my hands like stewed tomatoes. Each container had the name of the benefactor written on white cotton adhesive tape stuck to the underside. I put the clean dishes, plants, cards, holy cards, guest register, and other remembrances in Alexander's room, closed the door, dragged myself down the hall.

I met Jeff going into the bathroom. He tried to give me a hug. "What happened to your hands?"

I spread my fingers in front of my face. "Dishes."

"Jesus, Lu. They looked burned."

I shrugged, jammed my hands into the pockets of my robe.

"Where are those dishes we need to return?

"Bedroom."

"I'm going to run them back this afternoon."

"Now why would you want to drive all over hell's half acre with those dishes?" I snapped. "We don't even know half those people."

"I can check with Mom. Don't worry."

"Suit yourself." I couldn't wait to get back in bed.

The house was quiet when I got up later for a drink of water. A faint yellow twilight cast distorted rectangles against the living room wall. I turned on a lamp and sat down on the couch, stared out the window until the streetlights came on. Jeff still wasn't home. Oh, that's it. Taking the dishes back gave him an excuse to get out of the house. I plodded back to the bedroom.

I'd been in bed for two days by the time Jeff went back to work Thursday afternoon. I slept around the clock. By Friday, I didn't care if I ever woke up.

Alexander is gone. It settles on me. The weight of it pushes me flat against the floor.

The Lobster opens the door. "Okay. You're out tonight." I roll from my side onto my knees, draw my hands up under my body. From my hands and knees, I can get up slowly. My legs work, but I can't feel them.

"It's eight-fifteen. You've been transferred to Hall 9. You need to be there before night check. If you're not showered and ready by eight-thirty, you're not going." The Lobster backs up, pushes the door fully open with her body, stands in front of it while I pass. She covers her nose and mouth with her hand.

"Gee, we're really going to miss you, Luanne."

Chapter 10

I reach toward the nurse as two attendants drag me through the door. Nurse Judy waits at the nurses' station. "I'll take her, thanks. Welcome to Hall 9, honey." I crumble at the nurse's kindness, slump against her chest and sob. Every bone in my body aches, my mind is numb with drugs and shock.

"It's okay. We have your room ready. There's a stack of letters and cards for you." Nurse Judy puts her right arm around my waist, holds me by the forearm with her left hand. She unlocks the door to Room 15. "Heidi, you asleep? New roommate." Nurse Judy snaps on the room light from the hallway.

Despite her night medication, Heidi pops up. "Sweet Jesus, Luanne?"

"Heidi." I'd never been so happy to see someone in my life.

"Holy shit, you look like death warmed over."

"Lucky for you, they made me shower." I sit on the bed trying to gather my thoughts, but I can't think of what to say. I'm shaking from the inside out. I tremble so violently, I put my hand down to steady myself. Nurse Judy lowers my shoulders to the pillow, pulls my legs onto the mattress, covers me with the sheet and blanket. She hands me my meds.

"I put an extra blanket on your bed, Luanne. You're shaking. Sleep well, we'll talk tomorrow. Heidi, we should let Luanne sleep now."

"Sure, sure. Night."

"Night." I whisper. The thin mattress with the starched sheets feels clean and fresh. Two blankets to warm me up. "Heidi, my baby died." The words hang in the darkness. Heidi snores. I sink into sleep.

The next morning I sit in the dayroom on a chrome couch with brown plastic cushions, sort through the stack of envelopes. All six of my brothers and sisters sent cards, joking cartoon people wishing me well. Guess Hallmark hadn't yet developed a line for cheering up mental patients, like *"Heard you cracked up. Get well soon"; "Wishing you a speedy release from the loony bin."* I slide a card from a gilded envelope, from Father Barnes, our pastor, with a holy card and a small medal of St. Christopher. It probably should be St. Jude, patron saint of lost causes.

Five letters from Jeff, three from my mother.

November 29, 1968
Dear Luanne.
They wouldn't let me say goodbye. I hope you're doing okay. They gave me a list of rules. I'm sure you know this, but we're not allowed to visit you for thirty days. No phone calls. I miss you so much. I love you and pray you are well. I went to my folks for Thanksgiving, but also stopped in to see your family. They were all together at your mom's. Everyone sends their love. I'll write later.   Love, Jeff

It doesn't sound like Jeff, but then again, I'd never gotten letters from him before, never gone anywhere without him. Maybe that's why he sounds so distant, so matter-of-fact.

He sends a twenty dollar bill in his Christmas card along with a brief note.

I'm waiting for news from the hospital. They said you could write, why haven't you written to me? I pray every day that you are okay. I called the hospital, and they said you were doing well and they would schedule a visit as soon as you were ready.
It's a lonely Christmas here. I'm working as much overtime as I can so the guys can spend Christmas with their families.   I love you. Jeff

I open the rest of the Christmas cards. Mom's card bulges with a folded letter, most of it chatty news from home, details about the weather. The part that I can't get past . . .

...I called the hospital several times. They said you didn't sign a release, and they can't give us any information about how you're doing. Jeff said they told him you were doing well. I'm so glad to hear that. Molly and I are waiting to hear when we can visit. Love, Mom

I feel my chest cave in. I gasp, curl into a ball and rock.

"Luanne?" Nurse Judy rubs my shoulders. "What is it?" She pats my back, waits for me to stop crying.

"My family...Jeff, he tried ...oh my god ... " I can't stand the thought of the hospital withholding information, scaring Jeff and my mother. I leave my body. I float up above the dayroom, bump against the corner, look down at my own misery.

"It's okay. The rules can seem harsh, I know. Thirty days is a long time without a visit. Luanne?" Nurse Judy shakes my shoulder. "Luanne. Can you hear me? There are no letters allowed on Hall 5, then you were in protection ...I'm sorry, honey."

I hover, suspended like a helium balloon. Somebody tugs at my string. "Luanne? Luanne?" Nurse Judy continues to shake me.

Reconnecting with my body, I look at the nurse. I think of Jeff. If only I could feel his arms around me. "Can ...could ...my husband visit me now?" I wipe my nose on my sleeve.

"Discuss it with Dr. Murray. When she okay's it, I'll put in your request. The hospital will contact him. One week on Hall 9, and if you're doing well, you can have a visitor."

I sit up, examine Nurse Judy's face. I can't help suspecting her. "Thank you."

"It'll get better. Hall 9 is safer, quieter. You already know Heidi."

"Are my other friends here?"

"Now who would that be?"

"Isabel, Beth, Autumn, and Estee?"

"Isabel Jackson transferred in this week. I don't think so on the other three."

"Oh." My gaze drifts through the frosty windows to the frozen world outside. I imagine sinking into the snow, gracefully moving my arms and legs, creating an angel.

"What happened, honey? Do you want to talk?"

"My baby died. I ...I ...it just hurts so much." I hold my stomach, lean forward. Nurse Judy puts her arm around my shoulder.

"I'm sorry, I'm too upset." My voice squeaks out the words.

"It's okay." Nurse Judy squeezes my arm, waits silently for me to speak. I stare into space. Finally, I begin fingering the envelopes. "I don't want to be here."

"Luanne, you stay right here, read your letters. I'm going to get your friends."

Soon Isabel trots across the floor of the dayroom, Heidi behind her. "You okay, Lu?" The cushion hisses as Isabel plops down next to me.

"Yeah. Just reading my letters." I adjust the pages. "Listen to this."

I hope you're not mad at me, Luanne. It's been almost six weeks and I haven't heard from you. I pray every day that we made the right decision about the hospital. Your mom agreed, we all thought you needed help. You almost died, we had to do something. I love you and can't wait to hear from you. Please write to me. I called the hospital on December 18, thirty days after you were admitted, and they called me back just before Christmas and said you couldn't receive visitors yet. I'm sick with worry. Your mom wants to drive up there and see what's going on. I told her we have to follow the rules. Please, honey, write to me, or call if you can. Love, Jeff

"Can you believe it?" My voice cracks.

"Bastards." Isabel says

"They can't do that! They can't keep your family away forever. When they get here, tell 'em what's been going on," Heidi says.

Chapter 11

I settle into my usual seat in Dr. Murray's office, a wooden chair with curved arms, Early American, like my dining room set at home. "I'm not sure I can make it."

"Protection is tough," Dr. Murray says.

I start to cry, reach for a tissue. Crying hurts my head. I close my eyes, push off, swimming down for my thoughts. "It's like being dead. Only you can still feel — cold. I have to get out of here."

"Do you think you're ready to leave the hospital?" Dr. Murray asks.

I study her face, wonder if the question is some sort of trick. I figure there must be rules, secret rules, and if I follow all of them, I can leave the hospital. I see the names in the *Observer*. People do get out, it's right there in black and white. If I could just figure it out …Finally, "I'm afraid to go home."

"What are you afraid of?"

"People looking at me like I'm crazy …going home and not finding Alexander there …Jeff with that look on his face."

"What look?"

"Pity? I'm not sure. Like he's miserable, and it's my fault."

"Is Jeff getting help, too?"

"How would I know? I just got his letters. I haven't heard from anybody in almost seven weeks. Did you know they kept all my letters from home?"

"Yes. It's one of the rules."

"Nurse Judy said I could have visitors next week if you give your approval."

"Who would you like to see?"

"My husband. My mom."

"Anybody else? Family members, friends?"

"Maybe my sister, Molly. She still lives at home."

"Anybody else?"

"What are you getting at? Am I supposed to have lots of visitors? I don't want anybody to visit me here!"

"There's no right answer, Luanne. I just wondered if you felt close enough to anyone else."

"That's not it. I'm embarrassed ...Jeez." I pluck another Kleenex from the box. "I'm not even sure I can talk to anybody from home. I'm afraid I won't know how to chat about things, you know, normal things."

"Is there somebody in your family who could help you with that?"

"Nobody in my family ever had this kind of trouble."

"Everybody has problems."

"Not my family. If they do, they don't talk about it."

"So you're saying your family has never had a problem of any kind?"

"My dad died. That's the worst thing that's ever happened to our family. And my oldest sister got pregnant in high school. I guess that's no big deal, but it sure seemed like it at the time."

"What about Jeff's family?"

"They're nice, but sort of rigid, German and Finnish."

"Is Jeff like that, rigid, as you say?"

"Jeff's a nice guy. Everybody likes him. He loves his parents, stops over to visit them, helps them out. Jeff wants to please."

"It sounds like you think that's a bad thing."

"Maybe ...I don't know. I guess it's a good thing ..."

"How do you feel about Jeff visiting?"

"I don't know what to say to him."

"Why is that?"

"He let me down. I can't imagine how he could dump me off here. It's unbelievable, really."

"In what way?"

"I'm not crazy. But he brings me here, locks me up like an animal? My Lord, I'm plenty good enough when I'm all together, and when I need him the most, he gets rid of me."

"Can you talk to him about that?"

"I don't want to hurt his feelings."

"I see. Maybe I can help you with that. And when you're ready to begin transitioning home, we can offer you family therapy."

"Without my little boy, I don't have a family."

"Have you remembered anything more, Luanne?"

"Not really, snippets of the funeral home, the service …not much else. I'm still trying to accept …he's gone." I grab a wad of Kleenex and hold it to my face. "None of the letters say anything about it. It's like nobody will tell me what happened. I know I tried to kill myself. Jeff told me about that."

"What did he say?"

"That Saturday he had worked afternoon shift at the foundry. It was just thirty minutes before the shift-change whistle put him out of his misery."

"What kind of foundry?"

"Jeff said, *If hell had a basement, it was there where the blast furnace melted dune sand into engine cores for General Motors.* He pretty much hated the job. His eyes and ears were protected, but the sand found its way most everywhere else. From what he said, he and Bill Murphy shoveled their last pile in the core molds when the foreman tapped Jeff on the shoulder and motioned him out. A young police officer, his hand on his nightstick, stood by the drinking fountain. He nodded and waited for Jeff to pull out his earplugs."

"Go on."

"I guess the cop asked him if his wife was Luanne Kilpi. Told him a young couple had been smoking weed in Ojibwe Park when they spotted me floating down the river."

"He must have been terrified."

"Yeah. The cop said I was at St. Mary's and Jeff ran out the loading door to the back parking lot before he realized he had carpooled with Bill. I asked him why he didn't ask the officer for a ride, but he just shook his head. Said he sprinted all the way to St. Mary's in his steel-toe boots. He must've been scared, running all that way on such a cold night."

"I'm so sorry, Luanne."

"I didn't do it on purpose …"

"What?"

"Try to drown myself. I'd never do that ...I can't even believe I did. Everything is so unbelievable to me. I want to talk to Jeff about it when he visits."

"That might be a good idea, Luanne."

"If I can work up the courage."

The attendant walks me back through the tunnels to Hall 9. I replay my meeting with the doctor. I shouldn't have complained about Jeff. He's doing the best he can. For God's sake, what happened? I can't get my head around it. The guilt is overwhelming. Jeff lost a son, too, then his wife tries to kill herself?

Chapter 12

There are no mirrors. I'm not sure why. I smooth my hair. I've barely felt human, let alone attractive, in almost two months—good grooming and life in the disturbed ward are not compatible. Make-up, hair products, anything personal just isn't allowed.

I close my eyes, imagine myself twirling in front of the mirror in a rainbow tiered crinoline, a skinny six-year-old, my bird legs disappear into huge black and white saddle shoes. At seven, a white organza Holy Communion dress made by my mother. A proud ten-year-old in a straw Easter bonnet and patent leather Mary Janes. And all the fads and fashions since then—a watch-plaid kilt with an oversized gold safety pin, knee socks and penny loafers, my school uniform, rolled up at the waist, a homecoming dress, burnt orange wool, with a carnation corsage pinned on the cowl neck, my first formal taffeta for the J-Hop, the green velvet prom dress that made me feel like a movie star. The homecoming queen finery and, finally, the wedding gown I designed myself, showing off my tiny waist, falling gracefully into a long train.

Today I imagine myself as I used to be. I have to, Jeff is visiting. I pick at the fuzzy pills on my emporium sweater. I haven't felt attached to my body in quite some time, even before the hospital. I think my body started to break away during those long nights, sitting upright in a chair, Alexander's moist head against my breast, my back aching with fatigue, my muscles tense with worry. When Alexander stopped shifting with pain, finally escaping into sleep, I tried to hold so very still, making my body his cradle. At first, it was by sheer will and necessity, now it's automatic. Before I know it, I'm floating up against the ceiling.

I'm terrified. Seeing Jeff will demand me to be aware in a way I haven't been since my breakdown. And the not knowing. Jeff is scheduled. Will Mom, Molly be waiting in the visitors' room? I feel the panic rise.

"What time is he getting here?" Heidi says.

"Visit's scheduled for 2:30. I'm not sure if my mom's coming, but they told me Jeff should be in the visitors' room by 2:15. Nurse Judy will come for me when he gets here. How does my hair look?"

"Looks good. Excited?"

"Nervous. Even with my meds, it feels like my skin is going to split open." Fear, plain and simple, raw nerves exposed like an aching tooth.

"It'll be fine." Heidi puts her arm around my shoulder.

"Does this sweater cover my butt? Jeans are so big." I hike up my Levis.

"A belt would help."

"A belt on jeans, can you imagine that? It doesn't seem that long ago I eased them to my thighs, fell back onto the bed, shimmied them past my hips, sucked in my breath, and zipped up. I loved how I looked in those tight jeans."

"Jeff probably did, too." Heidi said.

"Yeah ...now look at me."

"You look fine, really."

"Thanks." I give Heidi a hug. She's a good friend, but I can't tell her I dread the visit, she'll think I'm crazy.

Jeff charges to his feet when Nurse Judy and I come through the door of the visitors' room. He holds out his arms. I stagger, my peripheral vision falls away. I feel dizzy, hot. Jeff's face blurs, his smile, pain-filled eyes fragment, then blackness.

"Lu, Luanne, you all right?" Jeff catches me before I hit the linoleum. Nurse Judy takes my hand, turns my wrist, presses her finger on my vein as she tracks the second hand on her watch.

"Her pulse is racing. Let's get her over to the couch." Nurse Judy takes one arm, Jeff the other.

Slowly, I come back. "I'm okay, really ...just a little too excited." I turn toward Jeff, "Hi."

"Hi." He holds my hand, face ashen, beads of perspiration across his forehead.

"Sorry." Damn, this is what I feared.

"You okay, dear?" Nurse Judy takes my wrist again. "Pulse is settling down."

"Yes, thanks. I want to stay for my visit."

"Are you sure you're up to it?" Nurse Judy feels my forehead.

"Yes."

"Mr. Kilpi, please ring the bell if you need anything. There's staff behind that window at all times." She points to the glassed-in reception desk.

"Wow, you scared me." Jeff sits beside me on the couch and puts his arms around me, holds me close. I lay my head on his chest, pull my legs up beside me as I lean against him.

"Thought Mom might come," I say after a long silence.

"Your mom and Molly are at that canteen thing. They said you were only allowed one visitor this time."

"Oh no ...they came all this way."

"They'll come back, don't worry. How are you? You're so thin."

"Yeah, I know. It's the medicine." I don't want Jeff to know what I've been through. Why make him feel worse?

"Oh." He rubs my arm. It irritates my skin. "Hard to get any news from here. Are you feeling better?"

"I think so. I hope to be home soon. How have you been?" I look up into Jeff's face.

"Pretty good ...better now." His voice quavers. "Do you ...remember anything?"

"No."

"I've been so worried about you."

"I'm fine, really."

"Do you remember going into the river ...or before that?"

"No. I still don't remember what happened."

"All I know is that guy pulled you out of the river ...don't know anything before that," Jeff says.

"I didn't mean to hurt you."

"I know." He hugs me again. "Do you remember the funeral, or ...before that? The day the funeral director came to the house?"

"I remember picking out the casket, some of the funeral service ...nothing really about the day Alexander died."

"We woke up that morning, and he was gone." Jeff pats the back of my hand.

"You were on days, then? Who went into his room?"

"Ah ...we both did, I think."

"I just can't remember that. I miss Alexander so."

"Your mom and Molly were anxious to see you. I'm sure they'll be back the next time."

"Are you doing okay? It's only been a couple of months."

"I'm working a lot. We were wondering where your room was when we drove up. What part of the hospital is it in?"

"First floor, far north wing, facing the front." I didn't see it coming. Here I am, smack dab in the middle of it, avoidance. If we don't talk about it, it doesn't exist.

We talk about the holidays at home, Jeff's work, mutual friends. It's hard for me to hear about life outside the hospital. It's like watching a movie, life moving along, but I'm not in it. I nod, smile as Jeff talks.

"Rooms nice?"

"Well ...it's a hospital. My roommate is nice."

Nurse Judy escorts me back to the dayroom.

"Good visit, hon?"

I slump into a chair, exhausted, and stare out the window.

"What is it?" Nurse Judy asks. I don't have a clue how I should feel. Jeff is a stranger, speaks a different language, a language from my other life, the life outside.

"My husband ...he was so distant ...I don't know how to explain it."

"It's okay to talk about it, Luanne." Nurse Judy sits down beside me.

"I thought Jeff would understand, maybe even feel some of what I do, but he's shut a door on me."

"Each person handles grief in their own way," Nurse Judy says.

"I guess so ...You don't know how it feels." All of a sudden I'm mad.

"You're right, of course I don't."

"It's not supposed to be like this."

"Um-humm." Nurse Judy nods her head.

"Why would babies die? Alexander never even got a chance." I start to cry. Nurse Judy reaches into her pocket, pulls out a rumpled tissue.

"Here. It's clean." When I stop crying, she says, "Give it time."

"You sure time will do it? You know that?" I know I sound cold, but I can't help it. Time?

"That's how it worked for me," Nurse Judy says. "Time … time and prayer heals all wounds."

"Easy for you to say, you're the one in the white uniform. You're not the patient, I am."

"Yes." Nurse Judy is quiet. A couple of minutes pass while I tried to stop crying.

"I'm sorry. I don't mean to be rude. I feel so alone."

"You're not alone, honey. I've been there, too."

"You've been a patient?"

"No." She looks at me with such kindness. "I lost my baby."

"I'm sorry."

"It's okay. It was a long time ago." She stands up. "I need to get evening med trays ready. We'll talk again." She squeezes my shoulder, returns to the nurses' station.

Chapter 13

I've been out of protection only a week, and I'm not sure I can handle group therapy. But if I ever want to get out, I have to go. If you don't follow the rules, you don't go home.

Dr. Murray gets there just in time to begin the session. "Welcome back, Luanne."

"I can't take this shit." Isabel pulls her crew neck shirt down over her belly and squirms in her chair. "The first time I came here, they called it the *Blind Room*. Before that, I heard it was called the *Strong Room*. I don't care what you call it, it's torture. Some gals in there for months at a time. You tell me, could you be locked up like that and not go crazy?"

Isabel leans back and folds her arms across her chest. "Luanne, you look like you've come back from the grave."

"Thanks." Leave it to Isabel to make me smile.

"Progress is slow," Dr. Murray says to Isabel. "I understand your frustration."

"Bullshit."

"I know, I know. Let's move on. Who wants to start today?" Dr. Murray says. The usual ritual starts, with the group members looking down and fidgeting in their seats.

"I guess I could start."

"Go ahead, Beth," Dr. Murray says.

"My parents are pressuring me to leave the hospital. They don't think I belong here. I haven't even told them about what goes on ...the forced feeding ...stuff like that."

"Did they say why?" Dr. Murray asks.

"They noticed the bruise on my neck and asked the nurse supervisor about it. She told them about Margaret attacking me in the dayroom. I'm sure she didn't say all of it. But my mom cried."

"You don't tell them what goes on here? Why not?" Isabel asks.

"I ...don't know." Beth looks at her blankly.

"Keeping things from your parents, Beth, when did that start?" Dr. Murray asks.

"Well, I remember when my classmates used to tease me every day at school. I didn't tell my parents about that. Gosh, that was grade school."

"The kids teased *you*?" Heidi looks shocked.

"Yes. They used to call me *Lambchop*."

"*Lambchop*? Like the puppet?"

"Yes. You know what? I really did look like *Lambchop*. I had big bulgy eyes, thick bangs."

"Well, you obviously got revenge," Autumn says.

"What do you mean?"

"Ah, you're gorgeous?"

"Beth, you're a beautiful girl with great talent. I know you were a star at Interlochen Arts Academy. Harp and violin, right?" Dr. Murray asks.

"And voice," Beth says. "All of that is over now."

"What do *you* want Beth?" Dr. Murray asks. "Do you feel you want to leave the hospital? Your weight is still low. You haven't yet met your clinical goals."

"I don't know. I hate seeing my parents upset."

"Jesus Christ. Your parents?" Heidi says. "What about you?"

"Heidi has a good point," Dr. Murray nods.

"I'm okay," Beth says quietly.

"Yeah, right," Isabel rolls her eyes.

"I want to be a good patient. I don't want to bail out on you guys. But my parents aren't happy. I don't know." The group falls silent.

I don't know what to say. Beth is such a cute girl, kind and polite. Even after hearing her talk in group, I still don't understand the eating problem. I can't make sense of my own life, let alone Beth's. Feeling like you don't measure up, that I can understand. I should say something, but it seems like such an effort.

"It's not a big deal. It's stupid, really. I can't make the simplest decision," Beth says.

"It most certainly *is* a big deal," Dr. Murray says. "This is your life. You have to do what you think is best for you."

"My parents expect I'm going to Julliard, even now. I've been accepted, but I can't go."

"Why not?" Heidi asks.

"I don't deserve it."

"Of course you deserve it, kid," Isabel says. "Having all your talent, that's real special."

"You're right. I should be grateful. I don't know why I feel this way. I just don't know."

After about two minutes of shuffling and sighing, Estee speaks up. "I have no idea what you should do." She scratches her arms. "I'm pretty sure I'm crazy again. They must have done something to my meds.

"Are you doing okay on your medication, Estee?" Dr. Murray asks.

"No, I'm not. You're trying to poison me. We're all going to rot in here. I guess Luanne was the first to go. One minute she's here, they swoop down, snatch her up, drag her down to the bowels of hell."

We all stare at Estee, until Beth breaks the silence. "I want you guys to help me."

"What would *you* like to do?" Dr. Murray asks again.

"I want to get better, leave here some day. Not now."

"Well, there's your answer. Do you want me to talk to your parents with you, Beth? Try to explain again about your disorder?"

"You won't say anything to upset them."

"Beth, I'm on your side. The main thing *you* can do is try to get your weight up to ninety pounds. Then you can transfer to Hall 9."

"I'll try. Thanks."

"You *must* gain weight, Beth. Otherwise, you will stay on 5. You need to gain at least one pound this week. Do you understand?"

"Yes, doctor."

"Why don't you just eat?" Isabel asks.

"I don't know."

"It's not that easy for Beth," Dr. Murray explains. "She has an illness."

"I don't have any place to go." Heidi brings the focus to herself. "Livin' with my dad up above Randy's Party Store all my life, then bein' out on the street. I hated high school. Don't have no education. My mom's such a bitch. She don't want me."

"Maybe my parents could help you?" Beth says.

"Your parents?"

"Well, my folks have money. They could give you a loan or something."

"Oh Jeez Louise." Heidi shakes her head. "They're gonna give money to some whore off the street you met up with in the loony bin. Oh, brother."

"I'm just trying to help."

"The reason you're in my group is because I believe you're all going to get better and leave the hospital," Dr. Murray says.

I really wonder about that. I can see now that Estee is seriously ill, a real mental case. What if Dr. Murray says that to everyone?

"I just want to see my kids," Autumn says.

"Autumn, I'm going to request at the next clinical team meeting that you be allowed visitation with your children."

"Really?" Autumn shifts in her seat and looks around the group.

"Are you ready for a visit, Autumn?" Dr. Murray asks.

"To tell you the truth, I'm scared to death."

"What are you afraid of? They're your *kids*," Heidi says.

"I'm afraid to see the hurt in their faces. Afraid they blame me for what happened …"

"What did happen, exactly?" Isabel says.

"Jeez, well …well, that night he came over to pick up the kids for visitation. He was so drunk he could barely stand up…" Autumn pauses, leans forward, then back. "He yelled at them to get their coats on. When I tried to say something, he called me …a …terrible name …"

"Go ahead and tell us what he called you, Autumn," Dr. Murray says.

"A worthless cunt. That's what he called me that time."

"Jesus," Isabel says.

"He yelled and swore, on and on and on. I told the kids to go to their room, they weren't going." She reaches for another tissue. "I was scared to death, but I couldn't let him take the kids."

"You were very brave, protecting your children," Dr. Murray says.

"Thanks. The rest is kind of a blur … He was on me before I knew what happened,…slapped me around …"

"Oh, my gosh," Beth says.

"This happened all the time when we were married. Jim beating the living shit out of me. The bastard."

"Go on."

"I feel like I'm back there. Look at my hands shaking. I …I don't think I can go on. Sorry."

"That's okay, Autumn. Before we schedule your children for a visit, I'll help you prepare. Who else has something they would like to share?

"Me. I have something," Heidi says. "Whew …okay …well …oh, never mind."

"Go ahead, Heidi," Dr. Murray says.

"Well …Something really bad happened to me when I was doin' drugs."

"It's okay, kid," Isabel nudges Heidi with her shoulder.

"I don't have any eyebrows 'cuz they shaved off all my hair. My eyebrows didn't grow back." Heidi bites her lip.

"They?"

"The guys who attacked me." Heidi brings her hands to her face.

Dr. Murray reaches out and squeezes Heidi's arm. Beth snatches two or three tissues out of the box and hands them to Heidi.

"Jesus Christ. Did you call the cops?" Isabel asks.

"Hell, no. You kiddin'? They would've busted me for drugs. I didn't tell nobody."

"Men are pigs," Autumn says.

"Yeah." Heidi wipes her eyes with a wad of Kleenex. She takes a deep breath and tries to smile.

"Can you talk about the attack, Heidi?"

"No, no …not …I'm not ready."

"Whenever you're ready, we're here to listen."

"Yeah, thanks. Anybody else want to talk?"

"Well, I just want to say I love you," Isabel says. "I'll be your mother."

"Damn it. Don't make me cry again," Heidi says. "Gimme a break."

Chapter 14

I press my forehead to the glass around the nurses' station. "She swallowed something again." Nurse Judy Reinbold and two attendants hustle through the door toward the dayroom.

"Agnes, what did you swallow this time?" Nurse Judy asks.

"My spoon. From lunch." She lifts her state-issue, pokes around on her stomach. We all keep track of how many items Agnes swallows, even make bets on what she'll eat next. In the month of December alone, she swallowed fifteen coins, several pop bottle tops, a screw, a crochet hook, a needle, twenty-five beads from OT, bulletin board tacks, and one of the rings off the draperies. Now we can add a spoon to the list. I heard that since Agnes arrived at the hospital a year ago, she'd been in surgery five times. I figure surgery is reserved for the large or particularly pointy and dangerous items she swallows. Castor oil and stomach cramps escort the less damaging items through her system.

"A spoon?" Nurse Judy tips the patient's head, fishes around in the back of her throat.

"Did it go down?" She runs her fingers along her neck.

Agnes coughs. "Uh-huh. I feel it right here." She presses her sternum, coughs again, gags.

"You'll need x-rays, Agnes." Nurse Judy guides Agnes to her feet, and with her arm around the patient's shoulder, leads her out of the hall.

"There she goes again," Isabel says.

"Why does she do that?" Estee asks.

"Agnes just likes attention."

"Maybe she's trying to kill herself," Beth says.

"There's easier ways to kill yourself," Heidi says.

"Tried it?"

"Yeah, once. I O.D.'d. My dad kicked me out and I had no place to go. I screwed a guy for some quaaludes. Ate 'em down as quick as I could, chased 'em with cherry schnapps. The puke stain's probably still on the sidewalk in front of the bank."

"Do you think I'm trying to commit suicide? Like Agnes?" Beth looks down at her feet. "You know, the eating problem? I know if I don't eat, I'll …I could …die …but … I …just have to get off Hall 5."

"You *want* to eat?" Isabel asks.

"I don't know."

"Luanne, you tried to kill yourself, right?"

"Yeah. Like I said, I can't really remember."

"My mom's coming this weekend," Autumn says. "They won't let me see my kids yet. Mom said they made me some gifts in school." She sniffs and wipes her nose on her sleeve.

"I don't want to see nobody." Heidi picks at the skin along her hairline. Her eyebrows, drawn on by an attendant, are crooked. "I wrote a letter to my boyfriend, but I don't have his address."

"I didn't know you had a boyfriend," Estee says, scratching her arms and legs.

"Tripper. He's nineteen. He's lookin' for work, so he probably won't visit me. But he loves me like crazy. I met him in the park one night, and he let me stay with him in his trailer. It was a really nice place, had heat, real cozy."

"Were you out on the street?" Beth asks.

"Yup. I kinda' made the rounds with my friends, but I slept in the park a few times, had to."

"Thought you were living with your dad," Isabel says.

"Yeah, I was, but …I just couldn't stay there anymore."

"Why's that?"

"My dad was getting weird …I don't know."

"Weird?"

"He was drunk or high a lot …just weird."

"Beth, are your parents coming this weekend?" Isabel asks.

Beth pulls her turtleneck over her knees, sits like a crow on a wire. "Yes. But I have to talk to them about visiting so often. Dr. Murray thinks their visits upset me."

"Yeah?"

"They ask about my weight …she …ah, the doctor …thinks that's harmful to my progress. My mom always cries."

"Maybe the doc doesn't know what she's talkin' about. Ever think of that?" Heidi says, "I haven't had one fuckin' visit from nobody. Neither has Estee."

"I'm sorry. You're right. I'm lucky to have my parents," Beth says quietly.

"I don't really want to see my husband. I don't know why," Isabel says. "I guess I'm ashamed of how I treated him."

"When you were drinking?" Autumn asks. "Dr. Murray says it's a disease."

"Disease or not, I've got a lot of apologizing to do."

"To who?"

"My kids, my husband. Everybody, really. My parents, they don't understand …Jesus, I almost said my foreman."

"Foreman?" Heidi asks.

"At work. The guy who supervised us. But I don't owe my foreman an apology. He's still an asshole, whether I'm drunk or sober. Which is beside the point, I guess. I was the one who screwed up. They fired me. I was a complete fuckup for three years. A big fat drunk who didn't think about anybody but myself. My oldest boy told me I ruined his life."

"But you quit drinking, right?"

"I'm trying this time. I love my kids."

"I wish I had somebody to visit me." Estee's mouth sticks together at the corners as she talks. "My grandmother would come, but she lives so far away. She writes me every week."

"What about your folks?" Beth asks.

"My dad left when I was six, my mom is crazy, certifiable." She arches her back and kinks into a contortion, her clawed fingers slide back and forth across her spine. By this time everyone in our group has earned the privilege of wearing street clothes. Heidi and Autumn's come from the emporium of donated clothing in the basement of the patients' library. Estee is back in state-issue after her breakdown a few days ago. I'd been sitting in the dayroom reading my letters again when I heard the racket from the hallway.

"Who put this up? Who put this up here? Who put this up here?" Estee stomped her feet, pointed up at the bulletin board where a patient had put up a knitted peace sign she made in OT.

"Settle down," the attendant said.

"Heretics! Devil worshippers!" Estee shouted. "That symbol is blasphemy, drawn by the devil himself. Take it down, take it down immediately."

I hustled into the hall, placed my hands on Estee's shoulders. "Estee, come on now. The peace sign is a good thing, means peace."

"Can't you quiet her down?" Heidi looked toward the nurses' station.

"Peace symbol, my ass. Don't you see it? The communists love to see this crap spread all over the place—people sticking up their fingers in a vee—don't you see? Russia loves this shit, proves we're being taken over by atheists and dark angels."

"All right, all right, calm down now." The attendants took Estee by the arms, shooed Heidi and me back to the dayroom.

We stood at the door, watching. "Damn it. She's wigged out again," Heidi said.

The attendant stripped off Estee's clothes, bent her over a chair. After they injected her hip with a tranquilizer, they slipped a state-issue over her head, and sat her down. I was worried. Estee hadn't been making much sense lately, but at least she was quiet about it. Now she was ranting and raving. Within seconds, Estee's head began to bob.

When Autumn and I pick her up for dinner, she's lying on the floor, legs splayed, out like a light. We each take an arm, lift her, steer her down the hall to the dining room. Autumn guides Estee by the arm, pulls out her chair, and helps her sit down. A small stream of saliva runs down Estee's chin.

"What's wrong, Estee?" Isabel asks.

Estee shifts in her seat and scratches her arms, then jabs her hands under her thighs, and rocks back and forth. "The itching . . ."

"Can they give you anything for it?"

The kitchen workers set trays on the table.

"Why is the meat always gray?" Heidi pokes her meatloaf.

"Don't start. I'm trying to pretend it's Mom's," I say.

"I make a good meatloaf myself," Autumn says. "Estee, can I open your milk?"

Estee rocks on her chair as if she doesn't hear her. Autumn presses back the sides of the carton top and squeezes until a spout pops out. She hands the carton to Estee.

"Potatoes are fake." Heidi slides a tan lump from her fork. "Beans are mushy."

"Just eat for God's sake, Heidi."

"Eat your food, Estee." Autumn hands Estee her fork.

"I'm itchy. Can't ..."

"Jeez, Estee. Sit still." Heidi uses her finger to push the beans onto her spoon. "Can't she sit still?"

"No. She's miserable. And stop talking about her like she's not here."

"Is she?" Heidi asks.

"Is she what?"

"Is she here?"

"Fuck you," Estee mutters.

Chapter 15

I huddle in the courtyard with the rest, over six hundred men, women, and children evacuating Building 50 in the worst blizzard of the winter, eighteen inches of new snow, winds howling off the frozen bay.

Autumn shouts directly into my ear. "Where's the fire?"

"It must be here in Building 50," I holler. Sirens cut the night. The attendants yell directions above the wind. I look around—all these crazy people out in a blizzard. No wonder there is no tap and count as we leave the building. Now attendants mill through the crowd, counting, sticking adhesive tape on each patient's forehead as they cut us from the group. "Lift your face." An attendant slaps the tape against my forehead. When the last patient is marked and released into the counted, I hear the attendant screaming at the top of her voice.

"Nurse Reinbold, I think we have one missing."

"Who?"

"We don't know yet."

"Find out." She leans close to the attendant, shouts into her ear. "Where is the fire?"

"It's definitely in 50. I saw flames over the patients' library. Men's wing, I think."

I push through the crowd. Patients scream and wave their arms. Attendants wrestle to turn the faces of the patients, identify them. I hear one of the nurses yell, shake Nurse Judy's arm. "How long can we last out here?" She pulls her cardigan shut over the front of her thin uniform. "Some of the patients are in slippers or just socks. We'll freeze to death."

"Where's Estee?" I shout to Isabel. She shrugs and frantically swings her head around, searching the crowd.

"I thought she was right behind me," Beth cries.

I motion to an attendant. I yell, "We know who the missing patient is."

The attendant takes the news to Nurse Reinbold. "The lost patient is Estee Weisman."

I duck as an explosion shakes the ground, flames shoot up from the library roof. Patients standing in the courtyard scream and wail. Fire trucks round the corner of Cottage 21. As they pull up, shiny black figures spill from the doors like ants, shouting orders, running to their posts.

"We need more manpower, more hookups."

"Willy, grab any extra coats or blankets we got. These women are half naked."

"There's a patient missing. Ground floor, Hall 9."

"One missing."

"Del, we got at least one rescue. First floor."

"Get the squad in there."

"Any missing? Any missing? Any missing?"

"Another one, second floor, back."

"Any missing, any missing?"

"We need more men, more equipment."

"All we got are volunteers, Benzie, Antrim and Leelanau counties, that's it."

"Get 'em here. Call the station. Tell them to put out a 410."

"Storm's pretty bad."

"Get 'em here! We don't have room for no pussies. Get the damn help. Now."

"Jack, where's the rescue team?"

"We got three men in the north wing."

"Start them pumps."

"Start pumpin', for Christ sakes, get them pumps started!"

Nurse Judy puts her arm around my shoulder.

"Luanne, when did you last see Estee?" I try to tell her we were all sitting in our place by the window when the alarm sounded. I thought we went down the stairs together. It's hard for her to hear me above the voices of the firemen and the screams of the patients. A man runs up to her. He brings his face close to hers.

"Judy, are you okay?"

"Carl! Thank God."

He grabs her forearms. "We got people coming from all over the hospital, bringing coats and blankets." He looks out over the group. "Some of these ladies don't have shoes, and them thin smocks..." He wraps a blanket around Nurse Judy's shoulders, briskly rubs her back. "Your uniform is like tissue paper." He shouts to another attendant, "Joe, where are them blankets?"

"Plows and trucks can't get through. Fire trucks got the roads blocked. I just got word we're evacuating this group north to Cottage 21."

"On foot?" Carl asks.

"Only way to do it," Joe says. "We can't wait—these gals won't last much longer out here. With the spray coming off the hoses, they'll turn into icicles."

"Carl, can you lead the evacuation?" Judy says. "I need to stay here and see if they've found the missing patients. Luanne, this is my husband, Carl. He'll lead you all over to 21."

Carl takes me by the arm and waves goodbye to his wife as we struggle through the deep snow in the courtyard. He instructs the patients to line up by twos. We follow orders, clutching warm clothing around us. Carl motions the line through the iron gate of the courtyard, away from the back of the building.

"Okay, ladies. Start walking. Hold the hand of the lady next to you. Walk quickly, but do not run."

As the line clears the rear wall of Hall 19, I see the fire running along the attic, the entire length of the south wing. I come to a dead stop. The patients behind me trip over my heels. My knees buckle, and I fall into the deep snow.

"Lady, what's wrong. Keep moving," Carl pulls me up by the waist. I put my arm around his neck and point up. "Look!"

Silhouettes of men set against a glowing background fill the second floor windows. Their arms are raised. I can't see their faces, but I can imagine them.

Chapter 16

When I wake up the next morning, I rise up on my elbow, scan the cots set up in the halls of Cottage 21. Drugged, most of the refugees still snore. I think I spot Beth asleep a few rows down.

"Beth, are you awake?"

"I am now," she says. She blinks her eyes. "I thought I might be having a nightmare. I guess we're really here."

"I'm going to find the others, see what's going on." I weave through the cots toward the dayroom. Autumn is asleep near the nurses' station. Women are gathered in the dayroom waiting for breakfast. Isabel sits on the floor, dragging on a cigarette. She's talking to Estee.

"Estee, you're here!" I hug her around the neck, practically sit in her lap.

"Yeah," Estee croaks.

"Where were you? Where did you go?" I glance over at Isabel. She shrugs her shoulders.

"I had to be saved, Luanne. I met the test. God sent angels." Estee stands up, speaks as if she were giving a sermon, hands punctuating her story. "The siren blared. *I'm coming,* I said. I moved toward the sound, the empty halls wispy with smoke. I was terrified, and I yelled, *Lord, why have you forsaken me?* Tears streamed down my face. Smoke snuck under the doors, burned my eyes. I heard the voices of the damned screaming from below.

"Then I ran, my arms straight out, toward the double doors. They flew back on their hinges as I hit them hard with the palms of my hands. Smoke billowed in from the hall. I staggered back, wiped my eyes, stumbled through the entryway, found the wall, pressed my body against it, slid along slowly. There had to be a way out, a way up. Hell was not far below, I could sense it, feel the heat. I took it slow, one hand pressing the plaster, the other flailing in front of me.

"I couldn't see, so I reached for the hem of my state-issue, wiped away the tears and soot. I kept blinking. Then I saw it, a red eye glowing through the smoky haze. Terror gripped my chest, my heart pounded like a piston. *Be gone, Satan. I cast you out in the name of God Almighty. Cast ye down, demon.* I yelled as loud as I could. I wanted to run, hide, but I knew I must meet the challenge. God was testing me. I had been chosen, Luanne.

"It took all the faith and courage I had, but I moved forward, toward the glowing eye. I remember blinking and blinking, my eyes burned. The smoke coated my tongue, I swallowed, coughed. *I cast ye down.* I screamed out the words, and each tiny step moved me closer to the demon. I would face it, stare it down. Then I made a cross with my arms as I slid along the wall. I could feel God with me.

"Suddenly, the red eye expanded, transformed itself. It glowed its message of salvation—*EXIT. Thank you, Lord. Thank you.* I laughed with joy and fell to my knees in prayer. Then I heard his voice, '*I am with you now, Estee.*' I stood under the *EXIT* sign. My hand touched the doorjamb, then the knob. I turned it. The door opened, revealing a staircase, steps ascending up."

Estee drags me down next to her, as she kneels on the floor of the dayroom. "Thank you for showing me the way, Lord. I am so alone."

She's a tough act to follow. All I can say is "Ah, okay."

"I am blessed now. Lord, please save my sister, Luanne. She's pure of heart, Lord." Estee's voice raises as she rolls her eyes toward the ceiling. She takes my hands, squeezes them tightly. "It is God's will. Fire and brimstone, Luanne."

As soon as the *Observer* comes out, I run to the nurses' station and grab a copy, rush to the dayroom with it.

THE OBSERVER
Traverse City State Hospital. The paper by and for patients and staff
April 4, 1969

SEVENTY-SIX SOULS LOST IN FIRE
Reports were released this week from the Traverse City Fire Department. The March 26th fire at the State Hospital claimed the lives of seventy-five patients, seventy-three from Ward 20, Men's Wing, and three patients from Hall 12 and Hall 16, all in Building 50. One staff member, Nurse Supervisor, Judith A. Reinbold, also perished in the fire.

THE OBSERVER
April 4, 1969
Page 3

CAUSE OF FIRE UNDER INVESTIGATION
Chief Barry Mead, Traverse City Fire Department, fought the fire, March 26 in Building 50. The fire fighting effort lasted two full days with the help of firefighters from five counties. Crews from as far away as Cadillac battled the blaze. Chief Mead indicated that the cause of the fire has not yet been determined, but it appears that a cigarette may have ignited the curtains on the second floor of the men's wing.

"Is that a picture of Nurse Judy and her husband?" Autumn asks.

"Yes, at the last Christmas Party." I wince at the sight of Nurse Judy with her husband. They look so happy.

"Hey. Remember when I told you I thought the attendant was my dad when I first came in? Well, here he is right here." I point out Carl in the paper. "Nurse Judy's husband, Carl Reinbold."

Isabel scans the paper. "They don't say a word about the faulty elevator."

"Here's an article by Father Fred, *God's Divine Plan.*"

74

"God's will be done," Estee says.

"Here's the names of the victims." We lean in to read down the list.

"Creepy," Heidi says.

Estee closes her eyes, bows her head. "You don't have to worry about them. I talked to the victims. They told me they're happier in heaven than they ever were at the hospital."

Chapter 17

The announcement scratches and crackles from the wall speaker. "Patient Luanne Kilpi to the nurses' station."

"Now what?" Being summoned, plucked from the safety of my circle of friends, jolts me. I feel a surge of anxiety.

"You better go," Heidi says, her fake brows knitted with worry.

"Jeez, what?" I push back my chair, step over Estee's legs, walk slowly toward the nurses' station.

"Luanne, your visitors are here. An attendant will escort you to the visitors' room," the nurse supervisor says.

"Visitors? I ...nobody told me ...who?"

The nurse checks her paperwork. "The order says *three approved visitors*, that's all it says."

I feel dizzy, disoriented. Life in the hospital is so routine, the only surprises are bad ones. My mind ticks like a roulette wheel, tries to match the message with its meaning. "I'm not ready." As I glance back at my friends, I long to be back in the circle, a little girl hiding behind her mother's skirts.

"Are you declining the visit?"

"No, no ...of course not ...ah ..."

"Do you need a few minutes to get ready?"

"Um ...yeah ...hold on." I take a deep breath and hurry to the safety of my friends.

"I'm getting ...I have visitors."

"That's great!" Heidi says. "Jeff?"

"Three. My mom and sister, probably. This sounds stupid, but I'm scared. I don't want to go."

"It'll be okay," Autumn says.

"Christ, I look like a tramp." I pull at the sides of my baggy sweat pants.

"Here, let me smooth your hair, tuck it behind your ears." Isabel stands and circles me, primping. "Autumn, take off your shirt and give it to Luanne."

Autumn starts unbuttoning her blouse, holds it out to me and then slips my ratty t-shirt over her head.

"Beth, your stretch pants," Isabel says.

"I ...I don't feel comfortable taking off my pants."

"Here, sit down, slip them off. Luanne, give Beth your sweatpants. We won't look." Isabel turns her back.

"Thanks." I button and smooth the cotton print shirt, adjust the black pants around my waist. "Good?"

"You look great," Beth says.

"Good luck," Estee adds.

Jeff, Molly, and Mom are lined up on straight-back chairs against the north wall, away from the other patients and visitors. They stand up in unison when I come through the doorway as if somebody pulled a lever under their seats.

Mom steps forward, gives me a hug. "We were so worried. Thank God you're okay." Jeff hugs me next, then my sister Molly.

"Yeah, I'm good," I can feel my knees shaking.

Jeff pulls a chair over, and motions for me to sit down. They scoot their chairs into a tight circle.

"First we heard about the fire, then they said no visitors for two weeks." Mom dabs at her eyes with a tissue. "My God, you're so thin and pale."

"I called right away. They said you were not on the list of injured or ...passed away." Jeff reaches for my hand, squeezes it.

"The other section is all burned," Molly says. "Did you know anybody who got hurt ...or ...died?"

"Yes. Nurse Judy. Remember her, Jeff?"

"The one who helped us when I visited?"

"She died in the fire."

"Gee, that's too bad." Jeff leans forward and rubs his palms together.

"The day I came in, an attendant reminded me so much of Dad. It helped make things easier. Then again, he helped me during the evacuation. I just found out he was Nurse Judy's husband. They were such a nice old couple."

"Man, you're skinny! Maybe I should spend a few weeks here," Molly says.

"I don't recommend it as a weight loss program." I manage a weak smile.

Mom flashes a look over her shoulder, leans forward in her chair toward me. "These people are …ummm …really mental, aren't they? I mean …look at that one over there."

"Mom!" Molly says.

"What are they doing here to help you?" Mom asks.

"I see the doctor a few times a week for therapy, I go to group. They reduced my medication twice already. I'm getting better."

"Is your memory coming back?" Jeff asks.

"Bits and pieces."

"Do you need to remember everything to get out of here?" Mom asks.

"I don't think so. My doctor said it could take a long time. Or it might never come back. Not fully."

"You might never remember that morning?" Jeff asks.

"What morning?"

"The morning Alexander …when we found him."

"No. We're going to have to work on that. Right now, we're trying to piece together the night I almost drowned. I don't remember that either."

"Did they say how long you'll be here?" Molly asks.

"Dr. Murray thinks another six to nine months."

"That long?"

"That's what she said." I feel myself leaving, floating up toward the ceiling. What do they expect? I'm a patient in a mental hospital, no different than the woman Mom pointed at. Do they expect an instant cure, a few zaps of electro maybe? I feel ashamed, grotesque.

"How's school?" I turn toward Molly. I can see myself mouthing the words, smiling. But I'm not there.

Molly starts talking, rattles on—who's going steady with who, the lucky girls who've been asked to prom already, what trouble her classmates are in, details of the last basketball game. Mom adds news about the family, church, and the local gossip. Between the two of them, they keep the awkward silences at bay.

"Our time's almost up. I'd like to spend a couple of minutes alone with Luanne."

"Oh, sure, Jeff. Of course." Mom jumps to her feet, Molly behind her. "We'll see you again soon." They hurry past the other patients and visitors, eyes riveted on the door.

"I just wanted to spend some time alone with you."

"It's good to see you, Jeff."

"I love you, Luanne." He kisses me.

I don't want to, but I feel myself pull away. "Love you, too."

"Are you okay?"

"Yeah, pretty good. How are you doing?"

"Okay."

"I feel bad leaving you with all the bills, the house..."

"I don't want to bother you with stuff, but I'm working at getting the bills paid, working a lot of overtime. The mortgage is getting a little behind, Dad's helping me," Jeff says.

"I ...I just can't think about that ..."

"No ...of course not. Sorry." Jeff stuffs his hands in his pockets, scuffs his feet on the linoleum floor.

"I'm sorry, too."

When I get back to the dayroom, the same feelings creep over me. Separation from myself, observing from the ceiling of the visitors' room. *Why didn't I talk more?* Jeff is suffering. Alexander and Jeff, they're the innocent ones. The baby grew inside *my* body. There must have been some seed, some cell, hidden deep inside— some contamination. Now Alexander is gone and I'm trapped, locked inside a life I don't recognize, don't want.

They'd be better off without me.

Chapter 18

THE OBSERVER   *May 23, 1969*

Page 7

BUILDING 50 CLOSING
Superintendent Dorsey announced this week the
closing of Building 50 would begin this month.
Cuts in state funding, fire restoration costs, and
the addition of the Arnell-Engstrom Children's
Hospital, now under construction, have led to the
decision. The closing could take up to two years,
said the Superintendent.

A steady stream of vans and trucks takes supplies and furnishings to the storage buildings. As Building 50 begins to close, Heidi and I are hopeful we'll be moved to the outlying cottages. They crack the windows in the dayroom—the smell of spring is unmistakable. Autumn, Isabel, and I volunteer to unload flower trucks from local nurseries, a project created when the hospital greenhouses closed. We are picked up in front of Building 50 by a white van. I recognize the driver, Carl Reinbold.

"Afternoon, ladies. I'm Carl and I'll be supervising you today. I got one stop and then we'll be on our way." We head down *Red Drive* toward Building 35. We pull up in front where an attendant stands on the porch with a patient.

The man makes a break for it. He stumbles down the walkway from the porch, sweeping his arms in front of him like searchlights.

"Grab him, Carl," the attendant hollers from the porch.

Carl leans into the handle to brace himself for the short hop to the curb. He lurches up the lawn like a lumber wagon on a rutty road. We all stare out the van windows. The patient veers off the sidewalk, slipping and high-stepping his way across the grass. His hands hit the tree first, but momentum carries him forward, his face smashes against the bark. He springs back and lands among the scattered chestnuts.

"You okay?" Carl presses his hand into his right thigh, lowers onto his left knee next to the patient. The patient's eyelids hang at half-mast, revealing a dark black line across a pinkish background. I've seen this before—blind patients without eyes, removed so they'll be easier to care for. The patient grunts, raises his hand and waves it.

The attendant runs up. "Is he okay?"

"Seems to be. Scraped his nose and forehead, though," Carl answers.

"Cripe. He's just getting out of the infirmary. What's his problem? Darwin, you okay?"

The attendant pulls the patient to his feet, brushes off his pants. Tears seep from the patient's sunken eye sockets.

Carl leans against the trunk and strains to his feet. Carl seemed so strong, I hadn't noticed he was crippled. He guides Darwin into the seat in front of me. Poor guy, crazy and eyeless both.

"Take it easy. You'll be back in your room in no time." Carl pats the patient's knee.

"I'm thirsty," Darwin says.

"Well, hold on and we'll make sure you get a drink." Carl turns the key in the ignition.

It's a beautiful spring morning, sparkly white trillium wink in the mossy foliage on the wooded hills behind the hospital orchards. When we step from the van, I see a small group of men loitering near the east side of the abandoned dairy barns. We women wait on the west side, in front of the large barn doors. It's a chilly afternoon, but the sun is brilliant. The river rock foundation is warm, radiating heat into my shoulders. Some of the women lift their faces and close their eyes.

"Okay, ladies. Here comes the truck. Step back against the barn until the truck stops completely." Carl leans against the foundation.

"What trucks do we take the plants to?" Autumn asks.

"Just wait for my instructions," Carl says.

Carl tells us to form an assembly line from the large panel truck to a point where pickups back in and load. The doors of the truck swing open. We start our work as the first pickup backs in.

"One flat at a time?" Isabel asks as she passes Carl.

"That's right. Take your time."

After I slide my first tray of snapdragons into the pickup, I stop in front of Carl.

"You're the one who helped me during the fire, right?"

"Not sure," Carl says.

"I'm the one who fell, you held me up the whole way to Cottage 21."

"Yeah, that'd be me. I remember that, sure."

"My name is Luanne Kilpi. I remember you from the first day I came in here. You took me to *Receiving*."

"By golly. I remember now. Sure, sure. How are you doing?"

"Better. Nurse Judy was your wife?"

"Yeah, that's right."

"Sorry for your loss."

"Thank you." Carl looks away, as if he is checking the loading process. I can see his eyes tear up.

"Nurse Judy helped me a lot on Hall 9."

"Is that right?"

"She was a special person."

"Yup, yup, she sure was. Well, we're running behind here."

The work crew of patients returns to Hall 9 just before four. Most of us make it to the shower room before the dinner bell. I shower quickly, return to the dayroom for a smoke or two. On my way, I notice a signup sheet on the bulletin board.

"There's a group going up Old Mission Peninsula tomorrow to gather rocks for the flower beds. Anybody interested in going?"

"I'll go," Isabel says.

Autumn says, "Does that mean we can skip our work shift?"

"The bus is leaving at two. I think the idea is you get your work shift over by then," I say. "The signup sheet is on the bulletin board."

"I overheard one of the nurses talking about the *Toap House*."

"What's that?" Beth asks.

"Toad House?" Isabel asks.

"No, p ...pa, pa, p ...*Toap House*."

"Hell if I know."

"How was it used?" Estee asks.

"Something about Marge saying she was at the *Toap House*."

"Marge, the retarded girl?" Heidi asks.

"I guess so. I don't know any other Marge in the hall," Beth says. "I heard the nurses laughing about Marge and the *Toap House*."

Chapter 19

Dr. Murray starts our session with, "So, how are you doing, Luanne?"

"Not so good …well, good and bad. I volunteered to unload the flower truck. It was nice to get outside."

"Yes, it's wonderful to see spring arrive. Do you enjoy gardening?"

"My dad was a gardener."

"You might consider working on our gardening crew this summer."

"How do I do that?"

"I'll recommend that your work shift be changed from housekeeping to garden crew."

"Thanks, I'd like that."

"Carl Reinbold supervises that I believe."

"Did you know he's Nurse Judy's husband? I mean …used to be."

"Yes, the Reinbolds were some of our oldest and most valuable employees I hear. Way before my time. I think they've been here almost sixty years. I worked quite closely with Nurse Supervisor Reinbold. And I know Carl, too. He's a very nice man."

"I feel sorry for him. He's crippled."

"Unfortunately, Carl was attacked by a patient in the tunnels years ago. He used to supervise the entire dairy operation at the hospital, but since his injuries, he's kind of a jack of all trades."

"Losing his baby, and then his wife. Do they have other children?"

"As far as I know, the Reinbolds do not have children. Where did you get the idea that their baby died?"

"Nurse Judy told me."

"Are you sure, Luanne?"

"Yes I'm sure. We were going to talk more about it but …we never got the chance."

"I see." She scribbled something in her notes.

"Don't you believe me?"

"Yes, I believe you, Luanne. Now when you came in, you said you weren't doing very well. What's happening?"

"Night terrors, but they happen during the day, too. These flashes of memory, all of it bad."

"We could increase your medication."

"No, I'm just starting to feel a little bit normal."

"Any suicidal thoughts?"

"No."

"We talked about this before. We want you to get well, so we have to balance your medication with your ability to handle things as they come up. We don't want to sedate you, but we want to make sure you won't get desperate again. Make sense?"

"Yeah. I'm miserable, but I think I can handle it."

"Why don't you tell me about some of what's coming up for you."

"I know I did something wrong, but I don't know what."

"Wrong? You mean trying to kill yourself?"

"That too, but I keep thinking there could be something I should have done ...you know, about Alexander."

"Go on."

"I've run it through my brain a million times, every detail. Every talk with every specialist, every trip to Detroit for radiation, every chemo appointment."

"You remember these details?"

"I do now. Yes. I remember about when he got sick. Then, after his surgery, Alexander started to get better, gained some weight. The cloud lifted and spring came. The nightmare was over. But then it came back. It came back worse than before."

I remember holding my breath through every endless day of bad TV, sitting next to Alexander, his world reduced to the couch because he was too weak to walk. Every long night, rocking him as my back turned to stone and my legs went numb. What had I done wrong?

"Tell me about Alexander getting sick."

"It was just a regular checkup. I planned to talk to Dr. Costello about thumb-sucking and blankets. Just a couple of days before, I noticed Alexander's stomach looked lopsided."

"Lopsided?"

"Yeah, when I looked at his belly straight-on, the right side was just a little bigger than the left. He had no symptoms. But I asked the doctor about it anyway. At first he seemed puzzled, but when he asked Alexander to lie back on the examining table, he said, *Oh, I see.*

"He called the nurse and talked to her for a few minutes in the corner of the room. She looked concerned, nodded her head, and wrote something in the chart, then left, closing the door behind her. I didn't know *what* was going on.

"Doctor Costello continued his examination, and then the nurse cracked open the door of the examining room and asked to speak to him. He excused himself. He was gone for such a long time, I had trouble keeping the baby entertained. When he walked back into the room, the nightmare began."

"What did he say?"

"I'll never forget it. He said, *Mrs. Kilpi, your son has a mass on his right side. I've contacted Children's Hospital in Detroit. They have scheduled Alexander for surgery tomorrow.* I didn't know what to think. My brain wouldn't work. I remember saying that my husband had to work tomorrow. Sounds stupid now. Then the doctor said, *Your son needs surgery right away. They are the best equipped to handle a case like his.*

"We got to Detroit before sunup that morning. The date is stamped on my brain, September 12, 1966. The car crept along the dark streets of the slums downtown. Trash swirled along the sidewalks, swept against the doors of boarded up buildings. I'd never even been to Detroit before and it seemed very big and scary.

"Alexander's blanket hung loosely across his lap as he slept against my chest. Later that day, it rested on the gurney next to him until the anesthesia took hold, waited for him in his room until he returned. It snuggled against his skin as he whimpered. The blanket went along to radiation therapy. Alexander clutched a corner of it as they taped his tiny body to the cold glass. *Hold very still, do not move,* I heard the doctors say before they pulled the heavy metal door closed behind them. I could see Alexander through the glass. He petted the satin binding on his blankie as the machine growled, its glowing white eye opening and closing with a whir as it clattered over him."

"Poor little guy."

"I know, I know …what he went through …Kleenex?" Dr. Murray handed me several tissues.

"I remember the day I took Alexander in for chemotherapy. I sat in the waiting room, Alexander on my lap, his blanket spread over his legs. Without warning, a great geyser of runny bright green vomit spewed into the air and splattered down. The amount was unbelievable given how tiny he was. It pooled between his legs and formed a puddle in the middle of his blanket.

"The waiting room full of mothers and children froze in mid motion, everyone stared. Time stopped, restarted when Alexander began to cry. Somebody called the nurse, she came running out with a little three-cornered plastic pan, held it out to me, stood there for a few seconds before she put the pan down. She folded Alexander's blanket carefully to avoid spilling the stuff onto the floor. It's hard to go back …Alexander was so good about it . . .braved the three inch needle without his blanket to help ease the pain …I …"

This time I sobbed. Dr. Murray patted my hand. The pain was so overwhelming.

"I'm so sorry, Luanne."

"Six months later, blankie made its final trip with Alexander in his cardboard casket."

Chapter 20

THE OBSERVER   *May 23, 1969*

Page 4
SPRING CONCERT AND DANCE
We have a real spring treat for you dancers! Mr.
Jack Barden will be performing in the auditorium
on May 31ˢᵗ. Mr. Barden is a master on the
Hammond organ, and he promises to provide a
lively evening of dancing. Cupcakes and punch
will be served. Dancers, please remember you must
change partners for each dance.

"Tonight, ladies and gentleman, we are proud to have Jack Barden and his Hammond Organ!" Everyone cheers and claps.

Mr. Barden walks on stage in a black tuxedo with a red cummerbund, and shiny patent leather shoes. His short hair stands straight up in the front, held in place by butch wax. He sits down at his stool, inches it up to the keyboard, and breaks into *Wake Up Little Suzie* by the Everly Brothers.

Autumn, Isabel, and I line up for cupcakes and punch. Beth and Estee hide by the stage curtains just off the back of the refreshment table.

"Dance?" A gnome with red hair and bad breath pokes my shoulder.

"No, bud. I'm getting food. Maybe later." He swaggers down the line only to be shot down each time he asks. Finally, he twirls onto the dance floor, his left hand extended straight up and his right hand bent out in front of him, smiling at some imaginary partner.

"I've never seen people enjoy dancing so much," the woman pouring punch says. Her name tag reads *Jill Farley, wife of Dr. Ronald Farley, Chief Psychiatrist.* "Don't forget your napkin," she says to a stubby man in a plaid shirt.

"Yup. You see all kinds of dances goin' on." Carl puts out more napkins.

I come to the head of the line and take a cupcake. "Hi, Carl."

"Well, hello there," he says.

"I'm Luanne."

"Yup, yup. I remember you."

"This is my first dance."

"How do you like it?"

"Ah …different." I take a cup of punch and walk back to join my friends, hiding out by the curtains. The first dance of the night ends, and the male and female patients split to opposite sides of the room.

"Thank you. Thank you very much," Jack Barden scoots back from the bench, bowing from behind his organ. "Now I'd like to try some psychedelic soul from Sly and the Family Stone." He stoops, takes baby steps as he pulls the bench behind him. Barely recognizable, *Everyday People* begins.

"Mrs. Farley. Good evening." Dr. and Mrs. Cho approach the table.

"Evening. Are you folks chaperoning tonight, too?" Mrs. Farley asks.

"Yes we are, but we're on our way out. Mrs. Cho isn't feeling well." Dr. Cho looks at his wife. "Su Lin, you remember Jill Farley, Dr. Farley's wife. She's one of our volunteers."

Mrs. Cho bows her head.

Dr. Cho takes Jill's hand in both of his. "Bless you. If it weren't for our volunteers, I don't know what we'd do. Some charitable group is always sponsoring our little hall parties and outings."

"This is Carl Reinbold, works here at the hospital," Jill says.

"I'm very pleased to meet you." Dr. Cho nods at Carl, takes his wife's arm and walks briskly toward the door.

"His wife looks like a China doll," Carl says.

"Yes, he came to the US from China for his education and then sent for her when he got his job as Medical Superintendent here. They have two of the cutest kids you'll ever see. She doesn't speak English very well beyond the basic niceties," Jill says.

"It must be hard for her living on the hospital grounds."

"I think it is. Their house is connected by the tunnels. Rumor has it they've had a couple of uninvited guests."

"I heard that, too. Grapevine."

"I want to tell you how sorry I am about Judy," she says. "I don't know what to say. How are you doing, Carl."

"Not so good. Can't sleep."

"I'm sure you miss her."

"Yup, I miss her. I sure do." He shakes his head as he neatens the stacks of napkins.

We finally get sick of hanging back and push onto the dance floor. We form a circle and dance the Pony to a song that vaguely resembles *Bad Moon Rising*. I notice Carl smile as he watches us clowning on the floor.

After several dances I sit at the end of the refreshment table and watch the dancers. Raylene Cline, one of the social workers, comes up behind Carl and I hear her say, "Carl, do you have just a moment?"

"Yup, sure do."

"Sorry to call you away at a social event, Carl, but I want you to report to Hall 6 first thing tomorrow morning."

"What's the problem?"

"Happened a couple hours ago. Another patient attack on staff."

"What happened?"

"Steve Phillipon was sitting at the desk catching up on his paperwork. Of course, the patients were all doped up, locked in their rooms. He told me it felt as if somebody was watching him. He got up and looked around a couple of times, nothing seemed out of place. He had a file open on his desk when a drop of water fell onto the page. He looked up to find a patient drooling from the ceiling."

"What?" Carl says.

"I don't have all the details, how he got up there. But he was wedged in between the steam pipes and the ceiling. When Joe looked up, the patient said, *I've been watching you. They told me to*

90

kill you. He pushed the emergency alarm as the patient sprang down. It took a couple of minutes for the attendants to arrive, but by that time, the patient had him by the throat. Could've killed him."

"How in heck did the patient manage to get up there without somebody seeing him? What about night check?"

"Don't know. They're looking into it."

"Steve okay?"

"Pretty shaken up. I wonder if you can meet with him and be a support person for him as he recovers."

"I'm not exactly a good example of how to recover from an attack," Carl says.

"I think you could be helpful, Carl. Would you be willing to meet with us in my office tomorrow morning?"

"I guess."

"I'm going to recommend that Steve talk to somebody who's walked in his shoes, so to speak. He may or may not want the help."

"Sure, I can talk to him if you want, if the guy thinks it's helpful."

Chapter 21

THE OBSERVER   *June 1, 1969*

Page 10
SELF RESPECT
Some people are walking around the hospital
looking like vagabonds. There is no reason not to
be neat and clean. Ladies, please do not show up
at the canteen or events with your slip showing or
your lingerie straps sticking out from your dress.
Don't look like a common streetwalker. Have a
little self respect.

At Heidi's urging, I make a trip to the emporium in the basement of the patient's library looking for summer clothes. "I want to go upstairs after. Dr. Murray approved a library card for me." I sort through the swimsuits.

"I'll go up with you. Do you need a card for magazines?"

"Not sure."

"I'll be over there, lookin' for shorts."

"I'm going to try on a swimsuit, if I can find one." I hold up a purple one-piece with a pleated skirt. They all look like old lady suits. A far cry from my bikini—not really a bikini, but a two-piece Jeff talked me into buying. I smile when I think about how he raved about me in that suit. I have to admit, I felt pretty sexy in it. But I hadn't worn it since Alexander was born. Jeff didn't understand why, but I did—I'm a mother now. I put the suit down. Used to be a mother.

Heidi and I head upstairs to the patient's library with our brown bags stuffed with clothes. "I just want to get a couple of books. I shouldn't be long," I tell Heidi.

"Our passes are good until two o'clock. I'll check out the magazines."

The library is huge, a scant fifteen or twenty rows of bookcases standing in the middle. The shelves are almost empty. I make my way along the first row, run my finger down the spines of the books. I pull out *The Adventures of Huckleberry Finn* and flip through it. I'd read it in sixth grade. I meander through the bookcases, pulling out a book here and there. I decide to re-read *Wuthering Heights* and take it up to the desk. Heidi waits by the door. She points at the ceiling.

When I look up, high above me the domed ceiling glitters with a wide gold inlay border, circling a giant fresco of angels sitting among clouds, looking down from the heavens. Astonished, I drop my book.

"What's the matter?" Heidi asks.

"That mural ..."

"Cool, huh?"

"See that angel with his finger pointed up?"

"Over there?" Heidi points.

"No, the one toward the edge. He's smiling."

"Yeah."

"That's Alexander."

Later that week, I walk to the canteen for cigarettes and I notice the maple branches birthing small brown nodules with tightly closed yellow buds. I love spring, but I can't help thinking about Alexander, how he loved to play outside and ride his trike. Beyond the lawns, wild flowers dot the hillside behind the fire house, popping up through remnants of snow. I see Alexander's smiling face, holding up a bouquet of wildflowers, the stems barely peeking out from the bottom of his fist. Twilight still comes early and tints the sky chartreuse. Flocks of starlings circle for their night roosts among the trees. Foot traffic is heavy; the canteen just reopened after months of renovation. I spot the Lobster crossing the courtyard, probably on her way to her break.

I've heard the Lobster grumble and complain the entire time the canteen was closed. Rumor has it that starting the Tuesday after Memorial Day, Doris Lobsinger orders an ice cream sandwich and a Coke every day until Labor Day. In the winter, she walks through the tunnels to order hot coffee and a slice of cherry pie. I notice the Lobster's tight uniform. Her waistband measures years of breaks.

The canteen buzzes with staff crowded around the soda fountain counter, some seated on the coveted red vinyl swivel stools, others standing behind them. The room is thick with cigarette smoke and chatter. I stand by the window, smoking a cigarette, waiting for an attendant to ask me to leave. Patients are allowed to purchase items in the canteen, but we are not allowed to loiter.

I watch the Lobster standing in line for her order, scanning the tables for a seat. Carol, an attendant from Hall 9, motions her over. The Lobster balances her drink and ice cream, plops down at the table with other staff from Halls 5, 9 and 19. I stand about two feet from the table. I turn my back to them and listen. It's a great way to find out what's going on around here. Listen to staff conversations.

"Okay. I got a story for you." The Lobster pauses to swig back a thick Coke bottle. "Yesterday one of the retards on Hall 9, you know her, Carol ...Marge. She comes up missing from her walk outside. Supposed to start her work shift and she's nowhere to be found. Around three o'clock, she strolls in with her skirt on backwards." She smiles, looks around the group. A couple of the aides chuckle.

"Well, you know the punch line. She's back at it. It's spring and she's spreading her legs out in the Soap House for any staffer that comes along."

"The old Rag and Soap House on *Yellow Drive*?" Dr. Murray asks.

"That would be the *Toap House*. When we know she's been out having sex, we just say, *Hey Marge, been out to the Toap House?*" The Lobster gulps her coke. The others stare into their coffee mugs.

"This is Marge from Hall 9?" Dr. Murray asks.

"Yeah Marge, the retard with the harelip."

"She's having sex with staff members in the Soap House?"

"That's what they say."

"Marge has the mental ability of a five year old. She's a child. She's being raped by staff members? "

"Well, now wait a minute. Nobody's forcing her, she likes it."

"That's ridiculous. As I said, mentally, she's a child."

"Ah, well …I don't know that much about it. It's just kinda' like a rumor. Ah, I don't really even know if it's true."

Dr. Murray shoves back her chair and slaps her napkin down on the table. "I'm going to check into this."

So that was it. I smash out my cigarette and leave. As I walk back, I think about Marge. Dr. Murray is right, we all think of her as a little girl, so innocent and loving. Damn it.

Chapter 22

THE OBSERVER   *June 15, 1969*

Page 3

SUMMER CARNIVAL JUNE 28^(TH)
Plans for the Summer Carnival are well underway.
Volunteers are still needed to set up. Activities
include: dunk tank, three-legged race, shot-put,
penny scramble for the kids, high-jump, egg toss,
and ball roll for the women. Booths will sell
popcorn and candy. Everybody come on out and
have some summer fun!

Good afternoon," Dr. Murray says. "I walked across the grounds today — the flower beds are gorgeous. Do any of you work in the gardens?"

"Isabel and I do."

"Great work." Dr. Murray sits in the last empty chair in the circle.

I've never seen the doctor look so healthy, relaxed. Her cheeks flushed against a deep tan and scores of freckles sit elbow to elbow on her face. Her hair is held off her neck by a leather barrette, damp wisps surrounding her head. "I hope you girls are getting outside. It's so beautiful up here in the summer, isn't it? Who would like to start today?"

"I'd like to start," Estee jumps in.

"Go ahead."

"I just want to tell you all how much I appreciate your support during my relapse. It's been a month now. I ...I'm getting back to my old self."

"I'm glad you're doing so well, Estee," Dr. Murray says.

"I don't have visitors, so I need all your support."

"Can your family visit?" Beth asks.

"They all live in the city, New York City. My grandma writes to me, though."

"Now what happened to your mom?" Isabel asks.

"I guess she moved to California, nobody knows where she is. My dad brought me up here to the hospital, but he's moved now, too. I don't really know where."

"You've shared that your mother is mentally ill, Estee. Do you know what her diagnosis is?"

"Paranoid Schizophrenic."

"Do you remember her, before her illness?"

"From old pictures, mostly. My mom was so pretty. Before they went out to the clubs, my dad danced her around the living room, spun her around, they both laughed. She was so happy. Then she got sick."

"What do you remember?"

"Well, I remember my mom would always pick me up at my grandma's after work. One day she just didn't show up. Everybody panicked; all the relatives went out looking for her. They called the police."

"Was she arrested?"

"Not that time. I guess my dad found her in a nightclub with some strange men. When they got home, my mother screamed and threw things around, tried to bite and kick my dad. It was pretty scary. She went in the hospital the next day."

"I worry about my kids," Autumn says. "They remember what happened. It must have been so terrifying for them. They probably felt like you did, Estee — scared, you know."

"My mom came home from the hospital, but she couldn't work. She slept most of the time. Then, she'd start getting happy again, laughing and joking. Later I'd find out she stopped taking her medication. Pretty soon she'd stopped sleeping, called people up on the phone all hours of the night ... My mom had electro shock," Estee says. "They almost gave her a lobotomy."

"Sounds like she was pretty sick," Dr. Murray says.

"Eventually, she'd get all dressed up and leave the house and we wouldn't be able to find her. A lot of times, the police either brought her home or arrested her for indecent exposure or disorderly conduct. My dad stayed through three hospitalizations, then he left."

"Who took care of you?" Beth asks.

"My grandma. She lived in the same building. My mom was in and out of Bellevue. By junior high I was pretty much on my own."

"It must have been so confusing for you," Dr. Murray says.

"I just never knew whether she'd be there when I got home from school, what kind of shape she'd be in. When she started bringing men home, I'd stay with my grandma."

"My kids don't have a father either," Autumn says.

"Would you like to talk about it?"

"I'll try. Lord knows, it's on my mind."

"Go ahead, Autumn."

"Well, that night. The night he came over drunk. The night it happened. Like I said, Jim started losing it, getting madder and madder. We were in the kitchen. I sent the kids to their rooms. He was on me before I knew what happened. He knocked me down and kicked me. When I got up, he grabbed me by the hair and pushed me into the bedroom."

"Oh, no," Heidi says.

"He, he ...raped me." Autumn pushes the tissue against her eyelids. "I looked up. The kids were in the doorway." She snorts, gasps behind her hands.

"You must have been terrified," Dr. Murray says.

"Yes, yes I was." Autumn takes a deep breath. "After he was done, he held on to my wrist, made me lay there naked in front of my kids." She reaches back for her long ponytail, bites the end of it. "The kids just stood there in the doorway for the longest time ...like statues. Each one of them locked eyes with me and never wavered. We all knew what this was about ...we'd been through it so many times." Autumn starts to cry. She motions to Beth for another tissue.

"For god's sake," I say, "how can a human being act like that?"

"Jim was a monster," Autumn says. "A real monster."

"There was a guy at work like that ...well, not as bad as your husband, I guess. But I could've killed him," Isabel says.

"Why?" I asked.

"You don't know me drunk."

"No, but ..."

"I was miserable. What's the female name for jerk?"

"Bitch?" Heidi offers.

"Yeah, bitch ...a real selfish bitch."

"Do you know why you started drinking, Isabel?" Dr. Murray asks.

"Not really. Neither of my parents drank. Drinking was forbidden in our house. I was only eighteen when I married Bob. Then we had the boys, both of us working really hard to get our house. I guess I was too busy to drink."

"What changed?"

"I ...I've thought about this a lot." Isabel crosses her arms. "I started feeling old and washed up. Day after day at the plant. Boys were teenagers, didn't need me much. Bob and I sat around watching TV."

"Does Bob drink?" Heidi asks. "My mom and dad used to drink and do drugs together all the time. How's that for togetherness?"

"Bob drinks a beer once in awhile. He's not a drunk. I can't blame him."

"I don't wanna hurt your feelings, Isabel," Heidi says, "but my mom wanted drugs, not me. Same with my dad. Maybe your boys figured you'd rather drink than be with them."

"You didn't hurt my feelings. I already know what I did and I feel like crap about it."

"My dad, the old drunk, ruined my childhood, too," Autumn says. "But I have to say he would probably be mean anyway, beer or no beer. Besides, he'd never get help."

"This is my third time here. Believe me, I'm trying," Isabel says.

"You're all here in group to support each other. All of you have problems."

"I feel so embarrassed. So weak," I say. "What's the matter with me that I can't just handle things like other people?"

"You had a significant trauma, Luanne," Dr. Murray says.

"Holy crap, Lu. I don't know what I'd do if one of my kids died," Isabel says.

"I …it …Thanks," I whisper.

"I don't know what I'd do without my kids either," Autumn says. "God, I hope they'll be okay. Will they, Dr. Murray?"

Chapter 23

I edge the flower bed with a hand spade. "I found a patient passed out on the lawn yesterday. Thought she was dead at first—just overmedicated."

"They're lying all over the place. Jeez, I never even knew about places like this until I came here the first time," Isabel says. She pulls the weeds from the dry soil.

"In high school ...I think it was my freshman year, Sodality Club. Sister announced the freshmen would teach catechism to the people at the State Home and Training School."

"What's that?"

"Home for the retarded. Marlene Davis raises her hand and says, *Sister, how will we teach crazy people? How will they understand us?* We all cringed. Sister didn't like it when students talked out of turn. So, Sister says, *These people are retarded, Marlene. If you want to teach crazy people, you'll have to go up to Traverse* City.

"Later I asked my older sister about it, and she told me about the nuthouse up north. I remember that's what she called it—the nuthouse."

"It's embarrassing," Isabel says.

"You know, after the spring dance, I got to thinking about the retarded guy who asked me to dance. Man, this seems like another life, but he reminded me of the pupil I had when I taught catechism at the State Home."

"Yeah?"

"We went on a tour first—saw freaky-looking babies in iron cages with mismatched heads. Some of their heads were pointed, some way too tiny for the body, and some enormous like watermelons."

"I don't get it. Cages? They took you freshman kids in there?"

"I guess they were metal beds, but they had sides and a top, like a square cage. I remember my friend, Barb, her face went gray and she started to cry. Sister told her to go back to the van. I wanted to go with her, but I stayed frozen in the doorway with the rest."

"That's kind of heavy for a kid."

"But I remember thinking, I guess if you're retarded, you don't have to go to purgatory or limbo, you go straight to heaven."

"You Catholics—bizarre."

"Oh, that's not the bizarre part. I'll never forget the first night of teaching. I was scared to death. I remember Sister gave us a last minute pep talk. The retarded pupils filed in. Sister stood a red-headed guy in front of me. He was short but stocky, his blazing hair lumped and swirled into a permanent bed head."

"Cute."

"Sister introduced us—Reggie was his name. He was *very* glad to see me. He says, *I love you, Luanne,* and gave me this long hug."

"He was affectionate, like Marge on the Hall."

"Yeah, but remember, I was a kid. I dreaded Wednesday nights. Reggie gawked around, snapped at his bleeding cuticles. His stubby teeth looked like kernels of corn. He smelled bad, and he jumped on every opportunity to give me a hug. Me, barely a teenager, and Reggie a grown man."

"Yeah, I see what you mean."

"One week, I was going through the lesson. I talked slow like Sister told us. Reggie began to shake and thump under the table. Obviously, something was wrong, but I didn't know what, so I just kept teaching. The bouncing and racket caught the eye of Tim McKinney who was teaching at the other end of the table. He left the room and came back with Sister Thaddeus on his heels. Reggie shook, made low moaning sounds, had his head down on the table."

"Oh, oh. I see where this is going."

"I sat paralyzed on the other side, staring at him. I remember thinking he had spazzed into a fit. I was so relieved Tim McKinney had the sense to go get Sister. Sister Thaddeus shot across the room like she had roller skates under her habit." I smile, Isabel throws back her head and laughs.

"She took Reggie by the arm and escorted him from the lunch room. After the door clicked shut, we all looked at each other. Nobody said a word."

"Well, what happened?"

"Tim McKinney sat down in Reggie's seat. He leaned across the table and whispered, *Jeez, did you see that woody?*"

"Oh my god." Isabel slapped her knee.

"It's funny now, but it wasn't then. I remember I couldn't sleep at night worrying about it. As if it was the worst thing …I didn't realize how bad things could get."

"Yeah, when you're a kid your world is pretty small." Isabel picks up a limp stalk. "Does this petunia have a worm? One whole side of the plant is gone." She flops the wilted purple bloom back and forth in her hand.

"Something got at it. Who knows, one of the patients could have picked it, then just left it here." I scratch lightly around the base of the plants and sprinkle a pinch of dry fertilizer into the soil. I love getting out in the morning sun, digging around in the dirt. It reminds me of my dad. He loved his yard and his flowers.

He's been gone now for six years, and I miss him. I remember the way his eyes twinkled when he laughed and how his old work pants bagged out in the seat. He was always busy doing something, a real handyman. I always wanted to be just like him, building things, gardening, enjoying the outdoors.

Life was easy then, before Dad died. I have to smile when I think about my first building project, a clubhouse. I was only nine, so Dad wouldn't let me use the saw. I nailed different lengths of lumber together in a shaky square, tossed feed bags across the boards for the roof. Mom looked out the kitchen window, shook her head. The clubhouse lasted until the first rain.

I finish fertilizing, begin deadheading. We are working just below the porches of Hall 11 where patients crowd behind the heavy mesh, smoking cigarettes. I hear an attendant yell, "Get down from there right now." I look up to see a woman clinging halfway up the mesh like a monkey in the zoo. I pinch at the plants, trying to block out the commotion above me. The green thumb I inherited from Dad is good therapy.

"Jeff is coming to visit."

"Oh, yeah? Looking forward to it?"

"Not really."

"Why?"

"I don't know. I haven't seen him much, and when I do see him, we're like strangers. Feels really weird. I met Jeff when I was fifteen and he was seventeen. We grew up together. Everything changed when Alexander died."

"Well, maybe you two can get reacquainted, marriage counseling or something." Isabel puts her hands behind her on the grass, leans back.

"Maybe," I say half-heartedly.

"I cheated on Bob."

"You did?" I keep pinching and tossing the spent blooms into a pile.

"I changed after I got transferred to afternoons. The guys on the line were really fun. A group stopped at the Red Horse every night after work for beers, guys and girls both. The Horse had a band and I actually got up and danced."

"Keep going."

"Anyway, I started staying out later and later, lost interest in Bob and the boys. I started drinking pretty heavy."

"Is that when you came up here?"

"Yeah. Well, I started the affair with my foreman. This sounds awful, but it was no big deal, like when somebody asks if you want another drink and it seems so easy just to say, *Oh what the hell, why not?*"

"Really?"

"I know, I know, it sounds bad."

"So then you came up here?"

"Had to. I kept getting into trouble at work; mad all the time, drunk."

"You got better then?"

"No. After I got out, I was back drinking within a month. I pushed a girl on the line into moving equipment."

"On purpose?"

"Got mad. Just out of control. Foreman was a big flirt, and that day he hit on her. My union steward got me treatment again. It was either that or lose my job."

"Back here again, right?"

"Up here for the second time. I'm not proud of it, but I got into trouble again after that. The thing with my foreman was over, but I couldn't get that through my head. I don't know what got into me, but I put a dead cat under the wipers of his truck and left a terrible note. Shit, I don't know what I was thinking. My union steward tried to help, but they fired me. Twenty-nine years at the plant. I was a year from early retirement, Luanne."

"A dead cat?"

"Yeah ...well, it was run over in the parking lot. I was drunk. Seemed like a good idea at the time."

"Are you over the guy now?"

"Yes, I am. But I need to tell Bob the truth. If Bob forgives me, I think I could make it work. I really don't want a divorce."

"Maybe you should talk about this in group. I have no idea what to tell you."

"Yeah, I know. It's just so embarrassing."

"Everybody makes mistakes. I started going steady with Jeff at fifteen. I never had much of a chance to see anybody else. By the time I was a senior in high school, I had an itch to date Vaughn Lawler. He was always flirting with me, asking me out, teasing me about getting rid of Jeff. I kissed him once."

"I never cheated on Bob before, never even thought about it. I can't blame it on the booze. Could've been a mid-life crisis or something."

"Maybe."

"About ready to wrap it up here?" Isabel repositions herself onto her knees and begins dropping the hand tillers and planting spades into the pail.

Chapter 24

I look up at Building 50, the tall windows of the abandoned wings like the empty eyes of ghosts.

"Sad isn't it?" Carl walks up behind me with a pail of garden spades.

"Oh, hi. You think it's sad?'

"It's the end of something. I helped dismantle the old girl, packed up remnants of her early splendor, faded carpets and chipped china, took them to storage. Burned a lot of history in a pit out behind the barns."

"I guess you've been here a long time, huh?"

Carl eases down onto the lawn next to me. "My wife and I started here about the same time. My dad had his heart set on me takin' over the family farm, but I applied here, just on a whim mind you. I been here ever since."

"No kidding."

"How are you doing?"

"Maybe you can give me some advice."

"What's that?"

"Should these be thinned? They don't seem as big as the other ones."

"Yup, I think that would do it. Can't grow, too cramped."

"I hate to pull out perfectly good plants."

"Well, here. Let me help. They can use them plants in the other beds." Carl tries to kneel, but ends up sitting on one hip, stretching his legs out on the grass.

"Somebody told me there used to be a big farm here and the patients worked on it."

"Yup, yup. It was really somethin'. That's why I applied here. I wanted to marry Judy and have a place of our own. The pay was good, and I got to breed topnotch milkers. Blue ribbon, every one of 'em.

"Dairy cows, then?"

"Yup. We had the best senior herd sire anywhere around."

"I think I saw his grave over there by the barns."

"Well, he ain't really buried there. It's like a memorial to the ol' boy. Admiral Walker Colanthra. Reminds me of the time ..." Carl takes off his hat, wipes his forehead, and laughs. "There was a lot of shenanigans goin' on around here then. Well, still is, I guess. Just once, I broke the rules ...You won't tell on me now, will ya?" He winks at me. "I smuggled out a little bull juice from the Admiral. Judy's hands jumped onto her cheeks when I pulled that vial of semen from my pocket. *Lookie here. Milk of the gods,* I told her. I can hear her now, *Carl, are you out of your mind? We'll both lose our jobs. It's taken me five years to become a nurse supervisor.* She was pretty riled up. I tried to tell her the ol' Admiral isn't gonna miss it. Well, long story short, the spunk didn't take. I think God was tryin' to tell me somethin'."

"That's a great story."

"I loved that job. One of my lowest days, nothing like losing Judy of course, was the day the dairy operation closed up. I watched as the last of the heifers were loaded on the truck for auction. I tell you, I reached in my back pocket, snapped the dirt from my bandana, wiped my nose and eyes, stared down the road until the last puff of dust disappeared over the horizon. And I wasn't ashamed of crying either, not a bit."

"Why did they close the farm?"

"Some damn ruling came down from the State, ruined everything. Excuse my language."

"Oh."

"I guess they liked me well enough. I started out as a farm hand and in five years, I was supervisin' the whole thing. Let me tell you, it was A-number one. You could eat off the floor in those barns. And the architecture—you don't see that anymore. Barreled ceilings suspended by arched maple beams. Every milker knew her own stanchion. When they came in from grazing, they filed in like they were finding their favorite pew for Sunday services. I loved walking down the rows of chewing heads, the mooing and snorting of the old girls as the milking machines hummed and slurped."

"My grandpa was a dairy farmer. But his barn was just a plain one. I always thought the cows were cute."

"I never thought of them that way, but you're right, they are cute, specially the little ones. Like I said, I never loved any job more than that one. After my accident, I did a lot of jobs."

"Is that what's wrong with your leg? An accident?"

"Well, not exactly…Oops, there's the bell. We'll have to talk another time. Holy moley, time flies.

"Was that the lunch bell? Thanks for talking to me, Carl. I love your stories. Here." I stand up and extend my hand. "Grab my hand."

"Thanks. Darn leg. Worse every day."

"Walking to 50?"

"Yup. Canteen."

"Hall 9 for me." I gather up my tools and walk beside Carl, chatting about how the planting season in Traverse City compares to mid-Michigan where I grew up.

Carl and I stop at the back entrance. "I'll be seeing you."

"Probably tomorrow."

I come to group late, my t-shirt soaked with sweat, hair plastered to my forehead.

"You're late, Luanne," Dr. Murray says.

"Five minutes," I answer. "I was talking to Carl Reinbold, my supervisor. Sorry." I wipe my forehead and sit down.

"Just this once. Next time, I'll have to make note of it in your file."

"Thanks. It won't happen again. I was outside, pulling weeds. With Isabel on home leave, I'm falling behind."

"You work too hard," Heidi says.

"It's fun, really."

"Who wants to start?"

"Five guys attacked me …I got gangbanged," Heidi blurts out. She brings her hands to her face. "It's just so hard to say it."

"Go ahead, Heidi," Dr. Murray says.

"Bastards. I …I knew one of them." Heidi sniffs. "Real nice guy, I thought. Can I pick 'em or what?" She shakes her head.

"Anyway, Kurt told me he wanted to party. We were drinking …he said he knew where we could get some good grass, maybe acid. Told me to meet him at the beach. I live in Benton Harbor, near Lake Michigan. That's where it happened." Heidi reaches for a tissue.

"He was a friend?" Beth asks.

"A friend? He was a party buddy, a guy I'd screwed a few times for drugs."

"Oh."

"See, that's what pisses me off. Just because I'm a whore, don't mean I don't have feelings. I can still get raped, ya' know. They got me high, alright? Then they stripped me naked, held me down while they each took a turn. Five guys."

"Of course, you have feelings, I didn't mean that," Beth says.

Heidi blows her nose. "I know, I know," she says. "They raped me …And was that enough? No. Some smartass got the idea to shave my head and body. I guess so I'd look like fresh meat. Then a couple of 'em screwed me again …They left me on the beach …like …like a dead carp or something." She works to catch her breath as her chest rises and falls in short jerks.

I'm stunned. "I'm so sorry, Heidi. I don't know what to say."

"You were a victim of a brutal crime," Dr. Murray says, her eyes glistening. "I'm so happy you're still alive. You will make it, Heidi. I promise you."

"Could somebody else talk?" Heidi asks.

During a long pause, I'm thinking I should try to share something, but my problems seem so small compared to Heidi's. No, this isn't a contest. What I want to talk about is important. "Well, I have a letter from Jeff I'd like to share." I reach into my jeans pocket and pull out a crinkled letter, unfold it, start to read.

May 23, 1969

Dear Luanne-

You seemed really depressed when I saw you last month. I'm sorry I haven't been up there as much lately. I've been working a lot. It doesn't seem like you're getting better. I drive all the way up there and you barely talk to me. I tried to give you a kiss last time, and you didn't even kiss me back. It doesn't feel like you love me anymore. It's been very hard for me since you've been in the hospital. I'm coming up to visit you June 5th. I hope you're feeling better. Love, Jeff

"If I'm well, he loves me. If I'm not ..."

"I don't think that's what he's saying," Beth says. "Sounds more like he's asking if *you* love him."

"But don't you see? That's what he does. He tries to make it about me, my feelings. I don't even know right now how I feel. I'm sick."

"Did you kiss him back?" Heidi asks.

"I think so. I don't remember."

"Do you love him?"

"Probably. I don't have many good feelings about anything right now. I'm scared. If I don't get well pretty soon, I'm afraid he'll leave me."

"No, that's not it," Autumn says. "He's just lonely, needs a little reassurance."

"I guess." What about my loneliness?

"Just try to get well. You can't worry about him," Beth says. "Just tell him you love him. It'll be okay."

I don't really believe Beth. What does she know about marriage? She's never even had a date. Jeff and I had a great marriage until Alexander got sick. "I hope it's a nice day. I'd like to take Jeff out on the grounds, just the two of us. Really talk."

"Must be nice," Autumn says. "They won't let me out unless I'm supervised. Nobody wants to babysit me."

"Maybe if you were willing to share today, Autumn, that might help in getting you off the restricted list," Dr. Murray says.

"Hey! It sounds like your tryin' to bribe her. She don't have to talk if she don't want to," Heidi says.

"Of course not. I encourage all of you to share. It helps you recover."

"That's okay. I'll go."

"You told us about that day. The day Jim came over drunk and became violent. He raped you in front of the children," Dr. Murray says.

"Yeah. We were on the bed. He was …done with me. Finally he started snoring and I could feel his grip loosen. I eased my wrist out from between his fingers and got up. I grabbed my robe, motioned the kids to back away from the doorway. Once I got out of the bedroom, I whispered to them to go to the neighbor's house and stay there until I came for them. They didn't want to leave, but they did what they were told." Autumn rubs her hands on her thighs, rocks in her seat.

"Please go on."

"Once the kids were safe, I went to the kitchen counter. I opened the utensil drawer. The poultry shears were right on top. I went back into the bedroom …oh, sweet Jesus …I …I sized up Jim's chest, and stabbed him with all my might." Her face went rigid and her eyes clouded over. "That was it. He opened his eyes and said, *you killed me*, and then he died. I keep seeing Jim's eyes pop open. His voice is so calm. *You killed me*, over and over. I don't even have to be asleep. He comes into my head, y*ou killed me*."

"Just try to stay with the pain, Autumn. Don't be afraid of it," Dr. Murray reassures her. Autumn cries softly. I feel the horror she's lived through. Sniffs and coughs around the group make me think others do, too.

"I wish I could've killed the bastards who raped me," Heidi says.

"I didn't know what I was doing," Autumn says. "It was like I was another person or something. I hate myself for doing it. If it weren't for the kids …"

"You did something violent, Autumn. I understand why you did it, but that's why you are on restriction. You're making good progress. It won't be long."

"Thank you, Dr. Murray."

"I'm in the same boat," Estee says. "I can't go out unsupervised either. But it's because I'm on to them."

"Yeah?" Heidi rolls her eyes.

"I know what's going on."

"What?" Beth asks.

"Sending radio beams to the star planets. I can see them at night through my window. They're coming from behind the old barns."

"I see."

"One of these days, I'll get out on the grounds. I know right where to head."

"Where?" I ask.

"Goddamn it, don't you listen? Behind the barns, I told you!"

"Okay, Estee. I'm sorry, I didn't hear you."

"Maybe you're in on it."

"Now that's not true." I try to calm Estee. I don't want to see her go back to Hall 5.

"I saw you and that attendant guy."

"Just now? Outside?"

"Yes. Walking, talking. I saw you through the window."

"That's Carl Reinbold, the gardening supervisor. Nurse Judy's husband."

"Oh my god. They got Nurse Judy, Luanne. Now they're after you."

"Okay, okay. I'll be careful."

Estee swings her head to glance over her shoulder. "You can't be too careful."

Chapter 25

I recognize him immediately, even from the back. Jeff stands looking out the west windows on the far side of the visitors' room, his hands crammed into the pockets of his Levis. Jeff loves summer and it shows. His hair is longer and sun streaked. When he turns, with his dark tan and the blond highlights in his mustache, he's handsome in a surfer sort of way. I feel a tingle. I walk up beside him, put my hand on his waist.

"Hi." He gives me a quick hug. "You look great. Wow, you seem so much better, Lu."

"Thanks." I feel my cheeks go red. I feel safe, almost childlike, standing in the nook his arm makes around my shoulder. "I thought we could walk around the grounds while we visited."

"Well, yeah, sure. It's a beautiful day. Is that allowed?"

"Yes. I've earned privileges since you were here last, a ground pass." I smile up at him as we walk side-by-side toward the nurses' station, close but not touching. We stop and I pick up two passes. The attendant unlocks the door and holds it open for us.

Since spring arrived, I've spent as much time outdoors as I can. No matter how many times I stand at the open doorway, I always close my eyes briefly, take a deep breath. The sun is high in the sky by the time we step off the porch. Jeff slides his aviator sunglasses on.

We stroll along the walkway under the large oaks, a warm breeze turns the leaves. Colorful finches glide on the air currents, chirp loudly as they dive for winterberries. I proudly point out my gardening masterpieces as Jeff and I make our way through the grounds toward the Willow Lake reflecting pool.

Jeff brings me up to date on what the family is doing, gossip about our friends, reports on the Vietnam War. Danny Ortez, one of my favorite dance partners in high school, has been killed. I think back to three years ago when Jeff received his draft notice. He could have been over there, even killed in the war, but he was granted an eleventh-hour 3A deferment when Alexander was born. Jeff always mentions the war as if he thinks about it often, as if he has to remind himself he's safe. Is he safe? Could they take him now that Alexander's gone?

"Luanne, there's something I have to tell you."

"Okay." I straighten on the bench, turn toward him, bracing for any news that might be bad. He faces the pond as if he is addressing the ducks.

"I had to sell the house."

"What? Why didn't you talk to me?" I slump back on the bench like a rag doll.

"It just happened. Dad was worried, and I agree with him, that the neighborhood was going downhill."

"Oh my god," I whisper.

"We needed the money to help pay the hospital bills, Luanne."

"Where are you living?"

"I got a little apartment in a complex out by the mall. It's a lot cheaper, just a studio."

"Where's Alexander's stuff?" Panic burns through my body. The last thing I remember of home is closing the door to Alexander's room. Now I feel as if I'm floating in space, with no connection to anything.

"I packed up everything. I had to."

"I ...don't understand. How could you sell my home out from under me? Dr. Murray and I talked ...talked about how you and I need to pack up Alexander's things together. I guess I won't get that chance." I stare past the pond into the blurry distance.

"I'm sorry. Six months now ...you barely speak to me. You still don't remember things ...I'm just trying to survive, Lu."

"I know, I know."

"Do you even love me anymore?" He rubs his hands up and down his thighs.

"Maybe this isn't the best time to ask me that."

"Is there anything else you're upset with me about, Lu?"

"Other than selling my house without telling me? No."

"I filed for divorce."

"Okay."

"Is that all you can say?"

"What am I supposed to say? You put me in here, now you're leaving."

"I don't know what to do. I don't know if you'll ever come home. I said I filed. Things could still work out between us."

"I don't know how."

"I talked to a friend at work and she said I need to think of myself, my own survival."

"She?"

"Yeah, a girl on the line. She's nobody, a casual friend. I've been totally faithful."

He sounds a bit too self righteous. "I see." My heart bangs in my chest. We sit silently and stare out over the glassy pool. I search my mind for something to say, but I can't focus. I leave my body. "I guess I'd better get back."

"Okay." He stands up immediately. We walk along the front of Building 50, toward the visitors' parking lot.

"You don't have to come back with me. Why don't you just give me your pass, then you can get right in your car and leave." I put out my hand, palm up.

"Lu ...Luanne, I'm sorry. I don't know what to do." He reaches into his shirt pocket, hands me the pass.

"Hell, you're the sane one and you still don't know what to do, Jeff? You never do." I turn, hurry up the path, eyes riveted on the ground. When I hear the old Mercury fire up, I clench my fists. As soon as I round the corner of the building, I slide onto the grass, my hot cheeks against its cool comfort. I lie there under a locust tree.

"You all right?" Carl reaches down and touches my back.

I turn over and sit up. "I think so." I pull a Kleenex from my pocket, blow my nose.

"What is it?" Carl sits down beside me.

"My husband ...he's leaving me." I release a jerky sigh.

"Sorry." He picks at the grass.

"Why does everybody leave?"

"Don't seem right."

"No," I say. "How do you get over it?"

"Don't know. Maybe you never do."

"Did you? I mean, your baby, and then your wife."

"Baby?"

"Nurse Judy told me she lost her baby."

"She told you that?"

"I'm sorry. Maybe I shouldn't have said anything."

"My wife must have liked you. To be talking about things like that."

"Yes, I think so. She was kind to me."

"You gonna be all right then?"

I watch Carl limp down the walkway, reach into his back pocket, pull out a white handkerchief. As he disappears behind the north wing, I lie on my back so I won't look like I've fallen in a heap, put my hands under my head, cross my ankles, and close my eyes. The grass tickles the back of my arms, the soft humming of bees takes me to another place—a place where children don't die and loved ones don't throw you away when you're on the fritz.

Chapter 26

Have a seat, Luanne."

"Thanks."

"Well, how did your visit with Jeff go?"

"Good."

"How is he doing?"

"Good."

"Would you like to talk about his visit?"

"No, not really."

I take a drink of water, shift in my seat, play with my hair, look out the window.

"Okay, what would you like to talk about?"

"Jean, on our hall, is shitting all over the place."

"Yes, Luanne, I know about that."

"Can't you do something about it?"

"We're working on it."

"This place is unbelievable." I shake my head.

"Did Jeff say that?"

"Jeff? *I'm* saying it. This place is gross, unfit for human beings ...it's like a nightmare. I ...I ...want ..." My voice grows thin as I began to cry. "I ... Why ...why, can't he love me?"

"What happened, Luanne?"

"He's ...leaving ...me." I bring my hands to my face and wail. "I'm all alone."

"Go ahead and cry, Luanne."

"Here we go again ..." I sob.

"Again?"

"My dad. Alexander. And now Jeff." I reach for a tissue. "The Kleenex box is empty."

Dr. Murray walks to her desk for another box of tissues, and when she returns, I sit straighter, try to regain my composure.

"Is this a punishment?"

"Loss is a part of life. You can't avoid it."

"Screw that."

"I didn't say it was easy."

"I hate him."

"He's let you down."

"Let me down? He's locked me up and thrown away the key. He can go back to his nice little life and I'm stuck here with the cuckoos."

"Yes?"

"What am I going to tell my family?"

"The truth."

"What's that?"

"Something like …Jeff abandoned you when you needed him most?"

"Yeah. I guess so. I just feel …so …embarrassed."

"Embarrassed?"

"A loser. Nobody …My dad …he loved me. But he died…"

"Yes. And your mom, and brothers and sisters love you."

"Yeah. I'm not as strong as I thought I was …Maybe God is testing me."

"Do you believe that?"

"I'm not sure."

"Sometimes strength is vulnerability, the ability to face challenges, pulling through difficult times."

"I guess so …a kid in my neighborhood drowned when I was little. I always wondered why."

"Sometimes things don't seem fair."

"My dad, cripe, compared to the other girls' dads, he's a saint. I have a good family. Not like the others. I feel like a big crybaby."

"You're not a crybaby."

"At my dad's funeral, I wondered how I'd get along without him. I loved him a lot. Sometimes it's still hard to believe."

"It sounds like you don't believe you're lovable."

"Lovable? Ha."

"Think about Alexander. How much you loved him and he loved you. You were a good mother. You have the capacity to love and be loved."

I cry for a long time. "Something went wrong. It couldn't have been Alexander. It must have been me." Flashes of Alexander, his eye swollen shut, a thin little gnome with tufts of fuzz where his curly blond hair used to be, smiles at his third birthday. His little white teeth look so out of place. Jeff crying and running from the room.

"It was hard to see him suffer. Just a little guy who had no chance to grow up."

"I know."

"See what I mean about God?"

"What's that?"

"Why would He give us this beautiful baby and then take him away?"

"I don't know, Luanne. I really don't know."

"Did I ever tell you how smart Alexander was? He was reading when he was two years old." I try to smile, but it hurts too much.

Chapter 27

Weall went to the concert Saturday night." I want Dr. Murray to know about Autumn's attack.

"How was it?" Dr. Murray asks.

"Great. A starry night, good friends, and *Wild Thing*. Couldn't ask for more," Isabel chuckles.

"A rock band, huh?" Dr. Murray smiles.

"You should have seen 'em dance."

"I brought it up because I'm worried about Autumn."

"Oh?" Dr. Murray looks at Autumn.

"Now why would you be worried about me, Luanne?"

"That thing with the June bugs."

"I hate the sticky bastards. Dr. Murray, those suckers were as big as poodles!"

"What happened at the concert, Autumn."

"They attacked me. The size of them, their buzzing. The sickening crunch of them under foot made my skin crawl."

"Autumn, you were shaking all over," I say. "We had to throw a blanket over you for the whole concert. When I asked you about it, you told me it was a flashback."

"Was it a flashback?" Dr. Murray asks. "Something you need to talk about?"

Autumn's eyes glaze over. "I was nine years old that summer night. My dad starts drinking when he gets up that morning. When I checked the fridge, the case was almost gone. I heard him yell, *Kids, get in the Mexican wagon before I kick all your asses. I'm ready to go. Gotta stop at the store.*

"My mom was terrified of him, we all were. Mom started grabbing our popcorn and pops, *Everybody in the car.* She muscled open the back door of our old Chevy, its rusty hinges squawking. We lined up quietly in the back seat. I sat in the middle between my younger brother and sister; it was my job to make sure they behaved themselves. The combination of beer and a captive audience might trigger one of my dad's tirades, accusing my mom of screwing the migrant workers over on the Johnson farm, or calling her a frigid bitch, a lousy mother, or a lazy deadbeat.

"He cracked open a beer, turned the key in the ignition. *Goddamn piece of shit.* The back of his neck turned red as he pumped the accelerator. Finally, the engine caught. The Chevy shook and rattled to life. *There we go. That's my girl.* He fawned over that old Chevy like he did waitresses and party store clerks. He never used that voice at home.

"We headed out to the fairgrounds. In the summer, a giant movie screen was set up outdoors and the audience sat on blankets under the stars. It was like a drive-in without cars. He slammed on the brakes. *Goddamn it. I dropped my change on the floor and it fell right through that hole. Momma, get your ass out there and pick up that money. Kids, you get out there too.* He sat behind the wheel drinking while we scoured the road, our shoulders bent, heads bowed, trying to spot the coins in the dim light. Mom called out as each car approached. *Heads up, kids—car.*

"Jimmy was only four and afraid of the dark. He went to Dad's window. *Can I come in with you, Daddy?* He sounded like he was about to cry. My dad says, *Find any money?* I heard my little brother's tiny voice. *No.* Then Dad yelled for me. *Autumn, come get your brother before I whip his butt.* I pulled Jimmy to my side and told him he could look by the street light where it wasn't so dark.

"I'd just found a nickel when I heard tires screeching. I looked up. He was lying in the intersection, under the light. Mom ran toward the corner. Jimmy had been knocked clean out of his shoes. His toe stuck out through his dirty sock. Mom made a strange chirping sound as she held Jimmy's head in her lap.

"All I could do was hug my sister, Christy, and cry as we waited for the ambulance. The June bugs were thick under the lights—slick as ice underfoot. They bumped and buzzed and stuck to my shirt, their picky legs dragging across my shoulder.

"Every spring since, I brace for the time the June bugs come out. Knowing if I'd been smarter, my little brother would still be alive."

There's a long silence before Autumn starts sobbing, pounding her thighs, pulling at her hair.

"Autumn, you did nothing wrong. You were just a kid. You did the best you could," Dr. Murray tries to sooth her, but Autumn starts screaming. The attendant escorts her out of the group room.

After she leaves, we all stare at each other. Nobody talks. Finally, I say, "Maybe I shouldn't have said anything."

"No, it's okay. You did the right thing," Isabel says.

"I know how she feels. She didn't cause her little brother to die, but she feels guilty. I do, too," I explain.

"What do you feel guilty about, Luanne?" Dr. Murray asks.

"Not saving my little boy. Letting him die."

"You did everything you could, Lu." Isabel reassures me.

Estee speaks up. "I feel guilty for being like my mother— for being crazy. I'm causing my grandma such heartache. First, her daughter, now me."

"Guilt is a powerful feeling. We all just try to do our best by people. Take responsibility for what is yours, but try to let go of the guilt," Dr. Murray says.

"I could just eat and my parents would be happy. But I won't. Is that what you mean by responsibility?"

"No. You have a disorder, Beth. But you are taking responsibility by trying to get help. I would like to break earlier today. I need to go check on Autumn."

We all filed out the door, silent.

Chapter 28

I shimmy out of my shorts, pull off my t-shirt, tug at the straps of the saggy tank suit I picked up at the emporium. Beth stands at the end of the blanket, smears lotion on her face and neck. Her peasant blouse ripples and fills with wind. She tucks it into her chinos to keep it from blowing up. She kicks off her sandals, spreads her toes in the warm sand.

"Lotion?" Beth hands me her Coppertone bottle. I thump it on my palm, squeeze out a long ribbon of lotion and spread it over my legs and arms. I fold my thin towel, stuff it under my head. I lie back, close my eyes.

I stretched the rules and forged my friends' names to the signup sheet for a picnic at the hospital park at the base of the Leelanau Peninsula. I had to, the outing is popular, took only fifteen patients at a time. We could swim, walk the beach, and have a lunch of ground meat or tuna, donated windfall apples, and Kool Aid. Beth and I tan while Isabel, Autumn, and Heidi brave the cold water of Lake Michigan.

"It's cold." Isabel's voice drifts toward me.

"You get used to it," Heidi laughs and splashes.

Miniature suns appear under my eyelids, radiate onto my face, down my neck, and into my chest. It's like being touched by a magic wand. My breathing slows, my hands go limp against the blanket. Waves lap over sand, hypnotize me.

I hear a child laughing down the beach. Alexander. No, no, no. He's gone. I can see him, before he got sick. Kicking his chubby little legs, a picture of health. Jeff dips him in the water and smiles up at me. I smile back. He turns Alexander toward me …says in a baby voice, "Look at me, Mommy."

I see Alexander sitting on the beach, bringing two sandy fingers to his mouth, scowling. My mother rushes over and wipes his mouth and fingers with a washcloth before he begins to cry. Alexander is the center of attention that day, his older cousins fill his pail each time he dumps it, covering his feet with sand, watching him wiggle his toes. Each time his piggies poke through, he reaches for them, not realizing until he makes contact, they are his.

"Here I come," Estee yells. Autumn makes strange "oop, oop" sounds as she hops along, her hands slapping the surface. Heidi sits down. "I'm staying right here in the shallow water."

The shallow water. The shallow end.

When I was a kid, I swam almost every day at the community pool. Sometimes swimming until my teeth chattered and my lips turned blue, staying in until Mom called me out to warm up. No matter how many times I went back in, I'd hear Mom hollering from the bleachers, "Luanne. Don't forget. Stay in the shallow end."

"Why?" I challenged her.

"Because if you stay in the shallow end, you won't drown."

"If I do handstands, I will."

"Don't get sassy, smarty pants," she frowned.

Stay in the shallow end—it's safe there. Mom promised me. I'd done everything right, everything she expected of me. But when the world turns upside down, there are no guarantees. Things happen …one day you're happy, then …wham. The white picket fence falls down, the house, as it turns out, is made of straw …the boogeyman comes …babies die. The rush of memories dissolve into pain. I use the techniques Dr. Murray taught me—stop the intrusive thoughts, distract myself.

It isn't working. Alexander's face. Grandparents singing happy birthday …Jeff breaking down, leaving the room. The sickening sweet smell of Puffs tissues, or was it the cake? …or death? Whimpering …

The weeks since Jeff's visit are tough. I resort to my old habits, closing down, pretending I'm fine when I'm not. I feel discarded, lost. And the realization—I still believe Alexander is coming back. Jeff sold the house. Our baby will come back and his toys will be gone — his tricycle, his Playskool bus, and all the rest. And worse yet, he won't be able to find me.

I tried to explain to Dr. Murray that, of course, I know Alexander is really gone. I know I will never rock him, feel his soft curls on my cheek. But at the same time, I expect, somehow, he will come back. *Sweat runs between my breasts. Now I'm nothing, nobody.*

Ice cold water driblets land on my chest. I sit up.

"Why didn't you come in?" Estee asks. "The water is cold, but pretty soon you're numb and you can't feel it."

I know what that feels like.

Heidi squeegees the water from her hair with her hand. "Beth, did you bring a suit, or at least shorts?"

"I may roll up my pants and wade in later."

Isabel pulls at her shorts, spreads her legs, anchors her feet into the sand while she rings water out of each leg. "I didn't plan to get my shorts all wet. Now I don't have anything to change into." She plops down on the blanket, a large wet spot growing from under her seat. "Got any snacks?"

Beth pulls a bag from her beach tote, hands it to her.

"You guys working on the float?" Pretzels bounce around against her teeth.

"I'm on home leave that week," Beth says.

"What's this float thing?" Heidi asks.

"For Cherry Festival. They make it in OT. Then they need people to help stuff it with napkins. Sometimes, patients get to dress up and ride on the float in the parade."

"I hear it's a big deal." Autumn reaches for pretzels. "The hospital won a prize last year."

"Well, rippy skippy," Heidi says. "Whadda ya' expect? We got a shit load of people standin' around with nothin' to do. Workin' on a float is probably the best thing in their life."

"Oh, we've got stuff to do, Heidi," Autumn says.

"Yeah, I know, work. I keep tellin' you to get out of laundry. That's the hardest job they got."

"It's part of my treatment plan, my work assignment."

"Ask for something else."

"I tried. They said I need supervision."

"Dr. Murray says I may be ready to leave the hospital soon," Beth says.

"Did you say leave?"

"No kiddin'? That's great, kid," Isabel says.

"We'll see." Beth gets up from the blanket. "I'm going to stick my toes in."

"I'll go with you." I slowly get up off the blanket, pull my swimsuit into place. We walk to the edge of the water. Beth extends her leg, dips her toes.

I look out over the lake and feel as if I might simply walk in and disappear. I hear water lapping, feel the cold wet sand on my feet. A flash of stars in a night sky...muffled voices ...splashes ...a hand on my arm ...

Beth squeezes my arm. "What am I going to do with myself?" she says in a loud whisper. "I'm going home on family leave for a month. I could be discharged. The thought of leaving the hospital makes me nauseous." She twirls her brittle hair with her index finger.

"What do you mean?"

"My parents. They still think I'm going to Julliard in the fall. Oh god, why can't I just get out on my own?"

"It'll work out."

"No, it won't. I can't let my folks down like that. What am I supposed to do, work in a factory, end up looking like Isabel?"

Chapter 29

It's eight o'clock, time to report for gardening duty. We meet at the tool shed to check out gardening tools and pails. Those of us who tend the gardens have daily duties of deadheading, weeding, watering. Because we are some of the most trusted patients, we are allowed to spend hours outside carrying buckets of water to our beds, grooming them to perfection. The gardeners transform plots of straggly seedlings into beautiful jewels, shining against the stark buildings of the hospital.

"Good morning, Carl."

"Morning."

"My bed's good on weeds. I won't need tools today."

"Interested in an extra job?"

"Well, sure. What?"

"Helper."

"What's that?"

"Goin' with me while I make my rounds, check the beds, anything else I might need help with. It won't require any more time on your part, unless you want it to."

"Yes. I'd like that."

"Might as well start now. You hand out the tools, I'll check the list. All the patients are equipped and working in their beds when we leave to pick up compost on the east end of the hospital grounds. I really need the help these days," Carl says. "This bum leg and now my back's goin' out. I'm fallin' apart since my wife died."

"Sorry, Carl. You must miss her a lot."

"Yup, yup, sure do. She's been with me a long time...was with me. If it weren't for Judy, I wouldn't have survived my accident."

"Was it an accident, Carl?"

"Nah, not really an accident. Got attacked by a patient. Almost killed me."

"What happened?"

"It happened a long time ago, almost twenty years now. Well, let's see ...I was on the last half of my double shift. I traded with Joe Doremire. I shouldn't have—meant sixteen hours straight. But, I had trouble saying no, even to the likes of Doremire. Anyway, I dragged to my dinner break, counting the minutes until 6:30. I liked getting off the ward. On graveyard shift, the dining hall was my only option. I strolled along through the tunnels. Thankfully, I knew the way with my eyes closed. I was one of a pack of moles—employees scurrying through the network of tunnels running under the hospital. I hummed to myself as I headed down the straightaway just before the left turn to the dining hall. I didn't hear a thing until the sound of metal hitting bone."

"Oh my god."

"Yeah, it was pretty bad. A loud whooshing roared in my ears, like surf crashing on rocks. I thought I heard the sound of distant voices, but I couldn't open my eyes. Then I went unconscious.

"The voices rose again. This time, I could make out what they were saying, but I couldn't talk. I heard the guys talking, *Hey. Hey, you okay? Is he alive? Check his pulse. I got a pulse. He's breathing. Who is it?* I guess I was bleedin' so bad, they couldn't recognize me. We all got our name inside our back collar, but they told me the blood was as thick as tar and they couldn't make it out. Finally identified me by my key number. *Lord have mercy, it's Carl, Carl Reinbold. Carl, can you hear us?* By this time I heard them, tried to move my lips. The effort sent me back into blackness. I woke up two weeks later on the third floor of Munson Hospital with my wife Judy by my bedside."

"How could a patient be down in the tunnels? What was the weapon?"

"Thought it might be a pipe, definitely something heavy. Broke my jaw, cheekbones, fractured my skull. Right kneecap was in a million pieces, shinbone broke in a couple places. They never did find out how the patient got in the tunnels. Patients aren't allowed down there, at least not without a staff escort."

"That sounds terrible."

"Yup. Had a rough time. Then, when I started to mend—with Judy's help, of course my mind started playing tricks on me. I was scared all the time, couldn't sleep, nightmares. Then I started calling in sick, just couldn't face people. They sent me to a psychiatrist and he put me off work. I ended up taking nerve pills. I was out for almost two years. And when I came back, they made me a rover."

"Rover? What's that."

"Kinda like a …well, a grunt, like in the army. They tell you what to do and you do it."

"So, you got to do a lot of different things."

"Can't say as I liked it much. Never knew when I came in to work where I'd be and what I'd be doin'."

We pass the old Soap House on our way to the tool crib.

"Hold up." Carl stops by the front door. "Looks like that door is open, should be padlocked."

As we peer in, I squint, adjusting to the dim interior of the boarded up building. Draped over a stack of pallets, an old blanket catches the sun, the window slats paint glowing stripes on the drab wool. Is this where it happened? I look at Carl.

"What's in there?"

"Nothin'." The door is loose from the hinges, the corner of it buried in the dirt outside the building. Carl lifts and pushes, the door scrapes the ground as it resists returning to the doorjamb. "Gotta' report that door broke."

"I heard something about this building."

"What's that?"

"One of the retarded patients in our hall had sex here."

"Happens."

"Don't you think it's wrong?"

"Yup."

"I heard some girls had babies."

"Um-humm."

"What happens to them?"

"Some go to Stillwater first, then they go to good homes."

"What's Stillwater?"

"Children's Asylum. All the babies from here go to Stillwater."

"That's not right! Those poor babies, nobody wanting them." I feel the tears on my face.

Carl puts his arm around my shoulder, "People want them babies."

"Who?"

"They're wanted, believe me."

Chapter 30

THE OBSERVER   June 10, 1969
Page 9
Leaves:
Weekend passes: Joe Flynn
                    Janice Fox
                    Rebecca Gomez
                    Randy Sheets
                    George Littlehorn
                    Luanne Kilpi
Home care:
                    Beth Shaffer
                    Gordon Fife
                    Allen Tilsway
                    Isabel Jackson
                    Ramona Duncen
                    Byron Potts
Transfers: Robert Fountain
Discharges: Candace Reynolds
                    Corado Selvadoni

I didn't notice the rentals before."

"Verna Fowler sold her house to a slum lord, so did Jackson Davis."

"Since I've been gone?"

"No, Luanne. They've been rentals for a good two years now," Mom says.

"I never noticed." We turn down Haley Street. "Who's parked out front? Molly got company?"

"No. It's your family."

"Who?"

"Just Margo and Charlene." Mom turns into the driveway.

"Mom, I wish you hadn't done that." I swallow hard.

"Don't be silly. They've been worried."

"I won't go in."

"You're here for a home visit. I thought …"

"You thought …what about me?" I panic, stiffen in my seat, my hand on the door handle.

"Calm down. They'll think you don't want to see them."

"I don't want to see them, Mom, I don't!"

Mom clutches the steering wheel and stares through the windshield. "I don't know why you're acting this way."

"Never mind. Tell them I took a short walk and I'll be back in a minute." I ram my shoulder into the door and get out.

"You won't run away or anything …I'm sorry."

"No, I just need some air. Just tell them that."

I start down the street. It's scary enough coming back for my first home visit, now I have to face my two older sisters, both of them living the American dream, husband, children. I feel like I'm seven, the little sister pest, the mistake. I hear Dr. Murray's voice in my head. *Maybe something good could come from this tragedy.* It made me furious when the doctor said it, but maybe she's right. Maybe this will bring me closer to my family. What if I've been the one who's made the judgments, not giving *them* a chance. I'm a grown woman now, not the annoying brat tagging along, sneaking their clothes, bugging their boyfriends. My pace picks up, I feel a little stronger. I don't have to compare myself to them, always coming up short. It isn't their fault.

I feel disconnected, as if I'd been beamed up by aliens and dropped on the wrong planet. Somehow I cover eight blocks, two blocks in each direction, and come down Haley, approach the house. I take a deep breath and open the front door. "Hi."

Mom's voice sounds strained. "In the kitchen."

Charlene and Margo are sitting at the Formica table drinking coffee, talking in whispers. "There she is." Margo gets up and gives me a hug. "You look great."

"It's so good to see you, Lu," Charlene says.

"Good to be home." I pull out a chair and sit down.

"Coffee?" Mom asks.

"Sure, Mom. Thanks. Where's Molly?"

"Cheerleading practice. She'll be here soon."

After the initial awkwardness, we settle into a familiar pattern, updates on their families, Christmas pictures. Then, the announcement.

"Lu, you'll never guess. Charlene and I are both expecting."

Slurping of coffee punctuates a long silence.

I try to respond, but my voice catches in my throat. "Gee ...congratulations."

"I hope you're not hurt. We were afraid ..." Charlene says.

"Hurt?" My response piggy-backs the end of Margo's sentence. "No ...no, that's not it. I'm happy for you." I can't help myself, the tears roll down my cheeks. "I'm sorry. I think I need to rest." My chair bumps back from the table, almost tips over as I get up. I flee the kitchen and drag up the stairs, bracing my hands, sliding them along the cracked plaster of the stairway. I open the door to my old bedroom.

I haven't been upstairs since Jeff and I got married. Mom moved her sewing machine into the room; stacks of fabric line the wall under the window. Hangers of pressed skirts and slacks hang on the rack in the closet—alterations ready to be picked up. Molly must have traded beds, taken the double, given Mom the single for a guest room. Skirts and slacks, dresses, suits, shiny pins at their hems, lay in neat stacks across the bedspread. There's a card table set up in the corner. I slide aside the pattern my mother has pinned to a length of black cotton fabric. I carefully lift the piles from the bed and set them on the table. I drop onto the mattress, pull the pillow from under the spread, jam it under my head.

I walk toward the narrow beam of light, my hand reaching the knob, pushing the door open. A large wicker basket sits in the middle of the room. I hear a faint squeaking coming from it. I look in.

Kittens. Fuzzy, glue-eyed kittens. I pick up a frowzy gray one with dark tiger markings. I hold it to my cheek, nuzzle it in my neck and scratch it behind the ears.

The meowing behind me grows louder. I turn back toward the basket. The kittens are getting out, crawling over the sides, jumping to the floor, scurrying into the hall. I pat the back of the kitten cuddled against my neck. I grab the kitten under its armpits, hold it away from my body. But it isn't a kitten at all. It's a baby, some kind of baby with pointed ears, yellow eyes.

It scratches my face, jumps down, runs into the hallway with the others.

I step into the hall, the kittens are running. I'm horrified to see the hall ends in nothing, just a black hole. The kittens are falling off the edge. I try to run but I can't. Their pitiful mewing fills my ears. The kitten baby is almost to the hole. My legs won't move. I see Jeff standing in a far doorway. Maybe he can stop the kitten. "Jeff, the kitten. Stop the kitten." He stands there, not moving.

"Luanne?" Mom opens the door to the bedroom. "Luanne, are you all right?"

Chapter 31

I haven't felt right since I got back from my home visit."

"Right?" Dr. Murray asks.

"I'm afraid, jumpy, sort of."

"Did something happen?"

"Well, my mom invited my sisters. That was pretty upsetting."

"How so?"

"They're so normal …I felt really uneasy." I look up sheepishly. "I wouldn't even go in at first."

"In the house?"

"Yeah, but then I took a walk, and when I got back, it was going okay. Then Margo told me they were both pregnant."

"How did you feel about that?"

"Teed off."

"It made you feel angry?"

"Yes."

"Go on."

"I just lost Alexander, and they go out and get pregnant? Don't you find that strange?"

"Strange?"

"Yes. Like they were trying to spit out a couple of kids to make up for the loss."

"Whose loss?"

"I don't know. The hole made in the family? I don't know. I just felt they were being insensitive."

"So you're saying they shouldn't have children because Alexander died?"

"Yes! I mean, no. I guess …I don't know. It made me mad. Just forget it."

"Are you mad now, Luanne?"

"Yes. You're not helping me. I feel depressed."

"Does your depression seem worse?"

"I don't know. It's not really like depression, more like I'm restless; my insides are jumping around, like I'm looking for the enemy to pop out of the dark."

"What are you guarding against?"

"I'm not sure. Something inside me feels afraid ...or maybe worried, is that anxiety?"

"Sounds like it. Anxiety is fear, but the scary thing is not always apparent."

"I did have a nightmare when I was home."

"Tell me about it."

"Well, there were these kittens in a basket. I picked one up and it looked like a baby."

"A human baby?"

"Like a human baby's body, but it had pointy ears and yellow cat eyes. It scratched me. Then the other kittens started crying really loud, and they got out of the basket and ran out of the room. When I went into the hall, I could see they were falling off into a black hole, as if the hall just dropped off into a cavern or something."

"What about the other one. The kitten with a baby's body?"

"It ran into the hall, too. It looked like a regular kitten as it ran away. I chased after it but I couldn't move."

"How did you feel in the dream?"

"Scared. Helpless."

"Helpless?"

"Yes, I wanted to save them, but I couldn't do anything. I kept hearing them mewing. Then I saw Jeff standing in a doorway. He was between the kitten and the hole. I called to him. That was it. I woke up."

"How do you feel about Jeff?"

"I can't even think about that."

"Luanne, I'd like to try something here," Dr. Murray says. "Would you mind?"

"What?"

"I want you to close your eyes and try to imagine the end of the dream where Jeff stands in the doorway."

"What?"

"Just humor me a minute. Would you be willing to try it?"

I sit back in the chair. "Now what?"

"See if you can visualize yourself in the dream, like you're watching a movie. Let me know when you have a picture of yourself in your mind."

"Okay. I can see myself."

"Now I want you to pretend you're acting out the dream, and you will be playing all the parts."

"I don't understand."

"Don't worry. I'll guide you. First, I want you to see yourself in the dream."

"Okay."

"Can you see yourself?"

"Yes."

"Now let's give Luanne something to say. What would she say?"

"Ah …I don't know."

"Go ahead, Luanne. Talk as if you are the Luanne in the dream."

"Ah …Jeff, catch the kitten!"

"Okay, good. Now you're Jeff. What does he say?" Dr. Murray said.

"I can't catch him."

"Okay, now back to Luanne. Go back and forth a few times."

"Why? Why can't you help?"

"I don't know what to do."

"I told you what to do. Grab the kitten before it falls into the dark."

"What kitten?"

"The one running past. Can't you see him?"

"Luanne, what does the kitten say?" Dr. Murray asks.

"I'm going to play, and you can't stop me."

"Now back to Luanne," Dr. Murray guides me.

"Here kitty, kitty. Don't go there, kitty. It's not safe, you'll fall."

"Kitty says?"

"You can't stop me."

"Jeff says?"

"I hear something. I hear the kitten crying."

"Kitten?"

"I'm going over the edge. Help, help."

"Luanne?"

"Jeff, why didn't you stop him?"

"And then Jeff says …I can't do it."

"Go ahead," Dr. Murray encourages me.

"I can't do this …" I open my eyes, cry.

Dr. Murray hands me the box of tissues. "That's alright. You did a fine job. Can I ask you something?"

"Okay."

"Did Jeff help out much with Alexander?"

"Yes, of course he did."

"Could he have done more?"

"No …I don't think so. It's so hard to remember exactly."

"Are you feeling guilty about something, Luanne?"

"Yes. Yes, of course I feel guilty. I'm the mother. I should have been able to help Alexander."

"How?"

"I don't know. Done something."

"You did everything you could. Alexander was leaving, and there was nothing you or Jeff could do about it. You did the best you could."

"I…we…"   I can't hold it together. I put my hands over my face and cry.

"Anything else, Luanne? Will you try to forgive yourself?"

I reach for a Kleenex, blow my nose.

"No. I've had enough."

Chapter 32

I lean against the wall next to the pay phones and check the wall clock. At exactly three o'clock, the phone rings.

"Could I speak to Luanne Kilpi please?"

"Mom, it's me."

"Oh, hi. How are you?"

"Good. Can't wait to see you and Molly. Are you still coming?"

"Yes, we are. We have a room at a place called Dream Acres Motel in Honor. Is that close to Traverse City?"

"Yes, I think so. Are you coming Friday?"

"Yes. Can you get out for dinner?"

"I've already talked to the social worker and she said I could have a weekend pass. We can see the parade and go to the fireworks. And I'd love to spend one afternoon at the beach."

"That sounds good. The motel wasn't that much."

I walk into the visitors' room on Friday, carrying a paper bag with my swimsuit and a change of clothing. Mom and Molly sit by the windows. Mom clutches her handbag, stares straight ahead, her brows knitted and her lips thin as if she is bracing for a punch. She looks tired.

We walk to the visitors' parking lot. "I'll just throw my bag in the trunk." I wait by the back of the car.

"Are you allowed to drive? We don't know our way around." Mom takes the keys from her purse and hands them to me.

"I haven't driven here either, but it might do me good. I still have my driver's license, so I guess I can drive." I slam the trunk, walk to the driver's side.

"Molly, you sit in front with Luanne. I'll sit in back."

Mom doesn't wait for an answer. She opens the door and slides into the back seat. I drive down the winding drive of the hospital.

"Jeff's been seen all over town with that girl from work," Molly says.

"Oh?" So the girl at work was nobody, just somebody who worked on the line. Our divorce was in limbo. I'd been granted some kind of crazy person dispensation, so even though the paperwork was filed, it was frozen. I decided to leave it that way. Jeff's *friend* would just have to wait.

"Molly, Luanne does not need to hear about Jeff Kilpi." Mom leans up from the back seat, pokes Molly's shoulder. "I still can't believe he turned out to be so selfish."

"He's an asshole," Molly says.

"No need for that kind of language," Mom says. "Luanne, I ran into your friend, Jan, after Mass last Sunday."

"Yeah?"

"She's got two kids now …oh, I'm sorry."

"It's okay." But it isn't okay. My anger springs up. "I hope Jan knows she could lose those precious kids at any moment. See how happy she would be if one of her kids got sick and died, how badly she would want to go to church then."

"God is a comfort, Luanne."

"I'm mad at God right now, Mom."

"I know …I'm sorry. You'll change your mind."

Well, the visit is going swell so far. Jeff has a new woman to take my place, and my best friend turns out to be a baby machine. I hate it when Mom runs into people from my other life. But I'm not going to let it ruin my weekend. People talk; I have to let it go.

Mom leans forward again, puts her arm over the seat back. "Father Barnes is still reading your name every Sunday, asking for prayers. You're listed in the church bulletin in the *Intentions* section under your maiden name and married name, Luanne Iazetto Kilpi. That way, people know who you are. Who to pray for."

I tighten my hands around the steering wheel to keep from lashing out. I try not to think about how my family is reacting. I'm sure my mother keeps them posted. Lord knows, it's the least I can do, let Mom sugarcoat it any way she needs to.

Out of seven kids, nobody else got into deep water. Until I went nuts, the only gnarl on the family tree was Margo's teen pregnancy. After the rushed nuptials, Margo left for Grand Rapids with her new husband. I went along with Mom and Dad a few times to visit Margo and Ron in their upstairs apartment across from the John Ball Park Zoo. The apartment was stifling, the baby cried constantly, and Margo was as big as a barn. I remember thinking how rotten a cook Margo was. How did she get so fat? On top of that, Mom wouldn't let me go outside—afraid I'd be kidnapped and groomed as a hooker by pimps on the street.

"How are Margo and Charlene," I ask my mother, trying to lighten things up.

"I talked to Margo yesterday. She's due in a couple months. And your sister Charlene isn't far behind."

I thought about the day Alexander was born—Halloween. My water broke at work. I hid out in the employee bathroom until Jeff showed up with a change of clothes. We went home, I called Dr. Powell.

"Wait until your contractions are five minutes apart," he said. By dusk, the porch lights began to flick on as the neighborhood kids came trick-or-treating down our street.

I stretched out on the living room couch, my hands on my stomach, my eyes closed. "It's starting," I called to Jeff. He grabbed his watch and stood staring at it.

"Okay, it passed," I sighed.

"Still twelve minutes." He placed his watch on the coffee table and walked to the kitchen, brought back a basket of candy to sit by the front door.

I waddled to the door between contractions and passed out candy to several pirates, Frankenstein, a trio of ghosts, cowboys, witches, a cat, and a bum. Jeff stood next to me with his watch in his hand. By eight o'clock, the last ghoul had turned and left the porch, headed home to sort his candy. My contractions were ten minutes apart.

"If I have this baby before midnight, his birthday will be on Halloween. He'll be a little warlock," I smiled. Jeff laughed and kissed me on the forehead. Alexander Jeffrey Kilpi was born at 11:23 p.m., October 31, 1965.

"Charlene and Tony and little Mark were over for dinner Sunday. She's very uncomfortable with this heat," Mom says. "They send their love."

"Let's be honest, Tony never liked me."

"That's not true, Luanne. He likes you."

"Mom, I'm trying to be open about my feelings, more honest and up front. That's what I'm working on with my doctor. She said I set myself up for a breakdown because of my perfectionism and my inability to admit when I had problems."

"Okay. Yes, he can be a hothead. He's still mad because the back end went out on his new car when he pulled the homecoming float."

"It was the transmission, Mom. Not the back end."

"I remember hearing about that," Molly says.

"It's ancient history." I don't feel like repeating the story again. I'm getting tired of driving, my anxiety is building.

"Come on, give me the juicy details," Molly begs.

"Remember that baby blue convertible Tony had?"

"Yeah, of course. He took me for a ride in it."

"Charlene volunteered Tony to pull the Queen's float. The deal was that Bob Voisin would drive Tony's car."

"Who's Bob Voisin?" Molly asks.

"You know, Bob Voisin, captain of the football team … married Bobbie Carlsen …works at Bierlein's now."

"Yeah, yeah, yeah."

"Anyway, we're heading down Davenport Avenue when I start to smell something burning. Bob keeps looking back over his shoulder. He knows something is wrong. Charlene and Tony appear along the parade route, Tony looking madder and madder every time he shows up. I'm up there waving and smiling from my throne, and all I can think of is that we're burning up the four-on-the-floor in Tony's new Malibu convertible."

"Well, it was an expensive car." Mom says under her breath.

"What did you say, Mom?"

"Nothing."

142

"Finally, Tony can't take it any longer, leaps from the crowd, pulls Bob out of the car, and tries to drive it himself. By that time, the smell of his burning transmission precedes the parade by two blocks. The car seizes up about three miles from the football field, somebody calls the wrecker, and the Queen's float arrives for the game pulled by Tony's dead convertible chained behind Rhinehart's Wrecker Service truck."

"Oh my god. What did Tony do?" Molly smiles, put her hand over her mouth.

"I blocked out the rest," I laugh.

"Well, he was pretty mad, but he got over it," Mom says.

"Not really. Let's move on. What else have you been up to, Molly?"

"Not much."

"You just might end up as the Homecoming Queen like Luanne."

"Maybe," Molly raises her eyebrows.

"Former homecoming queen cracks up and gets thrown in an insane asylum."

"Oh, Luanne," Mom's voice trails off.

There's a long silence. I shouldn't have made the crack about the homecoming queen. I knew it would hurt Mom's feelings. I'm beginning to feel edgy. Too much information, things moving too fast. The Cherry Festival traffic is heavy. And it's starting to feel as if every car will cross over the center line and plow into us.

"Let's head out the peninsula to the beach. It's too crowded in town," I suggest.

"Sounds good to me," Molly says. "Okay, Mom?"

"Whatever you girls want is fine with me."

The traffic thins as we drive out Peninsula Drive. Mom breaks the silence. "I told Molly she should try to meet Mrs. Fowler's boy. I told you about them, didn't I? They moved into the apartment above old lady Martin. He seems like such a nice boy, friendly, and so polite to his mother."

"Mom, he's gay," Molly says.

"I know. That's what I'm saying. He's gay, happy, upbeat ...however you say it, he's a pleasant young man."

"No, Mom. He's homosexual."

"Oh."

Chapter 33

THE OBSERVER   *June 15, 1969*
Page 3
NEW PROGRAM FOR PATIENTS
Because of the hard workers in our Sheltered Workshop over the last four years, the hospital is expanding the program to include two businesses in downtown Traverse City, Murdock's Fudge and Sid's Grocery. For the first time ever, two lucky patients will be working off the grounds. Good luck!

"Luanne, I have a bit of good news for you," Dr. Murray says. "I presented your case at the treatment meeting yesterday, and the team has approved you to start a part-time job."

"But, I already have a job. I'm on the gardening crew."

"Well, this would be a paying job."

"Will it get me discharged sooner?"

"It could, yes."

"I wouldn't want to give up my gardening."

"It would be part-time. You can continue your work assignment, if you wish. The team feels you are ready for the next step, working toward discharge. I agree. I think you're ready. Luanne?"

"Is …is that back in the OT building?"

"That's the Sheltered Workshop, United Boxworks and Bugsy's Fly Fishing. And that's an option. The hospital supervises the workers, almost seventy-five of them. Their pace is slow, but their work is paid by the piece, so the companies are pleased."

"I talked to Grace on our floor. She has a friend who works there, Jimmy Wildfong."

"Jimmy's one of our old-timers. I think he's been at the hospital almost forty years. Some of the others, not that long, but most of them have been in the hospital awhile. We're trying to expand, give some of the newer patients a chance to work for pay."

"I'm interested. I think I could learn to fold boxes, but I'm not so sure about tying lures."

"Well, as I said, that's an option, but what I'm suggesting for you, Luanne, is a job outside the hospital."

"Really?"

"Yes, we've expanded the program this year to include two placements downtown. It's the first time we're sending our patients out into the community to work. I think you'd be perfect for the program, Luanne."

"You think I can do it?"

"Absolutely. You have retail experience and you're making very good progress in your treatment."

"I'd get paid?"

"Um-humm. I don't know how much, not a lot."

The thought of a job that pays something pushes me to take the risk. In occupational therapy, I'd torn rags for rugs used on the hall, hemmed dishtowels for the hospital linen closet. I'd done housekeeping before I got the gardening job. I worked hard, but never got paid.

The day is already sticky with heat, the kind of morning that leaves the meadows all misty, the first rays of sunlight setting the grasses aglow. The dew glistens on the thick lawns, held there by the humidity. On my way to Cottage 23, I stick to the walkways to keep my tennis shoes dry. Work crews of patients are setting up for the 4th of July Carnival near the bandstand. It's early; I haven't had much time to be anxious about my job interview.

Taking a deep breath, I step up the front stairs of Cottage 23 for my interview for the position at Murdock's Fudge. Even though I've been told the cottage is non-secured during the day, I wait at the door a good ten minutes before I remember there's no key man.

"Luanne? I'm Mrs. Braverman." A tiny woman with big hair stands up and holds out her hand. As I shake it, the woman smiles, her lips pulling back over large yellow rabbit teeth. "I see you have a recommendation from Dr. Murray for the job opening at Murdock's Fudge. Have you had any retail experience?" She smiles again, and motions for me to sit down. I try not to stare at the woman's mouth.

"Yes. My first job was behind the candy counter at Woolworth's when I was a senior in high school. After graduation, I got a job as a sales clerk at JC Penney. I was there three years, two more part-time ...until my son got sick."

"You have the experience. How do you feel about re-entering the work force, Luanne?"

"Pretty good. I know I have the skills and experience. I'm a little concerned about how I'll handle customers who aren't very nice, but Dr. Murray thinks I'll do fine." Actually, the thought of working outside the hospital terrifies me, meeting people, trying to act normal.

"The job starts right after Cherry Festival, three afternoons a week and will start at $1.15 an hour. That will increase to $1.20 after your probation."

"That sounds great."

"From here, you will attend an orientation right down the hall. Then you are scheduled for an interview with the shop owner, Mrs. Dietz, tomorrow."

I calculate my pay, almost $15.00 a week, no need to rely on Mom for cigarette money. If Dr. Murray thinks I'm ready, I'll give it a try.

After my orientation, I walk back to Building 50 across the lawns, stopping at the flower beds tended by the other gardeners. I sit down on a bench and raise my face to the sun. I'm starting to feel lighter. After my last med change, I feel more alive.

Thinking back, I can see it first came in pleasant surprises like the time I laughed with Isabel over my high school memories. I can't exactly pinpoint when it started, but my thoughts are clearer. I've stopped planning ways to kill myself. But, with less medication, thoughts of Alexander's illness and death creep into my mind— flashbacks, night terrors, and rage. The kitten dreams are becoming more frequent.

Dr. Murray calls dreams "the royal road to the unconscious,"', but she says she can't take credit—she got it from Freud. Dr. Murray loves to explore dreams. Now she begins almost every session with "Any good bad dreams?"

I can't help but pinch off a few deadheads as I pass my flower beds. It's going to be a scorcher. My blouse is sticking to my back and it's only ten a.m. I ring the bell and hurry in to change into my work clothes.

The next day, I catch the hospital van into town for my interview with the owner of Murdock's Fudge. I wear a madras skirt and a white blouse from the emporium. The van lets me out at the corner and I walk half a block to the store. A bell jingles as I open the front door. The smell of chocolate makes my stomach lurch. An image of Alexander with a chocolate Easter bunny flashes in my mind. He was still eating last April, still looked and acted like himself, still laughed with excitement when he found his Easter basket.

"May I help you?"

"Yes. Yes, I'm Luanne Kilpi. Here about the job?"

The interview is short. Within ten minutes, I have the position. Mrs. Deitz shows me around the shop and talks to me about my duties. "Are you sure you can handle this, Luanne? I mean, we can't have you being absent. You know, when you're not ...not feeling well."

"I'll be fine, Mrs. Deitz. I'm never sick."

Chapter 34

Carl brings lunch and we sit down at a picnic table near the Willow Lake reflecting pool. We eat together on the days I'm not at Murdocks.

"I always thought I'd be passing the Reinbold wisdom down to my son someday, or daughter. Stewards of the land my dad called it."

"My dad loved gardening, too."

"Looks like you got his green thumb."

"Yeah."

"We got our work pretty much done for today, how 'bout we go over to the old barns. I'll take you on a tour, greenhouses and storage, too. You can see all old the farm machines. Heck, guess you'd call 'em antiques now. I been drivin' a Massey since I was seven years old. I remember Mother called and called to get me off the tractor and out of the fields to practice piano." Carl laughs, takes a bite of his tomato sandwich.

"I saw some really big machines at the end of *Yellow Drive*."

"Yup. Those are the snow removal rigs. We got a new Sno Cat last winter—Tucker 342. I'm backup driver when Stan Denny is off. Lordy me, that thing can howl. I wrestle the wheel, arms vibrating, jostling in the seat like I'm breaking a bronco. The Cat operates the same as my Massey, only difference is the tracks. The growl of the engine and the clattering of the steel tracks through the drive sprockets can be heard for two miles on a calm, crisp winter day. Over and above that, the grousers clack when I hit the plowed road. Man, I love driving the thing, as long as I remember my earplugs. Here, take one of these apples. MacIntosh."

"Thanks."

"'Bout ready?"

We drive down *Blue Drive* toward the abandoned barns. Carl tries one of his keys in the padlock. He leans back and slides the big door on its tracks. We step into a gigantic building, dust riding on beams of light through the cracks. Looks like searchlights coming from the ceiling. Cobwebs hang from the rafters and huge beams support barreled ceilings.

"Wow. Reminds me of a church."

"Yup, yup, it's somethin' alright."

"Where did the cows stay?"

"Well, there used to be a hayloft, a second floor, and the hay was dropped through that chute in the roof. See, right there. The cows were on this floor. They had their pens over against this wall, milking was done right down the middle here."

"How many were there?"

"There's two of these big dairy barns. Hundreds of cows, Luanne."

"And you supervised the whole thing?"

"Yup. Never had any problems …well, that's not exactly true. There was stealin' goin' on. A little semen here and there we could put up with, but then this guy Joe Doremire, he was a bad apple that one. He went a step further."

"What happened?"

"It was a long time ago."

"Can you remember?"

"Yup. I can remember alright. Seems like it happened yesterday. It was during second shift. I was off, but drivin' through after dinner in the canteen with Judy. There's a truck parked where it shouldn't be. I walked in and found a couple of guys by the calf pen. *Them the new heifers?* I asked.

"*Yeah.* Joe Doremire backed toward Ralph Langley.

"*Bill of lading?* I held out my hand for the paperwork.

"*Yeah, that's right. I'm taking care of it, Carl. No need for you to be here on your night off,* Ralph said.

"*Well, I'm here now. Let's see the paperwork.* Ralph looks at Joe. Somethin' was startin' to smell bad.

"*Give it to him, go ahead,* Joe said. Ralph handed me the stack of papers.

"*Ah, you'll see it's all in order,* Joe said.

"I ran my finger down the page. Then I stepped closer to the pen, pointing around to each calf, counting out loud. *We got ten calves in the pen, and the lading says ten, but the second sheet says twelve.* I waited for the men to answer.

"*We got ten here, Carl,* Joe said. *That's easy enough to see. Must be a misprint on that* second page.

"*Hummmm.* I walked over to the bulb hanging from the ceiling, held up the first sheet of paper. *Somethin' not right here. You boys got any idea why there's been erasing on this, the Number 10 written on top, here?*

"The men looked at each other. *Nope,* Ralph said.

"*No idea.* Joe shrugged and looked away.

"*Where's your vehicle?*

"*Why?*

"*Thought I saw a truck parked outside. Not in the designated parking lot.*

"*Don't know,* Joe said. *Listen, Carl, what's up your ass? We're here trying to do our* job. *Now why don't you leave and let us do it?*

"*I'm going outside and take a look at that truck.* I started to walk toward the back entrance.

"*Holy Christ, Carl. Ain't no big deal. Hospital's got more cows than they know what to do with.* Joe threw up his hands.

"I caught 'em red-handed."

"Did they get fired?"

"Nah. There was stealin' goin' on all the time. Even now, leftovers from holiday dinners, chickens, turkeys, whole sides of beef come up missing from the meat lockers."

"You mean they got away with it?"

"No. I didn't say that. I reported them and they were reprimanded. The day Joe Doremire got kicked off the farming operation, it was like pulling a rotten tooth. He got transferred, but he's still here—and he's still trouble."

Chapter 35

How was your leave, Beth?" Dr. Murray asks.

"A whole month. We missed you." I really did miss Beth. And I'm happy for her—she got a home leave and will probably be discharged soon.

"It ...I ...discouraging."

"How? Don't your parents own a big house on the lake?" Heidi always seems surprised at Beth's unhappiness.

"Home for the entire month of July. As soon as I got there, they suggested I play the piano, wondered if I would like to invite some friends up, watched every mouthful of food I ate. Unbelievable— they actually expected me to get into a swimsuit and participate in their pretentious summer rituals. Don't they know everyone thinks I'm a freak?"

"I'm sorry to hear it was so difficult for you, Beth," Dr. Murray says.

"I just wanted to stay in my room. But the first morning, my father cracked the door of my bedroom. *Why don't you come out on the dock, sweetheart? For goodness sake, open a window up here, it's stifling.* I'm freezing to death, even with a fisherman's sweater, sweatpants and wool socks. *We're all out on the boat. Come down, sweetie.* Thank God he left. I sat in my chair in front of the curved glass and watched them. Even with a wool afghan over my lap, I'm shivering. My fingertips are blue.

"I observed the show from my box seat. My parents entertained several couples on their cabin cruiser anchored near the dock. All the players wore beachwear, their bodies like burnt toast. The women wore large-brimmed hats, sipped drinks from tall glasses filled with crushed ice. Clones of my mother, they lined up across the bow on chaise lounges. The men stood at the stern, drinks in hand, watching the boats pass by, making comments about the women in swimsuits."

"Why were you so cold?" Isabel says. "Didn't you say you gained a little weight?"

"The weight started dropping off as soon as I got home. I tried to hide out in my room, but I walked a thin line with my parents. I watched my dad walk down the path, wearing his ridiculous captain's hat. When he reached the end of the dock, my mother looked up and mouths something. He shook his head.

"Later I strolled down the path, waved to them. They both smiled and waved, then their friends smiled and waved. A couple of women motioned me toward the dock. I flashed a smile, shook my head, sat down on an Adirondack under the maples. So, I was out of the house at least. That should've pleased them."

Dr. Murray folds her arms. "Beth, as I've said to you before, you are a master magician, adept at hiding inside yourself. It sounds like you were teetering on the brink of discovery."

Beth runs her hand over her downy cheek. "Yes. How long could I hide Jo-Jo the Dog-faced Boy under my sweater? I'm covered with fur on my back and stomach. I shave my legs, but shorts are out of the question. My legs are thin, very thin."

"Fur?" Autumn asks.

"Yes. It's a soft downy fur, quite thick, actually."

"It's called lanugo, the body's reaction to starvation, Autumn."

"Jeez."

"The last straw was later that night at a family cookout. My mother hits me with the big surprise. *Honey, guess what? I ran into Wendy Beal and Lisa Stoppert, and they'd love to see you. I invited them to spend your birthday weekend with us.* I can't believe it. They're not even at Interlochen anymore. I know she called them.

"*I ...I'm ...I guess ran into them is the wrong way to say it. I talked to them on the phone and ...* She talks a mile a minute. I ask her point blank if she called them.

"*Well, yes ...Your friends are still here, sweetheart, they want to see you. I ...I just wish you'd give it a try.*

"I totally lose it. I stumble, fall onto the lawn, roll back and forth, retching with dry heaves. I'm like a maniac."

"I don't get it. Wasn't your mother trying to help you?" Estee says.

"Are you kidding? Oh my god ...my friends ...see me looking like ...like some kind of ghoul ...carnival freak ...lunatic. I had to stop her."

"Okay, try to calm down, Beth. Take a couple of breaths."

"I yell, *Take it back. Take it back. Call them back right now. Please, Mother. Call them. Say you'll call them* ... It's kind of a blur, but I crawl across the grass and grab my mother by the ankle. *CALL THEM! Please ...please ...call them and tell them not to come. Daddy?* I'm desperate.

"My father is tending the shish kebobs. He just stares at me, tongs frozen in his hand. He comes over and rubs my back and assures me nobody will come. It's a close call." Beth leans back in her chair, her hands shaking, her thin hair wet with perspiration.

"Did this incident affect your eating?"

"Not really. To tell you the truth, I stopped eating."

"I thought you said your parents were watching you," I say.

"Well, it's not that hard. As usual, I shove the food around on my plate trying to create empty spaces, the appearance of a meal in the process of being eaten. I nibble on a mushroom, and when my parents are engaged in conversation, I slide a chunk of steak from my plate and put it in my pocket. I always have my pockets lined with waxed paper just for that purpose. Later, as they watch the neighbors waving from their boat, I snatch another piece of steak. Toward the end of the meal, I manage to add the third cube to my pocket. My father always overcooks the meat, so there isn't much grease to stain my clothes."

I've never heard Beth talk so frankly about how deceptive she can be. Maybe she won't be leaving the hospital after all.

153

Chapter 36

THE OBSERVER   July 28, 1969
Page 3
HOSPITAL TAKES TOP PRIZE
Winner of the grand prize for the best float in the Cherry Festival Cherry Royale Parade is the Traverse City State Hospital! Photo by Jerry Wade.

Page 6
WHITE COATS IN COMPETITION FOR THE CITY TITLE
Our men's softball team, the White Coats, have stolen another victory. They defeated the Bay Beachbums by two runs in extra innings. They are now tied with the Beulah Bombers for first place. Thanks everyone for turning out to support your team. See you at the tournaments!

Page 9
MORE FUN THAN A BARREL OF MONKEYS
The hospital community has been busy, busy, busy this summer. We had two great concerts at the bandstand, The Liberators, and Time Travelers. Marching bands played continuously on the front lawn of Building 50 during the Cherry Festival, and we have lots of opportunities for outings and field trips: Platte River Fish Hatchery, Sleeping Bear Dunes, Old Mission Point Lighthouse, and the hospital park. Our patients are the luckiest ducks in the north!

I'm riding shotgun with Carl on an outing to Old Mission Peninsula. He reaches from the driver's seat, pulls the handle. The folding door to the bus squeals open as Dr. Murray hoists herself up the steps, sits in the first seat behind him. As Carl explains it, excursions outside the hospital are perks designed to keep the patients socialized and, more importantly, to demonstrate to the community that patients are *just plain folks*, like them. Staff members take turns volunteering as chaperones.

Carl exchanges greetings with Dr. Murray, chats about the trip. The doctor pauses several times to warn patients to quiet down. The winding road bumps up against the beach of East Grand Traverse Bay, and ends at a small clearing where the hospital set up picnic tables with access to the water, away from the summer tourist spots. Dr. Murray sways down the aisle to check on a distressed patient. Jostled by the bumpy road, she staggers back alternating her hands on the backs of the seats to steady herself.

She sits at the edge of her seat, leans forward. I hear her say, "Carl, have you heard any rumors about a patient named Marge who was assaulted in the old Soap House?"

"She was in Judy's ward. Got pregnant two years ago."

"Is that right?"

"She had a couple stillbirths in the past, the way I understand it. There's a lot of that in the women's wards. This time, though, the baby lived …sent to the children's asylum, like the others."

Dr. Murray looks over at me as she leans forward again. "Carl, do you know who the father is? Who might have been having sex with Marge?"

I pretend to be sightseeing. I lean my chin in my hand and look out the side window.

"Way I hear it, a lot of guys." He pauses for awhile. Then he says, "But I know for sure Joe Doremire 'cuz he told me."

"Joe Doremire? Spelled like it sounds? I would like to turn his name in to supervision, Carl. I won't say who told me."

"Okay by me. Just isn't right. What's it matter now. Judy's gone."

"What did you say, Carl?"

"Nothin'."

Group meets the next day. With all the leaves and home visits, the group hasn't been complete all summer. But it will be today, everybody but Beth.

"Hello." Dr. Murray takes her spot in the circle.

"Having a good summer, Doc?"

"Pretty good, yes, Isabel."

We do our usual dance, squirming around a bit in our seats, looking down. Estee is asleep, her chin rests on her chest.

"Estee, are you with us?" Dr. Murray asks. "Estee?" She reaches over, shakes her knee.

"Huh?" Estee snaps her head up.

"Just want to make sure you're awake. I have something I want to say."

"Yeah, yeah. I'm here."

"There is no easy way to tell you this. I have some very bad news." Dr Murray's voice is husky with emotion. "I received word at team meeting yesterday that Beth died."

Chapter 37

My feet squish inside my sandals as I make my way along the walkway by the reflecting pool, past the abandoned shuffleboard court, grass and weeds crack the concrete. It seems at least ten degrees cooler on the front lawn of Building 50. I think about all the patients who have walked under these same oaks in the last eighty-some years.

As I come up to Building 50, I step back inside the pages of my favorite childhood book, *Nancy Drew and the Message in the Haunted Mansion*—Nancy locked in the tower of an imposing stone castle, with vines and moss covering the thick walls. I shudder at how real it seems now.

As a kid I was an ace detective, carrying my sister's old black leather shoulder-strap purse with the metal medallion on the front. It held all my sleuthing equipment: pad of paper, pencil, ink pad and rubber-letter stamp for messages, an old compass I found in the garage, and the white stretchy Easter gloves I wore when investigating a crime. My private office was the front coat closet, between the first and second rows of coats. The sign pinned to Dad's hunting jacket said: *Nancy Drew is __IN___*. Two paper squares, IN or OUT could be thumbtacked to the sign to indicate my presence at headquarters.

My mind wanders back inside Hall 5. I don't have a clue what will become of the women locked away in the disturbed wards. Who will save them? My heart skips several beats. I can't stay there long, in Hall 5. I've already filed it away in some back file cabinet in my mind. But I can't forget the patients hidden behind the brick walls and barred windows. No matter how many hall parties are given, dances and concerts planned, field trips taken, nothing will change for the chronics. It's like treating terminal cancer with a Band-Aid. They will die here.

I check my watch. It takes me about forty-five minutes to walk from Murdock's if I keep an even pace. This afternoon I reopened briefly to slice a piece of nut fudge for a little kid who pressed his face against the locked door. He had big blue eyes, just like Alexander.

I miss dinner, get back to Hall 9 by my six-thirty curfew. I change my clothes and head out to the west porch for a smoke with my friends, a predictable and welcome end to my work day. Summer evenings in Michigan are sticky, but a breeze off the bay helps. Moves the heat around, keeps the air circulating on the porches. The west porch is jam-packed. Autumn has wrestled off several women to save me a seat.

"Hi, gals. Nice night, huh?" I stretch out my legs and hold up my cigarette.

"It's a hot one," Heidi says.

"I'm leaving here in three weeks, and I gotta' tell ya', I'm going to miss you gals," Isabel says.

"Too many things changing," Estee says. "Autumn and I will probably be rattling around in 50 until they close it. Sometime before winter, I guess. They won't want to heat it past fall."

"Hear anything about your transfer to a semi-open cottage?" Autumn asks.

"Still on the waiting list," Heidi answers. "You hear yet, Lu?"

"No, as far as I know, we're both still on the list. It takes forever for these transfers."

"Hall 9 will be lonely with Isabel and Beth gone and you and Heidi in a cottage," Autumn says.

"We'll still see each other." Heidi nudges Autumn's shoulder with the flat of her hand.

"Yeah, the place is a regular social club," Isabel says.

"*Observer* says there's a rock and roll concert tonight at the Bandstand."

"The Who?" Heidi grins.

"Some local high school group, *The Blue Boys*. I'm going," Autumn ashes her cigarette.

"I'll go. Might be fun," I say.

"Count me in." Isabel leans back in her chair.

"How's the job?" Heidi asks me.

"Good. It took me a couple weeks, but now I feel like I know what I'm doing. Your program going okay?"

"Yeah. Once I get out of the Daily Living Program, Dr. Murray says I can apply for the Sheltered Workshop."

"I'm Carl Reinbold's helper on garden crew."

"You get paid for that?"

"Nah, I enjoy it. Carl reminds me of my dad."

"Yeah?"

"You know, I can't stop thinking about Beth," Autumn says. "Anybody heard anything?"

"Nothing."

"I don't think we're ever going to know what happened. Dr. Murray says Beth's parents won't return her phone calls. She wants to go to the funeral, if there is one, but she can't find out when it is," Isabel says.

"Nothing in the Traverse City Record Eagle either. Her being such a big star at Interlochen, doesn't make sense."

"Parents kept it out, probably," Estee says.

"I just keep thinking about her. Trying to imagine what happened." I can feel my lips quiver. "You know, something passes between people who suffer together. It forms a bond, like a sister."

"I sure miss her," Autumn says.

Isabel takes a long drag, noisily exhales, looks out over the lawn. "When you know somebody in their worst moments …and yours too, I guess . . ." Isabel wipes her eyes with the back of her hand.

"I got a sick feeling she starved herself to death," Heidi says.

Chapter 38

I received a letter Tuesday. It's from Beth's mother. She wants it read in group."

"A letter? Her mother wrote it?" Isabel asks.

"Yes. It's more like a story. But Mrs. Shaffer called it a letter, and asked me to share it with you."

Dear Friends:

I would like to tell you a story. I hope this will help you grieve for my beautiful daughter, Elizabeth.

Once upon a time, there was a beautiful young girl named Elizabeth. She was entranced by a magic spell and slumbered in a deep sleep—like Snow White. Her mother looked down at her as she slept. Her thick lashes almost to her cheeks. Shiny dark hair framed her face, draped luxuriantly across her shoulders. She wore an antique brooch pinned at her throat, centered on the high collar of her ivory silk dress.

Her mother bowed her head. No sorrowful dwarfs would file past Beth's coffin, no Prince Charming would kiss her awake.

A spray of red roses and baby's breath with a wide gold ribbon, Beloved Daughter, rested on the mahogany. Her parents had chosen the Sunshine Chapel in Cross Village just north of Harbor Springs for Beth's final appearance. They sat side by side on a velvet settee pulled up close, near their daughter's head. The pews were empty.

Elizabeth was interred at Lakeside Cemetery. The blue granite headstone etched with angels was especially designed by Wally Garner, the renowned stone mason and artist, now retired to his cottage on Walloon Lake.

A HEAVENLY ANGEL FLOWN AWAY TOO SOON

Beloved Daughter, We miss you.
Elizabeth Ann Shaffer
Born: August 12, 1950   Died: August 12, 1969

Her mother smoothed the cuffs of her daughter's dress down over her thin wrists. She kissed her forehead. My beautiful daughter—flawless. The funeral director had done a good job, despite all his complaints.

"Isn't she stunning dear?" Beth's mother said to her husband. "She hasn't looked this good in a long time." Satisfied, proud even, she knew it would turn out all right. The last few days had been difficult, but now her daughter slept peacefully.

May she rest in peace.
Sincerely,
Dorothy Shaffer.

"Okay, now that pisses me right off." Isabel crosses her arms.

"Why is that?"

"My god. Her daughter kills herself, and this woman makes it all about her and how beautiful her daughter is. That's sick."

"It doesn't sound right to me either," I say. "Beth was having a terrible time with her parents' expectations. Now her mother acts like they were all in some kind of fairy tale?"

"Dr. Murray, if a person dies, do you still have confidentiality?" Heidi squirms and crosses her legs.

"What do you mean?"

"Can you tell somebody else what they told you?"

"I think so. As long as it isn't malicious, and isn't gossip. This group is ruled by confidentiality, too. If you want to share something about Beth in this group, I think that will be fine."

"Beth told me she tried to kill herself last year. Her family was up here for the summer. It was right after her birthday party. She took a neighbor's dinghy—she said that's a small boat—and jumped overboard. She wanted to drown, but a guy—a captain from the Maritime academy—saved her. I guess the neighbor was gonna press charges against Beth. Her parents hired a lawyer. He said get her to the closest hospital, so they sent her here. Parents were so afraid of what their friends might think."

"I see."

"Before she left for home visit last time, she said goodbye to me. Said she saved up enough pills to kill herself. I begged her not to. She made me promise not to tell. I …I didn't think she'd do it. Now I feel like shit."

"If somebody wishes to end their life, there really isn't anything we can do. I feel badly, too, Heidi. I'm her therapist. Maybe I could have helped her more. I'm so very sad. Such a wonderful girl with a promising future …" Dr. Murray wipes her eyes with a Kleenex.

"She told me her mother was a drunk," Isabel says. Well, she didn't use those words, but I know a drunk when I see one."

"Beth faced a lot of challenges. I wish she could have made it. Anorexia is a very, very stubborn and deadly disorder."

"You said we'd all make it," Estee screams. "Now will you believe me? Who's next?"

Chapter 39

THE OBSERVER   *August 13, 1969*
Page 7

THE LAUNDRY SCENE
The laundry workers are proud of the equipment they have. They have two shirt presses, one flat work ironer for sheets and bedspreads, one flat work ironer for smaller items, five 400 pound washers, one press, one 100 pound washer, two extractors, ten dryers, one set of uniform presses and three sets of dress presses.
Some interesting statistics: They do 1,390 pairs of pants, 14 thousand sheets and spreads, 12,884 bath towels, 9,114 washcloths, 10,097 dishtowels, 5,939 bed pads, 2,538 pillow slips, 1,165 men's handkerchiefs, 3,200 dresses and 2,600 shirts per average week.

Summer drags its sticky feet—August in the laundry is like being dropped down an active volcano. Today, I work one of the extractors, taking over for Barbara who's sick.

Autumn is *behind the eight ball*—working the eight-roll flatwork ironer. The sweat slowly creeps from our armpits and necks, joins up at the center of our blouses. By midday our soggy clothes will stick to our bodies like cellophane. Autumn is one of ninety-five patients and eleven employees who got the short end of the stick and ended up in the laundry. I've only worked there a couple of times, and that's enough.

The bell for morning break vibrates above the clanking and groaning of the monstrous washers and dryers. I wait for Autumn as she takes her knee from the press lever, scoots aside while her replacement slides in behind the massive machine, the rollers whirring as the steam hisses and sighs. We hurry out the back door where workers gather on the porch. We crowd around the attendant with the lighter like pigeons in Central Park. The lucky frontrunners will squeeze in two cigarettes in the ten minute break.

I notice Autumn looking around the crowd, her glance falling on a handsome attendant. He winks and smiles.

"Who's that?" I ask.

"Attendant."

"Well, I know that. But he winked at you."

"Shhhhh. It's Rudy," Autumn whispers. "I'll tell you later."

I light a second cigarette and hang back to smoke as much of it as I can before the break ends. I watch as Autumn inches her way toward Rudy. She drops her hand and turns it palm up behind her back. Rudy presses a note into her hand; she closes her fingers around it.

When the three o'clock bell rings, I wait for Autumn by the front door of the laundry. I lean close. "Okay, what's going on?"

"We keep our distance on the job, but we've been sneaking around most of the summer."

"Are you nuts?" I say it, then pause, and we both laugh.

"We have a system."

"What does that mean?"

"He gives me a note. Tonight we'll meet behind the machine shop."

"Are you ...is he like a boyfriend?"

"I love him."

"He'll lose his job."

"That's what I told him. He said he doesn't care."

"What about you? They could keep you in here longer."

"But if I didn't have Rudy, I don't think I could make it at all."

"You have us."

"But I fell in love."

"How?"

"We met on break. There are a lot of private places around the grounds. We meet in privacy ..."

"Oh, I get it."

"He loves me."

"Wow. If you're happy, I'm happy for you. I just worry."

"That's what I said to Rudy, *Please don't break my heart.*"

"What did he say?"

"*Not a chance. I'm going to take you out of here and marry you.*"

"He sounds serious."

"I know what you're thinking."

"What?"

"I don't know how long they'll keep me here."

"Well?"

"He says he'll wait as long as it takes."

"I just don't want you to get hurt."

"Please be happy for me. I've found somebody who really loves me, no matter what."

"I *am* happy for you." I stop and give Autumn a hug. "And I know you had to kill your bastard husband. You had no choice. You deserve some happiness."

Chapter 40

I walk along with Carl through the cemetery. He limps gingerly, taking care to walk a straight path approximately eight feet from the rows of headstones. Carl pulls off his cap, holds it in front of him. "Hi, Judy. Garden's lookin' pretty droopy."

Briarwood is old, crumbling stones dating back to the early eighteen hundreds, a cool spot shaded by maples and beeches sitting on a slight hill on an acre just outside Lake Ann. The cemetery is small, and all the graves are full. Carl tells me he and Judy have the last reservations in the Reinbold family plot.

Carl stops at a long-handled green pump. He leans into the handle, the loud braying finally brings up a trickle of water which grows to a stream, falling on river rocks at the base. He grabs hold of the galvanized pail with his left hand, sticks it under the spout. Then he hands it to me while he fills a second pail.

Hobbling back across the lawn, the cold water splashing from the pail, Carl stops in front of Judy's headstone. He has planted the flowers around Judy's grave, and I help him maintain the little garden through the hottest part of the summer.

"Well, honey, the new children's hospital opened. It was a big deal. Governor Milliken came up." Carl stoops and rations the water around each plant. "Luanne's here with me today. You remember her, don't ya? We been spendin' quite a lot of time together." He smiles and sits back on the grass. "She'd be about the right age for our daughter, wouldn't she, darlin'? She's a fine young woman, just havin' a hard time." He chuckles to himself. "She's quite the little gardener. Gettin' better every day."

After deadheading the petunias, I sit under a maple to give Carl his privacy. He leans back on his elbows, stretching his bad leg with a groan. A breeze moves through the trees. He closes his eyes. He rolls onto one hip to pull his handkerchief from his back pocket.

It isn't easy for Carl to get up from the ground. But I know from experience, he doesn't want help. He leans against the stone and uses his arms and his good leg to push himself to a stand. "Guess you're still helping me, honey. Somebody I can lean on." He wipes his eyes and walks to the truck, bends over the tailgate. I start to get up to help Carl load when I see a man coming behind him. Carl turns just as the guy steps up. Carl seems to know the man. They start talking. I sit back down and listen.

"Joe. What are you doing here?" Carl asks.

"Wanted to catch you alone."

"You followin' me?"

"I know you come out to the cemetery every day."

"You got somebody here, Doremire?"

"No."

"Why you here then?"

"Like I said, I want to talk to you alone."

"Coulda' talked at work …Okay, what you got to say?"

"I know what you did."

"What?"

"Oh, the superintendent didn't say who told him, but it was you, I know it." Joe Doremire's lip curls. "Trying to get me fired this time, Carl?"

"I don't know what you're talking about."

"Don't give me that. You told the boss I screwed that retard."

"You're nuts. I didn't tell the superintendent anything."

"You ratted on me, Carl, just like before."

Carl pushes past Joe, walks back toward Judy's grave with the clippers in his hand. "You better go, Joe."

"If you say a word about our little deal."

"Don't bring that mess to the cemetery," Carl snaps.

"Now you listen to me, Reinbold. You open your mouth, you're the one's goin' to prison. Let's not forget that." Joe pokes Carl's chest.

"Rapin' somebody could get you in prison," Carl says.

"Now let's be clear on this. That's not gonna happen. Nobody cares about that girl. Besides, she wanted it."

"Bullcrap!"

"I'm due to retire. I could lose my job."

"You get fired, it'll be your own fault. You pulled so much crap over the years; they could've fired you a hundred times over."

"We don't need tattletales like you around. You'd think you woulda' learned your lesson."

"What're you sayin'? You mean turnin' you in for stealin' them calves?" Carl stops and turns toward Joe.

"It was pretty quick after you finked out on us that you had that accident in the tunnel, wasn't it?"

"Yeah …when the patient attacked me?"

"It wasn't no patient, Carl." Joe steps back a couple of steps.

"What are you saying?" Carl's voice climbs.

"You figure it out, you fuckin' snitch." Joe points his finger. "Now you listen to me. If you so much as mention my name …you'll be sorry." He pokes his finger into the air. "This time you won't get off so easy."

Carl brings the clippers up in front of him. "You? It was you?"

"I ain't sayin' that …but things happen to people like you— Mr. and Mrs. High and Mighty. You ain't so smug now, limpin' around like a cripple and your wife, there, in the ground."

Carl brings the clippers up over his shoulder, steps toward Joe. I rise to my feet.

"Judy?"

"Calm down there, partner. I don't know anything about Judy. I'm sayin' to keep your mouth shut. If you don't, you'll be sorry. That's all I'm sayin'."

"Hey!" I run toward Carl's truck. Joe Doremire jogs across the lawn and onto Heaven's Gate Road where his truck is parked behind a monument.

"Carl, you alright?"

"Did you hear that, Luanne? He's the one. Some of his boys the one's beat me up down in the tunnels." Carl turns back to Judy's grave. "Honey, did you hear that? I swear to god …if he had anything to do with you …I'll kill him."

Chapter 41

It's the first week in September. I groom my flower beds early before the sun catches fire. I hear the work crew of patients gathered by the bandstand, setting up for the Fall Carnival, the last major outdoor event of the summer season. I stand up and scan the crowd, my hand over my eyes to block the sun, still low in the sky.

Heidi scurries across the lawn with posters in her hand. "Morning, Lu. Man, do you ever give up? It's September."

"Best time of year for gardening."

Autumn comes down the walk from Building 50 on her way to her job in the laundry. "Morning, girls."

"Morning." Heidi motions Autumn over. "Don't tell me—laundry."

"Yup, hi-ho, hi-ho," she smiles. "How's the carnival going?"

"Busy. I'm captain of the ship of fools."

"Heidi!"

"Just kiddin'." Heidi is the volunteer coordinator for the carnival. Although she jokes about it, I know she takes her job very seriously.

"Garden looks pretty, Lu," Autumn says.

"Yeah, and her mother and sister are coming to the carnival. They'll be proud of you, Lu," Heidi says. "I gotta get going."

"Me, too. There's the bell." Autumn breaks into a trot toward the laundry. I sit down on the grass, and before long Carl comes by to help.

"Getting' that garden in tiptop shape?"

"Yeah, I gotta admit. I want to show it to my mom on Saturday."

"Well, course you do. It's a beauty. I'm proud of you."

"Thanks, Carl."

"Here, let me prop up those mums with a few of these sticks."

"There's the Lobster on her way to break."

"A lobster? Where?"

I laugh. "Doris Lobsinger. The Lobster, we call her. She's the one I told you about. The nurse who was so mean to me when I first came in."

"That so?" Carl shielded his eyes with his hand. "Well, by god, no wonder. That's Doris Doremire."

"Doremire? You mean like Joe Doremire?"

"Yup, sure do. She's his wife. Well, not now. They got a divorce. I can't tell you how many times the police were called to their house. He beat her, too. Just like Jeannie, his new wife. Yup, she married Vern Lobsinger. He's gotta be better than Joe."

After lunch, I go to Hall 9 for group and sit down next to Estee.

Dr. Murray starts, speaks across the group, directly to Estee. "Good afternoon. How are you feeling?"

"Really good."

I can hear her mumble under her breath, *That's it, play the game, fake it, fake it.*

"Have you been tired?"

"Yes, a little. I'm nodding off a lot." *The bitch is planning to keep you doped up. Do something!*

"The itching and dry mouth are starting to bother me," Estee says.

"Have you heard any voices, Estee?"

"Voices?...No." *Good job. She doesn't know what she's doing anyway.*

"No voices at all?" Dr. Murray asks.

"No, none."

"That's good news." *See? Told you ...ignorant cow.*

I can't hold my tongue. "Estee, Dr. Murray asked if you've been hearing voices."

"I know. The answer is no."

"Hearing voices. Like right now?" I don't want Estee going off the deep end again.

"Shut up, Luanne. I said no."

"I'm going to reduce your medication again, Estee. You should feel more alert, less groggy. By Saturday, you'll be in good enough shape to go to the carnival with Heidi."

Bingo! "Thanks, Dr. Murray. I really think I'm ready for that." *Yeah, you're ready all right. They can't keep you down. You've got things to do.*

Dr. Murray leans forward, looks directly at Estee. "You've had a setback, but you're on the mend. I'll see you at the carnival." Dr. Murray sits back in her chair. "Who would like to talk?"

"My parents locked me up here because I'm a pervert," a young woman named Fran speaks up.

"Go ahead," Dr. Murray nods.

"I love Jody."

"Who's Jody?" Heidi asks.

"She's my …girlfriend, I guess. We love each other. We tried to keep it a secret …my little brother saw us kiss. He told. All hell broke loose."

"You get locked up for that?" I ask.

"I'm a homo, I guess," Fran said. "My mom says Jesus hates queers."

"Is that being mental?" another patient asks Dr. Murray.

"Right now, homosexuality is a mental illness, yes. But I believe that will soon change."

"You don't get locked up for being a homo, do you?" I ask.

"I tried to kill myself," Fran says.

"Oh. Me, too," I say.

"And yes, you do get locked up for being a homo."

"My kids are coming up for the carnival," Autumn says. "My oldest is so mad at me. He's hard to be around."

"Just be patient with him, Autumn. His world is upside down right now," Dr. Murray says.

"I feel so guilty. My mom says I'm letting him walk all over me, just like Jim did. But he wouldn't be so mixed up if it wasn't for me," Autumn says. "I don't know what to do."

"Jesus, you killed his dad!" Fran shouts.

"You don't know jack-shit about it, you perv," Heidi yells.

"Ladies, please try to be respectful. Let's keep it positive," Dr. Murray says.

"Positive, huh?" I've had it. "That's a laugh."

"What's going on, Luanne?" Dr. Murray asks.

"Summer's over, gardening's done. I miss Isabel. Now I'm losing Carl. He's been . . .in the time we had working together …well, he's been like a dad, or an uncle, at least."

"It's okay to be friends with a staff, right? I mean if they help us get better?" Autumn asks.

"It's not allowed. Patients do tend to feel close to some of the staff, that can't be helped. But, not friends." Dr. Murray says. "Carl is a father substitute for you, Luanne."

"Yeah, I guess so. He's a nice old guy. He treats me like a real person."

Later, in the dayroom, I sit next to Estee. She holds up her cigarette for a light, and sits smoking. She isn't speaking to me. But she isn't silent.

"I hate feeling this way. I can't trust anybody—well, maybe Autumn," she says out loud.

"Autumn's my friend. She's never done anything to harm me, Luanne or Heidi either. They're my family now."

I look over at Estee, wonder if she's talking to me. But she isn't. She's having an argument with somebody, somebody who isn't there. "The carnival's coming up …It's going to be fun. I need that. I need it!"

Estee rocks and hums loudly—my guess, to drown out the voices.

Chapter 42

THE OBSERVER   *October 4, 1969*
          FALL CARNIVAL FUN
*Our Fall Carnival was a roaring success! Dr.
Murray spent a lot of time underwater thanks to
the hotshots who bought tickets at the dunk tank.
Huge amounts of popcorn and soda were sold, as
well as candy and caramel apples. Winners of the
contests are on page 11. Goodbye summer, see you
next year.*

We walk across the grounds on a cloudless, crisp Saturday.
The sky pulses with flocks of barn swallows enjoying the fading
days of summer, singing their songs high in the oaks. The dunk tank
booth takes center stage at the carnival, and Dr. Murray has once
again volunteered to be the one of the stooges. Carl and I are there
to help set up.

"Mornin'."

"Good morning, Carl, Luanne," Dr. Murray says.

"I been assigned to the dunk tank …supposed to reset after
each dunk and help you back up," Carl says.

"You're volunteering?"

"Yup. Gives me somethin' to do."

"I'm just here for an hour or so to help get things going," I
add. "Mom and Molly will be here at noon."

"Great. Luanne, you can get that stack of towels ready and
put a little more water in the tank. I don't want to hit bottom. The
hose is right over there by the back of the tent. Carl, how are you
doing?"

"Good, real good."

"I'm so glad to hear that, Carl."

Carl checks his watch. A stampede of patients will begin
right after the nine a.m. bell, time for Dr. Murray to get perched in
the tank. Carl holds her arm as she skooches out onto the platform.

The bell rings and patients and attendants spill from the cottages and hurry down the sidewalks, chatting and laughing with excitement.

Dr. Murray turns toward Carl. "Just thought you'd want to know. Joe Doremire was fired last week."

"Oh?"

"Yes. Thank you, Carl. I didn't mention who told me about the Soap House, but he got what he deserved. He's gone."

"He planned to retire this year."

"He lost his retirement."

"Well, he brought it on himself," Carl sighs, steps away from the tank.

Heidi and Estee walk up with tickets. Heidi gives Carl three and lines up for a winning shot. The balls flash by on their way to the target. The first misses completely, the second nicks the edge, and number three lands just outside the bull's eye. "Damn it! I need to save tickets for a caramel apple. Estee, you try."

Estee stares at Heidi. "What ...what do I do?"

"Here, give me a ticket. Carl, we'll take one." Heidi rips a ticket from Estee's roll, takes the ball from Carl and hands it to her. "Now throw as hard as you can at that bull's eye." Estee shuffles up to the front of the booth. She raises her arm, brings the ball up to ear level and throws it. It plops onto the counter, bounces, and lands in the dirt outside the booth.

"I'm not very good at this, I guess," Estee says weakly. "What? No, that's not it."

Heidi puts her hand around Estee's shoulder. "It's okay. You'll do better at other stuff."

You need a gun, not a ball, Estee mumbles.

I see Autumn coming down the path with her children. She's talking and laughing with Rudy. The kids chatter with excitement, all but the oldest who drags his feet, kicking up dust as he walks by.

"Carl, how's it going?" Rudy asks.

"Good, Rudy, real good. You?"

"Pretty good. I ran into Autumn here today. She works for me in the laundry."

"Nice day, huh?"

"Gimme' some money. I want to try it," Ryan says to his mother. "Give me some money," he demands. Rudy gives him a ticket. He throws the ball with such force, it almost hits Carl who stands behind the tank.

"That's quite an arm you've got there," Dr. Murray says.

"Yeah, right." He kicks at his sister.

"Hey kiddo, let me help you with your aim," Rudy says.

"Nah. Never mind." Ryan walks ahead, kicking stones into the booth canvases as he passes.

"Nice to see you, Dr. Murray. Good luck," Autumn says. "See you later, Lu." She puts her hand on the shoulder of her youngest, guides her down the path.

Just before noon, Mom and Molly meet me at the dunk tank.

"Mom, this is Carl, the attendant I told you so much about."

"Luanne can't say enough good about you, Carl," Mom says. "Thank you for helping her." She shakes Carl's hand.

"She's the one's got the good heart," Carl says, patting me on the shoulder. "She's a hard worker, this one."

"I'm proud of her," Mom says.

"Jumpin' Jesus, you look just like my dad," Molly says. "Man, that's weird."

"What did I tell you? And that's my doctor over the tank."

"Hi, Mrs. Iazetto, Molly."

Molly buys three balls. "Prepare to swim." She sends Dr. Murray into the tank all three times. They laugh as she mocks drowning.

"Please don't let her have any more tickets," Dr. Murray jokes as she rubs her hair with the towel.

"She's a powerhouse! Made all-state this year in softball," I pat my sister on the back.

"I'm proud of all my daughters," Mom says.

Chapter 43

Afternoon, Dr. Murray." I sit down for my session. "Good afternoon, Luanne. How are you doing?" "Okay, I guess." "Any good bad dreams." "Um-hummm." "Go ahead." "I'm at the beach. I see a kitten scratching in the sand. Like he's in a giant litter box. When I get closer, I can see the kitten is wearing diapers, like a baby."

"Go ahead."

"I bend over to pick the kitten up. He lets out with this loud squalling. He clings onto my shirt with his claws. He's starting to hurt me. I pull him away from me, and he's now the kitten baby. He reaches out and scratches me. I drop him in the sand. He scampers away, and climbs on top of a large sand hill. He's crying really loud. Then I hear Jeff's voice. *What's that?* I hear him say."

"Jeff's there?"

"No. Just his voice. I look around, but there's nobody on the beach. I go toward the kitten to see what's the matter with him. Suddenly the hill starts to move, and a hand comes up out of the sand. The hand grabs the kitten, who is mewing even louder now. Suddenly, the sand blows away, and Jeff's face appears. I yell at him to put the kitten down. He opens his hand, and the kitten is limp. *I'm sorry,* he says. That's all I can remember."

"How do you feel about the dream?"

"Very, very sad. And mad at Jeff."

"Have you had any new memories about Alexander's death?"

"Not really."

"How about his illness?"

"I remember almost everything about that."

"What?"

"I remember one night when the pain got so bad, we had to take him to the hospital. The nurses were giving him medication, but he was still squirming and crying out. I knew he was in pain. I kept asking them to give him something. Dr. Costello came in much later. I'm not sure why he took so long.

"When the doctor came in, he looked at Alexander, and then looked at his chart. He went to the nurses' station. I could hear what he said."

"What was that?"

"He was mad. Said Tylenol III was nothing. There was no excuse for the baby to be in pain …told them to get in there …give him a shot. After Alexander got that shot, he fell asleep."

"I'm so sorry," Dr. Murray says.

"My worst fear came true."

"That Alexander would be in pain?"

"Yes …I should have insisted …"

"Was Jeff there?"

"He wouldn't make any waves."

"Probably not."

"But I guess I wasn't any better. How could I sit there for three hours with my little boy suffering and not do something?"

"I think you said you tried. You kept asking for medication."

"Yeah, but I could've done more."

"You did the best you could."

"I guess so …"

"What else do you remember?"

"Alexander's eye was swollen shut with cancer. I took him in for his regular chemo appointment and they had a new nurse. She calls for Alexander and I bring him up to the nurses' station. She says something like, *Oh my, what happened? Did you fall down?* Everybody looks up. I want to strangle her on the spot."

"What *did* you do?"

"I said, *No, he didn't fall down.* But she just won't let it go. *What happened, honey?* She pretends she's talking to Alexander. Finally, I say *He's here for chemotherapy* and she shuts up."

"That's terrible," Dr. Murray says.

"I want to turn around and shout into the waiting room, *My little boy didn't fall down. He's not going to get better. My son's got cancer. He's going to die!*" I put my hands over my face and cry.

Chapter 44

roup is small with Isabel, Beth and Estee missing. I figure we'll be talking about Autumn's attack. I give her a hug before she sits down.

"How are you doing, Autumn?" Dr. Murray asks.

"Okay, thanks."

"That's quite a shiner you got." Heidi says. "Does it hurt?"

"A little."

"As I told you yesterday, Autumn, we're going to use our group time today talking about what happened. You can start whenever you're ready."

"I've been on reduced sleep meds for about a week, so I'm waking up from time to time during the night. Thursday night, when I woke up, I felt something. *Am I dreaming?* I rolled over, my eyes straining and bulging into the blackness of our tiny room. Someone breathed close to my bed."

"Eowww. How scary is that?" Heidi says.

"Very. I couldn't see. Just a dim gray light came through the transom. *What?* I sat up and pumped my heels against the mattress as if I were keeping myself from sliding down a steep hill. I pushed until my back hit the iron rungs of the headboard. *Estee, is that you?* I mean, who else could it be? The pillow flew at me before I had a chance to raise my hands. She pressed down on my face, bending my neck backwards over the metal rail. It felt as if my head would pop off. I kicked my legs wildly, my clenched fists stabbed at the darkness. Finally, my punches hit home, each one landed with a sickening thud, like tenderizing meat. Ugh, it was so awful. The taut pillow released, I gasped for air.

"You can't escape. You will meet defeat. The deep voice hissed into the darkness. I swear, it didn't even sound like Estee. I shouted at her to stop, asked her why she was doing this. Told her it was me, Autumn. She said, *You can't fool me. Your tricks won't work. Help me Lord. Give me strength to carry out your mission."*

"Man alive. I've got goosebumps." I could feel the hair on the back of my neck pop up.

"I shouted *Help! Help!* as loud as I could in the direction of the door. *Attendant ...Help!* Then I rolled, using my heels as leverage, reaching and pulling for momentum. I broke free from Estee's hold, dropped off the edge of the bed, and crawled under it.

"*I'm on to you ...invisible or not ...Almighty Lord, help me!*" Estee bumped into walls, tripped over beds, babbling some strange language I couldn't understand. I ...ah ...Jesus, ...I ...was so scared."

"Slow down, take a deep breath. You're shaking from head to toe," Dr. Murray says.

"The granite bedpan hit the floor with a loud clatter. Now they will hear the racket and come running. I crouched at the head of the bed, balled up against the wall. Nobody came. The room went quiet, the silence hung over the room like a shroud. I was frozen, my heart thumping in my chest so loud, I thought she'd hear it. I remember thinking, *Where is she?* I didn't hear a sound. I tried to slow my breathing as I leaned from under the bed. I ran the palm of my hand across the floor. When I felt the curved side of the bed pan, I made my move. I flung it against the door and screamed at the top of my voice, *Nurse, Nurse!*

"That's when she jumped on my arm, pinched at my skin, dragged me from my hiding place. *God is on my side. Vengeance is mine, sayeth the Lord.* She held my arm and just kept kicking me in the side. I thought I was going to die. Kleenex, please."

"Then what happened?"

"That's when the door burst open, the light flashed on. Two attendants stormed the room, grabbed Estee and twisted her arms behind her back. She's strong; it took four of them to pin her to the floor. They held her while she kicked and rolled. Two more attendants arrived with a straightjacket. I stood in the far corner, plastered against the wall, hands over my eyes. When Estee's voice got smaller and smaller down the hall, I covered up with my blanket.

"An attendant came in and gave me a pill. She told me Estee would be in protection that night, and probably transfer to Hall 5 tomorrow. Is she? Did they take her to 5?"

"Yes. She'll be there for awhile. How do you feel about this, Autumn?"

"Just terrible. I know she's sick, but I cried so hard last night I puked in my bedpan. I've been trying to sort my thoughts. I heard my dad's voice yelling at me when Estee was attacking me."

"Yes, not only was last night a trauma, it also triggered all the abuse you suffered from your father."

Four weeks later Autumn comes into group. "Estee's back."

"How is she?" I ask.

"Bad. I came into the dayroom from an afternoon walk. I headed toward our usual spot, and I noticed a small slumped figure backlit from the window light. I stopped for quite a while and stared. Then I crept forward, squinting into the sun. The figure turned her head. It was Estee alright. Her curly hair had been shaved; her mouth drooped on one side. Her white hands were clasped in her lap. She was shaking like a leaf. I asked her if she was cold. I rubbed her thin arms. They were no bigger than a twig."

"Oh, no. Is she able to come to group?"

"Not today," Dr. Murray says.

"She asked me for a cigarette, but her hands were trembling so badly she couldn't even hold it. I told her I'd get it lit for her. The attendant was a bitch. *Are you going to supervise her with this cigarette? She's a fire hazard.* Of course I'd supervise her. She was so pitiful."

Autumn wiped her eyes. "Her lips wouldn't even come together when she tried to drag on her cigarette. It burned out while she was still holding it. I took it and held her hand. She nodded off. Later, when she woke up, she had nothing to say. It's so sad."

"Estee is seriously ill. She's having a bad time right now."

"Jezz, what's with shaving her head? Monsters," Heidi says.

"She rubbed excrement on herself in protection. They had difficulty keeping her clean," Dr. Murray says. "I know it's heartbreaking to see her like this. We're doing all we can."

"What can we do to help?" I ask.

"Just be with her as much as you can. Don't expect too much from her, try to include her in things. She's been down before and has rallied. Let's keep our fingers crossed."

Over the next two months, Estee improves. The shaking and itching decrease, and her mind seems clearer. Dr. Murray reports in group that Estee's medication has been reduced. If all goes well, she will soon return to the world of the living.

Chapter 45

We look out over the field. The corn husks bend like withered old men marching across the frozen ground in the west twenty.

"Just don't have the inclination to plow 'em under this fall," Carl says. "In the spring, I'll put the old Massey up for sale—won't need a tractor if I'm not plantin'. Come with me, Luanne. I want to show you something."

I follow Carl as he limps along the path leading down to the stream, his boots sliding on the frozen meadow grass.

"A blanket of white's comin' soon. Winter time, this farm looks just like it fell off a Currier and Ives print. Then, I'll be stuck in the house, lookin' for somethin' to do. I want you to take this one last walk with me before the path blows over and closes up with snow. You'll be goin' home soon …Yeah, here it is. After twenty-three years, that small stone cross there hangs together by the sheer will of God."

I feel like I've been led to a sacred place. Behind the cross, the crystal water rushes over rocks, swirling the river grass, leaving tiny shards of ice, sparkling harbingers of the cold months ahead.

"Hello, my precious. Brought somebody to visit today." Carl bows his head in the clearing of frozen flowers. "Don't you worry; I'll be with you soon."

"Who is it, Carl? Who's buried here?"

"Our baby girl, Hope Marie Reinbold."

I step up beside Carl and put my hand on his arm. "I'm so sorry, Carl." I can't help it, I cry softly. I'm not sure if I'm crying for Carl, for his baby daughter, for Alexander, or myself. A deep sadness fills me.

"Here, take my hankie. I'm all cried out. When Judy died, thoughts of her up there in Briarwood Cemetery, little Hope out here by herself haunted me. I'm a foolish old coot."

"I don't understand. Why is Hope buried here and not Briarwood?"

"Well now, that's a simple question with a complicated answer. Let's go back to campus, have a cup a coffee, and I'll tell you why."

We stop in the canteen for coffee, and sit on a picnic table in a far corner of the hospital grounds, near the old barns.

"Luanne, I haven't told anybody this. But I think it's time I got it off my chest. Do you mind?"

"No. Please, go ahead."

"Hope was two weeks old that hot summer night, 1946. I spent the day harvestin' grain, ate a late supper, and fell into bed. The noisy old fan drew in the night air, blowin' the curtains into the room like dancing ghosts. Me and Judy sprawled on the bed, only our hands touching in our hot bedroom.

"Next mornin', I woke up early to tend to the milkin'. I looked over at Judy sleepin' beside me. She was probably exhausted from the night feedings. I stopped at the foot of the bed to say good mornin' to little Hope, asleep in her bassinet. As I bent to kiss her head, I noticed her labored breathing. *Was the room too closed in, blankets too much?* I touched my fingers to the baby's chest. Seemed like her heart was beatin' pretty fast.

"I gently shook Judy's shoulder and called her name. She sprang up. *What? What is it?*

"*Probably nothin'*, I said. I could see she was upset. *The baby's breathing seems off.* Judy rushed to the bassinet, snatching little Hope in her arms, bringing the baby's mouth up to her ear. She bolted from the room, into the bathroom. *Carl, run some cool water in the sink, she's burning up.* She checked Hope's pulse, took her temperature. *Temp's over a hundred. Mash up an aspirin in a teaspoon of water. Hurry.* Judy fed the aspirin mixture to Hope in a dropper, gently bathed her in tepid water. Even with this, the baby didn't cry. Judy was a nurse, and a darn good one. I knew she'd know what to do.

"After a few minutes she said, *Carl, we have to call somebody. The fever's not coming down.*

"*Call who?*

"The doctor, the hospital, somebody!

"We can't do that, hon. They'll put two and two together. We'll go to jail. Hope won't have a home.

"Lord help me. I don't know what to do! She wrapped Hope in a receiving blanket, sat down in the rocking chair. *Just wait for the aspirin to work, I guess. Heavenly father, please help our little girl.* She rocked frantically. *Get me a cool washrag, Carl.* She patted the baby's face, smoothed the damp cloth across her forehead, back through her curly hair. I sat on the edge of the bed, praying. By mid-morning, the fever broke, Hope's breathing slowed.

"She's sleeping like an angel, Judy said as she lowered her into the bassinette. I stood behind her, smiling. We hugged for a long time, hung onto each other for dear life. I asked Judy what happened, but she wasn't sure. Some kind of infection, cold bug …Looked like it was gonna blow over. I asked Judy if I should go to work. She wanted me there, just in case. I was glad to stay home. I didn't want to leave Judy alone with a sick baby.

"I needed to get to the barn before the cows blew up. I was done in a couple hours. But, it wasn't long after, Hope died. She just stopped breathing. Judy blamed herself, said she should have called the doctor. Or maybe she blames me, I'll never know for sure. I just remember her saying, *Our baby's dead, and it's my fault.* I never heard a woman wail and cry like she did. There was no comforting her, but I tried to assure her Hope went straight to heaven. Nothin' we could do, 'cept give her a proper burial. And we were on our own with that.

"Next mornin', we walked through the field to Judy's favorite spot down by the creek. We worked to clear a spot for Hope's grave, turnin' over the grass and removin' the clumps. I raked the soil smooth, Judy came behind me, stompin' the ground solid. When we were satisfied, we went back up to the house.

"I spent the better part of the afternoon in my workshop in the barn, buildin' a simple pine box, finished with a birch cross on the lid. Judy dressed Hope in her baptism gown. At sunset, we said our goodbyes and put the baby in her coffin. I carried her, Judy followed with a bouquet of wild flowers. I placed the tiny box in the grave as Judy read from the family Bible. We placed stones on the freshly turned earth until I could make somethin' more fitting for a marker.

"We sat on the porch that night well past midnight under a blanket of misty summer stars and listened to the frogs singing down by the creek."

Chapter 46

It's a Sunday morning in late October. Heidi and I walk down *Red Drive* from Cottage 22. We're meeting Estee and Autumn in front of Building 50 for Sunday services at the All Faiths Chapel on the east side of the hospital complex. September was unusually hot, and cool nights coaxed the leaves to turn. They fall away from their nodes and dance to the ground, sliding softly onto the cool grass. The wind whips them into eddies spinning across the lawn. We get to Building 50 with just ten minutes to spare before the chapel bell rings.

"Where are they?" Heidi paces in front of the door.

"They're usually here waiting."

We pace, sigh, and peer through the front door. At exactly nine o'clock, the chapel bell rings.

"That's it," Heidi says. "I'm supposed to be an usher today. I can't be late."

"You go on ahead. I'll talk to the key man; see if he'll let me in."

"Okay. See you later." Heidi takes off at a dead run across the lawn.

I ring the doorbell and wait.

"Good morning." I say when he opens the door. "I'm supposed to meet two patients out front. They have passes to attend church."

"Looks like they changed their minds."

"May I come in and check at the nurses' station in Hall 9?"

"Guess that's okay. Do you know the way?"

"Yes. Thank you." I hurry down the hall toward the elevator.

The bell dings as the elevator doors slide open on Hall 9, I step up to the nurses' station and press the buzzer. I wait a good five minutes for a nurse to come to the door.

"What is it?" The nurse's face is unusually red, a blue-white cast around her thin lips.

"I'm here to pick up Estee Wiseman and Autumn Bauer for church."

"Come in. Stay right here." The sound of soles squeaking across linoleum catches my attention, loud voices rising and falling, the words indistinguishable. I peer down the hall. The nurse joins a group of attendants gathered at the far end, near the bathrooms. A few patients hustle from the dayroom toward the commotion. I walk slowly into the hall, try to make out the voices, pick up the pace as I approach the crowd.

"What's going on?"

"A patient went berserk and has one of the bathroom aides."

"Who ...who is the patient?" I feel the fear spark down my arms. My stomach rolls.

"Don't know."

I push toward the door and stand on tiptoes trying to see over the heads of the attendants.

Autumn squeezes my arm. "Luanne, thank God. It's Estee. Come on. They're trying to talk her down." Autumn pulls me through the crowd. We stop just outside the bathroom door.

Estee stands in front of a line of sinks with her arm across the chest of a terrified aide. Her other hand holds a small curved knife against the aide's throat. Two attendants are negotiating for her to put the weapon down and release her prisoner.

"Where did she get that curved thing?" I ask Autumn.

"It looks like a leather tool from the Shop. I don't know how she got it, but they're sharp."

Autumn takes a couple of steps forward, talks to one of the nurses. The nurse whispers to one of the negotiators.

"Okay, Autumn. They said you can try to talk to her." She guides Autumn by the elbow, brings her within a few feet of Estee.

"Estee, it's me, Autumn. Put the knife down, sweetie. It's time to go to church."

"Ha! Now that's a clever one, isn't it," Estee shouts.

"Estee. You know me—Autumn."

"He takes many forms."

She pulls the aide closer. One of the attendants comes up behind Autumn and puts his mouth to her ear. "Okay, step back. I think you're making it worse."

"But, she knows me. I can help."

"No, she doesn't recognize you. She thinks you're the devil. Step back!"

Autumn and I stand against the wall and watch as the attendants try to enter Estee's delusion, manipulate it to their advantage. Nothing works. Estee's eyes are wild, black, darting around the room. One of the attendants sneaks along the back wall by the showers and approaches Estee from the rear. He has a large syringe in one hand, leather restraints in the other. Just as he steps away from the wall, she turns.

It looks like she's drawing a line across the aide's neck with red pencil. The knife moves slowly and deliberately across the aide's throat, curves upward toward her ear as Estee's hand finishes the arc. The aide makes a gurgling sound, clutches her neck as she crumples to the floor. Attendants are on her immediately, applying pressure, carrying her from the room where a stretcher waits in the hall.

Estee waves the knife back and forth in front of her body, stabbing at anybody who comes close. The attendants clear the room, pushing Autumn and me into the hall. I hear a scuffle from the bathroom as they jab me toward the dayroom. We stand with the others in the doorway as the attendants pass, dragging Estee by the straps in the back of the strait jacket. Her head dangles forward, her legs trail along the tile floor.

She disappears.

Chapter 47

THE OBSERVER   November 2, 1969
Page 11

Admissions:
Randal Fife, Marquette, Mi
Lillian Brayfield, Prudenville, Mi
Felicia Courtland, Grayling, Mi
Jeffrey Bednarczyk, Rosebush, Mi

Home Leaves:
Luanne Kilpi
Nadine Peltzer
Rhonda Knapp
Samuel Gray
Discharges:
Gerald Grisdale
Benedict Falmouth
Staff Terminations
Joseph Doremire
Bonnie Harrison
Judith McInerney
Valerie Petrowski
Retirements:
Bernice Laferty

I pick up the hospital newspaper and search for news of the aide who Estee attacked with a knife in Hall 9. I'm not surprised when I find nothing in the *Observer*. The hospital grapevine reports the victim is recovering at Munson Hospital.

I walk to the tool crib to meet Carl. We have fall cleanup to attend to. He's at the picnic table, behind the paper. "Hi, Carl."

"Mornin, Lu. I read Joe Doremire's name in the staff terminations. I guess he really got fired—just a few months before his scheduled retirement. He's gone."

"Do you think he might try to hurt you?"

"Nah. Haven't heard anything. No surprise visits, no threats."

"He could still be out there, Carl. Waiting."

"No need to worry. I'm fine. Besides, I've got more dirt on him and I'm not afraid to use it. Judy's gone and now it don't matter."

"What do you mean?"

"Well, I might as well back up a bit and tell you the whole story."

"Okay."

"It was early June, 1947 when Doris Lobsinger, then Doris Doremire, came under Judy's supervision. According to Judy, Doris paid her dues working in Hall 5, and despite her checkered work record, seniority finally won out and she transferred to Judy's hall.

"The nurses were taking their lunch in the staff dining hall. *Anything yet?* Judy's best friend, Bev, whispered to Judy. *Gramma visited last night,* Judy told her. We were trying to have a baby, and Judy had started her monthly. It was always a big disappointment.

"Later that afternoon, Doris was assisting Judy in the nurses' station, doling out tranquilizers into little paper cups for the three o'clock med line.

Ah …maybe I shouldn't butt in, Doris said.

What is it? Judy asked. *You tryin' to have a baby"*

What"

Calm down. I'm tryin' to help you.

Help me what? Judy set the medication jar on the shelf.

Would you like a baby?

Judy told me she was shocked. *What are you getting at, Mrs. Doremire?*

My husband and me …we know somebody wantin' to adopt out a baby.

Who?

Somebody here at the hospital. Ah …I can't say …baby's due this summer. I mean, her daughter's pregnant …due to give birth soon.

"*Oh? A newborn then? What agency?* Judy said she tried not to show her interest, but she was bustin' with excitement.

"*No agency. Cash and carry deal.*

"*Is that legal?* Judy started to get nervous.

"*Sure it's legal. Ah, there won't be no papers or anything.*

"*No papers?* Judy's no dummy, now she was really startin' to get suspicious.

"*Maybe it's not what you'd call totally on the up and up. Do you want a baby or not?*

"*Well, yes. Yes, of course. Let me talk to my husband.* Her heart took over at that point, and by the time she got home, she could hardly talk.

"I'm in the barn tendin' a sick cow when I hear her yellin' from the back porch. I pat the cow's flanks, stomp across the floor, stick my head out the barn door and wave to Judy. *Out here, hon. Got a cow with a bad foot.*

"Judy bursts through the door, still in her uniform. *Carl, we could get a baby! Doris Doremire, you know the new aide on the Hall? Well, she got me in the nurses' station. Apparently she overheard Bev and me talking at lunch about my period and all, and she says to me, You want a baby? and I said, What? And, anyway, she tells me she knows somebody who's going to give birth soon, wants to adopt out the baby.*

"*Whoa! Slow down. Here, sit.* I lower myself onto a bale of hay, pull Judy onto my lap. *Now, tell me the story.*

"I haven't seen my wife this excited since our wedding day. To tell you the truth, the prospect of a baby has my own heart pumping. But after hearing the story, I'm worried there is something shady about it. I have questions. *Doremire? Any relation to Joe Doremire?*

"*Her husband, I think.*

"*Joe in on this?*

"*I'm not sure. Why?*

"He worked for me at the hospital farm. Got transferred.
He's a bad egg, Judy.

"Will you go to a meeting? Oh, Carl, this could be the answer
to our prayers.

"She's so happy, I can't say no. *I don't know …*

"Carl, please!

Okay, sure. We can find out more about it. I hate to see Judy
get her hopes up. Joe Doremire has been a thorn in my side on
the farm since he came in as a hand. *But, Joe isn't the one havin' a*
baby.

"Judy and me met with the Doremires at City Park two
days later, after work. I wanted details. I tried to balance out Judy's
enthusiasm with a little common sense. She was so taken by the
idea of bein' a mother, she would have taken the baby no questions
asked.

"Joe's story was Doris's teenage niece got pregnant by a
boy from a good family. They managed to keep the pregnancy a
secret by keepin' the unwed mother to the house since school let
out. Their plan was to have the baby at home—pretend it never
happened. There's no birth record, and that's a problem. We have to
have the child's birth certificate to make her a legitimate member of
our family.

"That's your problem. Joe Doremire said. *Five thousand*
dollars for expenses, payable in cash when we give you the baby. I
told him we didn't have that kind of money. He stood up, *Come on,*
Doris. I told you. We're wasting our time. I looked over at Judy, her
face seemed frozen, like she was standin' in front of a firing squad.
I just couldn't hurt her. *No, no. Sit down, just a minute now,* I said.
This don't sound legal, I mean, how can we get a birth certificate.
We gotta' have a birth certificate.

"I told you, I don't know. That's why you're gettin' this deal.

"We could talk to a lawyer, I guess, I said.

"You crazy? No, I can check with a guy I know. Not wastin' my
time 'til I get an answer, though. You in? We got others interested.

"How long do we have …to get the money, I mean. I just had
to make this work, for Judy.

"Who knows? She ain't had it yet, but it could be any day now.

"Gimme a week to get to the bank, sell off some cows.

"I'll give you a week, if I got it. If the baby comes, the money is due.

"Fair enough. We'll need to see the baby, and a birth certificate, before we hand over the money.

"We'll contact you. Joe pulled his wife up by the arm, turned, and left."

"Wow. Weren't you excited, Carl? A baby." I'm so wrapped up in Carl's story, I feel like I'm Judy.

"Course, course I was excited, but I also felt like we were making a big mistake. To trust Doremire? Seemed like jumping into the ocean without a life jacket."

"Well, come on. Keep going. I know you got the baby, but what happened next?"

"When the phone call came, Judy and me drove to City Park with the money wrapped in heavy brown meat paper. I pulled up, and when I came 'round to open Judy's door, I spotted Joe. Sittin' next to him at the picnic table sat Doris, a small bundle in her lap. Doris stood when she saw us approach and handed the baby to Judy. After examinin' her, Judy carefully rewrapped the baby in the receiving blanket, held the infant to her shoulder.

"I tell you, Luanne, I've never seen a baby as beautiful. She was perfect, all the fingers and toes wiggling happily. Judy smiles at me with as close to bliss as I'd ever seen." Carl wipes his eyes.

"Did you give him the money?"

"Yup. I handed Joe the money. *It's all here. Where's the birth certificate,* I said.

"We don't have one yet. Baby came early. It'll take a couple more weeks, Doremire said.

"That's not what we agreed to. Here we go, I thought to myself. Chiseled already. He sure didn't waste no time.

"Carl, please. Judy was about to fall apart.

"Okay, okay. I know where to find you, I told Joe.

"And I know where to find you, Carl."

Chapter 48

The ghost trips leaving the porch. He steps off the sidewalk onto the crunchy lawn. Cochise and Roy Rogers brush past him toward the light.

"Trick or treat," they sing-song.

"Hi, kids." I offer the basket. "Take one." Tiny red fingers rifle the treasure trove, pull out a Slo-Poke and a licorice. "Bye, kids, stay warm."

I pull the door closed and return to the couch, squeezing in next to a hooker in black fishnet hose, a tight satin skirt.

"Looks like they're about done," she says.

"Should we turn off the porch light?" Mom looks up from her sewing.

"Let's wait," Molly says. "I can shut it off when Jess picks me up." She stands up and adjusts her tight sweater. Teetering on spike heels, she turns in front of me.

"Seams straight, Lu?"

"Perfect. Your make-up is hilarious. Where did you get the bright blue eye shadow?"

"Had it." She pushes her hand around on her ratted hair, patting the sides into place.

"Oh, there's Jess." Molly swings a fake fur stole over her shoulders. "Be home by twelve." She wobbles out the door, snapping the light switch as she leaves.

"I told her not to wear that get-up." Mom pulls her needle through the wool fabric of a skirt, lock-stitching around the hem.

"I think she's a riot. I'm turning in early, Mom, right after *Mission Impossible*. It's a long drive back up north."

"Is eight-thirty early enough to get up?" Mom asks.

"I have to be back in the cottage by one."

"Will you drive up?"

"Molly's going, right?"

"She can drive back, but I get nervous with her—she just got her license. She doesn't watch the road, drives too fast."

"I don't mind driving up, Mom."

I'm tired, so tired. So tired it feels like the mattress has flipped, and I'm caught between it and the box springs. I hear a faint crying. *Just a couple of minutes …just a little more sleep, then I can …*

"Mommy, Mommy." A tiny voice, so far away. *Just a second* …My arms and legs feel paralyzed, as if the wires between my brain and my body have short circuited.

" Mommy." A voice so small, like the squeaky bawling of a kitten.

I open my mouth to answer, but my lips are frozen. *Jeff …Jeff …Jeff, it's the baby, the baby …*I push against some kind of force. I roll from under it, and pull myself up. I drag toward the hallway as if wading through sand.

The house is dark, silent. A low light glows from the cracked door of Alexander's room. I push open the door, inch toward the crib. I grasp the railing, lean forward, peer down on the rumpled blankets, my baby …asleep …motionless. I lift the covers …fuzzy gray …round little paws …He opens his eyes, cat eyes, "Meow, meow, Mommy." The scream is in my throat.

The light switches on.

"Hey, hey." Molly shakes my arm. "Jesus, you scared the crap out of me. You're soaking wet."

"I …I …I killed my baby."

"What?"

"What's the matter?" Mom stands at the doorway.

"Lu had a bad dream." Molly's eyes fix on my face.

"Do you need a pill?" Mom asks.

"Ah …yeah. Bottle's by the kitchen sink." I bring my hands to my forehead, slide them back into my hair and squeeze my head as if I can force it to clear.

"Luanne?" Molly whispers.

"Sorry. It was a bad dream. I didn't take my pill."

"Jeez." Molly hugs me.

I drag into the kitchen the next morning, sit down at the table.

"You're quiet." Mom drops two slices of bread into the toaster.

"I'm groggy, Mom. Took my pill late."

"Bad dream, huh?"

"I guess so, I don't really remember. Mom, I don't think I can drive."

"Okay. I can do it."

"I might just sleep on the way up."

"That's fine."

"Are you sure?"

"Yes, I'm sure. It doesn't seem like you're up to it. Didn't you tell me your doctor thought you could be out by Christmas?"

"That's the plan. Why?"

"I just want you to be ready is all."

I sip my coffee. One bad dream and Mom is ready to keep me locked up. I turn to gaze out the back window at the chickadees on the bird feeder. No, she probably is just concerned. What was it Dr. Murray said? Sometimes you project your own feelings on somebody else. Is that what I'm doing? Was I doing it now? Projecting my fears and doubts on Mom? There's no question I fear leaving the hospital. The dream has shaken me, shaken me badly.

As soon as I say goodbye to Mom and Molly in the foyer of Cottage 23, I look for Nurse Delaney.

"I know its Sunday, but I was wondering if I could talk to Dr. Murray today?"

"She's not on call this weekend. Can I can help you?"

"Something happened over the weekend. I ...guess ...I could wait until tomorrow."

"You're not suicidal or anything?"

"I ...I don't know."

"I'll call Dr. Murray. She may want to talk to you on the phone. Or Dr. Webster is on call?"

"Thank you. I'd like to talk to Dr. Murray, if that's possible."
I go back to the dayroom to wait.

"Hey, how was your weekend?" Heidi drops into a chair beside me.

"Good."

"I wish I could get out of here for a weekend. Raylene Cline said she couldn't authorize a home visit 'cuz she called my parents and neither one wanted me visitin'. Now that's fuckin' great, isn't it? Get many trick-or-treaters?"

"Yes, we did ...cute ...Heidi, to tell you the truth, I had a bad weekend."

"What happened?" She leans toward me.

"I ...I'm confused, really."

"Something with your mom?"

"No ...no ...I had this dream."

An attendant walks into the dayroom. "Luanne, Dr. Murray is on the phone. She would like to talk to you."

I follow the nurse to the sliding window. Nurse Delaney unlocks the cubicle, disappears, then reappears on the other side of the glass. She passes the clunky black receiver through the window, the springy cord tethered to a square office phone. I have to bend over and lean forward to bring the receiver to my ear.

"Hello? Yes, Dr. Murray ...well, yes ...hate to bother you, but ...yes, that's right ...since I had this dream ...okay, thank you." I pass the receiver back.

"Dr. Murray is coming in to see me. She asked me to come to her office."

An attendant escorts me through the tunnels to the administration building. When I get there, Dr. Murray is waiting.

"Now, tell me what happened." Dr. Murray motions me to a seat.

"I ...I think ...well, I worry ...I might have killed my baby." That's all I can get out before my voice breaks. I reach for a tissue.

"Was it the dream?"

"Yes. I guess so ...well, the dream was very scary."

"Tell me about it."

I tell Dr. Murray about finding the kitten baby in the crib. I cry, stop several times to try to pull myself together.

"That's a terrifying dream. But it doesn't mean you killed Alexander."

"I think I heard him that night and I was too tired to get up."

"Okay. That's okay. That's understandable. Sometimes the body just gives out, overloaded with grief and stress."

"I think he needed me."

"Luanne, we don't really know if Alexander even called for you that night."

"I ...I think he did. I think he did ...I didn't go ...I was too damned selfish."

"Luanne, please listen. Even if you were too exhausted to get up, it's not your fault. You couldn't have done it differently."

"If he choked or something ...I could have saved him."

"Did he choke?"

"I don't think so ...he looked peaceful ...I guess that's what I'm afraid of ...afraid he choked." I blow my nose. "How do people survive this? Can some people do this? ...mothers ...who can handle this?"

"No, Luanne, nobody handles this. But they do survive it."

"I got mad at him that afternoon."

"You're just a woman, Luanne, not a saint."

"He wanted beans."

"Go on."

"He wouldn't eat and ...anything he wanted ...Campbell's pork and beans ...My hopes were up ...maybe beans would be it ...he'd eat. I heated them up ...then he said no ...he didn't want them ...I ..." I can't stand the shame, I sob, hide behind my hands.

"It's okay, Luanne."

"No, let me finish ...I dumped the beans out on the table ...I ...oh my god ...how could I have treated him like that ...getting mad, for Christ's sake."

"What happened?"

"My voice was all crabby ...told him to make up his mind ...he looked so hurt." I want to escape the memory. I grab my head, drop my elbows to my lap, pull at my hair. "What kind of mother does that ...Jesus."

"You need to forgive yourself for not being perfect." Dr. Murray touches my hand.

"Then he up and died that night." I snapped my head up. "I didn't have time to make it up to him. He died!"

Chapter 49

I jump to my feet. "Heidi, where were you? I barely slept a wink last night."

"Sorry. I should have told you, but I was afraid you'd try to talk me out of it."

"Where did you go?"

"Let's sit down," Dr. Murray says. "Heidi?"

"I hitched to a bar last night. Big mistake. I got plastered and ended up having sex, passed out ...Goddamn it."

I'm so relieved Heidi is back, I come over to her and kiss the top of her head. "I'm so glad you're back. You did the right thing."

"Heidi, we need to hear in detail what happened last night." Dr. Murray seems extra serious.

"I hitched to a bar outside of town called *The Buck Snort*. It's on highway 115 just two miles west of Mesick."

"Not that kind of detail, Heidi. Start with why you snuck out of the hospital and went to this bar."

"I'm not really sure. I overheard some attendants talkin'. They said the bar would be burstin' at the seams last night. I guess November fourteenth is the eve of huntin' season. I snuck out, hitched a ride with a trucker. As we pull up, a hundred fifty or so pickups fill the parking lot and spill down both sides of the road. The semi kicks up gravel as the tires hit the soft shoulder. *Thanks for the ride,* I holler up to the driver. *Be careful, little lady,* he says as he waves to me. The guy was really nice.

"*The Buck Snort* was somethin' else. Big door in the front with deer carved in it, antler door handle. A cloud of sweaty smoke smacks into me as I step inside the entry. I pretend to be reading some of the ads posted on the bulletin board so I can get up the courage to go in. I hear loud voices and laughter just beyond the inside door. I pause at the cigarette machine, look at the neat rows of colorful packs, bend over the glass, try to look like I'm pickin' out a pack while I study the place. *The Buck Snort* has a lot of deer stuff in it."

"That figures, Heidi," Autumn says.

"I never seen a deer as big as the one they have in there. His mangled head's hangin' there with a big sign next to it *Smuck the Buck.* Sign says *'Take a drink, ring the bell.'* The glass eyes stare from crumbled eye sockets. Antlers are decorated with key chains, necklaces, motel keys, and other doodads, one ear's pierced with tons of women's earrings, the other one's gone completely, the nose bent off at a forty-five degree angle, the fur rubbed off the face. All kinds of shit covered the walls and the ceiling, animals and guns and stuff."

"That's enough about the décor, Heidi. Tell us how you were feeling."

"Well, I was nervous, but I kinda sauntered up to the bar, pulled out a cigarette, and held it out to a red-faced man with a couple of day's stubble, wearing a red and black plaid hunting jacket. *Got a light? I says.*

"*Sure 'nough.* He jumps like somebody goosed him and smiles so wide he flashes his gums where his back molars used to be. *Buy you a drink?* He steps off his stool, motions for me to sit down.

"To tell you the truth, that was the moment I've been waiting for, praying for. After Beth died, the guilt got to me so bad I just wanted it to stop. I started thinking about drinking and drugging, talking to myself like it's so romantic, the highlight of my life and all. By the time Estee got transferred to Creedmoor, the craving for alcohol is all I can think about."

"Why didn't you talk to me about it, Heidi?" I'm thinking we talk about almost everything.

"I told ya. I didn't want you talkin' me out of it. Anyway, the bartend asks what I want. *Whiskey and water, straight up.* The first gulp rushes down my throat like hot heaven, sends a shiver through my body, forces my lips back over my teeth. From then on, I just keep ordering 'em.

"I try to talk to the guy who's buyin' me drinks so he won't stop. *Crowded, heh?*

202

"Deer hunters. Won't end 'til after Thanksgiving.

"Thought I'd been caught in a time warp when I walked in—all that junk up above. I wave my hand toward the ceiling.

"Owner got a lot of this stuff when the old Spikehorn Museum outside of Grayling closed. It's kinda like a bar-museum combo. We can swig back a beer and look up, take in Michigan history while we drink.

"I didn't waste no time gettin' drunk. I have to admit, I hung all over the guy, whispering sex talk in his ear. I know when I have a live one.

"I got grass in the truck, he says.

"This was better'n I expected. Far out. We head out into the parking lot, hangin' on to each other and stumblin' over the gravel like contestants in a three-legged race. He opens the passenger side of the truck and boosts me up by my ass. He punches open the glove box and pulls out a lump wrapped in saran wrap. He fumbles a joint from the plastic, lights up, takes a long hit, and passes it to me.

"Man, this is good stuff." His voice raises a couple of octaves as he exhales his words.

"Hell, it's home grown shit, full of stems and seeds, poppin' and sparkin'. I toke on the soggy tip, and that's all I remember. I wake up in the cold truck, naked, covered with an old blanket, smellin' like wet dog. When I sit up and look out at the full parking lot, lights roll from the windows of the bar, music pounds. I couldn't have been out that long, but my buzz wore off, my eyes burn, head feels fuzzy. I dress and stumble across the parking lot to the bar."

"Back into the bar?" I can't believe it.

"Where else was I gonna go?"

I just shrug my shoulders, shake my head.

"Yeah, so I go back in, wash my face, try to touch up my eyebrows. Then I feel this hand on my arm, *Dance?* He's a gangly guy, a checked shirt tucked neatly into his wide belt with a large metal buckle, dark jeans with a perfect crease, cowboy boots. I'm about to dance with Howdy Doody."

Everybody smiled at that one. Everybody but Dr. Murray.

"The floor was hip to hip—Howdy struggled with the fast dances, but he pulled me close for the ballads at the end of the set and came alive, swayin' and dippin' like an Arthur Murray graduate. He invites me to sit with him at his table, pulls out the chair for me, and this time I order a screwdriver and sip it.

"Mr. Doody is a nice guy, lives with his parents in Buckley, just outside Traverse City. His real name is Kurt, nineteen, a couple years older than me. He graduated from Buckley High in the spring and works as a carpenter's apprentice. We talk and dance until last call.

"Need a ride home?

"My plan was to run away, hitch downstate, probably latch on to some guy, and become invisible. But now I'm thinkin' nothin' will change. I'll still be a drunk and a loser, *and* a fugitive. The ol' shame just washes over me. This is the moment of reckoning, I can stick with my original plan, have Kurt drop me off at some made-up place, the next town, Mesick, up the road. Before I know it, my mouth opens and I say, *I do need a ride ...back to Traverse City.* I tell him the whole story, and he listens, noddin' as I talk. He asks if he can visit me in the hospital. I don't know if he'll actually show up, but I said yes. Maybe I'll have my first visitor."

"Heidi, you have to forgive yourself for the past," Dr. Murray says. "All of it. Your dad's drug addiction, your mother walking out."

"How?"

"Most of all, forgive yourself for all the things you did out of self hatred. It's time to move on."

"I know, I know ...I keep screwing up."

"It's the shame."

"Shame?"

"When you feel shame, you not only feel your behavior is bad, you believe *you* are bad. But you're not bad, Heidi."

"Yeah, I guess." She brings her hands to her face and cries. "Kleenex?" She sticks her hand out toward me, open palm. I slap a tissue into it.

"You going to protection?" Autumn asks.

Heidi lowers her hands, looks at Dr. Murray. "I don't think so."

"No, she's not going to protection. She will lose privileges, but no protection room," Dr. Murray says.

"Can I get off the hot seat? I need time to think," Heidi says.

"She'll still be rooming with me, won't she?" I ask.

"There's no need to change Heidi's room," Dr. Murray says. "And I have something to tell you, Autumn."

"Yeah?"

"You are going to be transferred to Cottage 21 before Christmas."

"Mary, Joseph, and the little baby Jesus. Thank you," Autumn says, clasping her hands in front of her.

"That's great," I say. "We'll be in the same dining hall, right, Dr. Murray?"

"Yes, that's right."

"I always dreamed of the day Estee and I ...we would leave Building 50 ...Now, I'm going, which is wonderful, don't get me wrong ...any word from her?"

"Autumn, we won't be getting any reports on Estee. She's at Creedmoor State Hospital in Queens, near her family. She'll be hospitalized for awhile. The State of Michigan could no longer fund her treatment. She's actually a resident of New York. I can get an address for you if you want to write to her."

"I just can't believe she's gone," Autumn says. "Yeah, I'll take that address."

There's a heavy silence in the room.

"We have time left—Anybody?" Dr. Murray asks.

"When I went home ...to my Mom's ...on leave, I had a really rough time."

"Your family?" Autumn asks.

"Yes ...well, two things. I had a meltdown about Alexander ...I've been working on that with Dr. Murray ...I really need my mom, but she ...doesn't get it."

"What do you need from her, Luanne?" Dr. Murray asks.

"Support, understanding. She thinks I'm a weakling ...She wants me to just snap out of it ..."

"What do you *need?*"

"I …I want her to tell me she loves me no matter what."

"She's never said she loves you?" Autumn asks.

"No …Well, she said it at Alexander's funeral. My little boy had to die first. That's pretty damn pathetic."

"Your mom has trouble expressing her love," Dr. Murray says. "Do you believe she loves you?"

"Yes. I know she loves me. But she can be tough. I've always thought she expects me to be perfect. Even with Alexander's illness, I had to handle it, buck up …seems crazy now."

"Yes it does," Dr. Murray says.

"I couldn't do what you had to do," Heidi says.

"Thanks."

"I can't even think about losing one of my kids," Autumn says. "There were times I wished I didn't have kids. I felt helpless. I couldn't keep them safe. I just wanted to run away and hide."

"I miss Isabel," I say. "With Isabel, I always know where I stand. She always makes me feel better."

"It's hard to let people go," Dr. Murray says.

"Monday was the anniversary of Alexander's death."

"You okay?" Heidi asks.

"I think so."

"He's in heaven," Autumn says.

"Yeah." I wipe my nose. "I'm going to go ahead and sign the divorce papers. I can't control what Jeff's doing. No point in trying to punish him."

"You're moving on," Dr. Murray says.

"Thanks. It scares me, but I've been thinking about getting out of here."

Chapter 50

I settle into my chair.

"Coffee or water?" Dr. Murray asks.

"Nothing, thanks."

"Okay, then. Let's get started. How are you doing?"

"I had another one of those nightmares."

"Awake or asleep?" Dr. Murray says, as she pours herself a cup of coffee.

"Awake. I walk outside, thinking about something ...I don't know what ...just so hard to think about it." I blink my eyes and look toward the ceiling, trying to keep control. I want to talk about it, but the words refuse to shake loose from my throat. The images haunt me in the quiet moments—before I go to sleep, working in the gardens, walking on the grounds—the horror creeps in and tries to take me over. To invite it in feels like making a deal with the devil. I try to swallow, my tongue so thick, it won't move. I make a strange sucking sound.

"Are you okay, Luanne? Water?"

"I ...just give me a minute." I try to swallow. Pictures flash in my mind—how the cancer invaded like some kind of alien, its fingers gripping Alexander's head, transforming his face. The huge purple bulge closing his left eye, then it filled his sinuses and showed up at the back of his throat. My stomach turns. I can actually smell Puffs tissues, the sickening perfume of death. I cry into my Kleenex.

"One of the things I remember is the pain on Jeff's face, and his parents and my mom and sister. They struggled to keep it together."

"It's so hard," Dr. Murray says.

"Alexander changed ...it wasn't easy to see ...I thought it hurt so bad because I missed him so much ...so cute and smart ...a sweet baby ...he wouldn't have a life."

"I understand."

"Now I think it's that I lost a part of me. The world shining brand new ...things would pop out from the drab background of life, light up, become new through the baby's eyes ...I miss that." I twist the tissue in my hand.

"Of course you do."

"A nightmare ...with no end. The suffering would be over ...but ...but then my baby would be gone." I can't stop crying. Dr. Murray gets up from her chair, kneels down in front of me. "It's okay." She takes my hands.

"And the guilt ...trying to figure out ...if somebody is dead. His eyes ...eye ...so different ...lens like a piece of glass ...nothing behind it ...just a ...blank."

"I'm so sorry," Dr. Murray says.

"They show people closing the lids ...in movies ... Alexander's eyelid ...it wouldn't move, stiff ...wouldn't close." I lean forward and wrap my arms around Dr. Murray's neck. I sob as the doctor holds me. When there are no more tears, I sit back and blow my nose again.

"I ...I ...can't think Alexander might have needed me that night ...I guess I believe he died peacefully ...in his sleep."

"It really sounds like that's what happened, Luanne."

"Do you think he realized how much I loved him? Can ...a child ...one so young ...understand I lost my temper?"

"Your temper about the beans?"

"Yeah ...it sounds crazy when you say it."

"These are things parents get angry with their children about all the time."

"Maybe their kids live ...so they can apologize, make up for it."

"Um-humm. I've been doing this for a long time, Luanne, and it still amazes me to what lengths loved ones will go in blaming themselves when somebody dies, especially someone they feel responsible for, like a child. You did the best you could under horrific circumstances."

I nod my head. "Thank you for saying that. The days before Alexander died were all the same, like sliding down a slippery slope. I really wasn't there at the funeral, I mean, I was there, but it was like watching myself from somewhere else. I saw myself greeting people, being concerned about their grief, cordial, pleasant. I'm not sure I even cried much. Now I know I had a breakdown."

"You were in shock. Now, these months later, the pain is fresh. And it hurts."

"When will it stop?"

"Soon now. You can't go around it; you have to move through it."

Chapter 51

I wait by the front door of Cottage 23. Heidi runs up beside me. "Sorry I'm late. Couldn't get my hair right."

"You look great. Phil isn't here yet anyway."

"Am I dressed okay?"

"Heck, yeah. Anything goes. I'm wearing jeans."

"I can't believe I'm going home for Thanksgiving. I mean, *your* home. Thanks." Heidi gives me a hug.

"I should be thanking you. This is the first time my whole family's been together since, well, since I flipped out. I'm nervous."

"Is Phil your youngest brother?"

"Yeah. He's out on the big boats all year. Now they're dry-docked for winter. Frankfort isn't that far from Traverse City, about twenty or thirty miles is all."

"I hope they like me," Heidi says.

"They will."

We pull into the driveway of Mom's house about eleven o'clock. It's snowed, and the streets in Saginaw are slushy. We take off our wet shoes on the front porch, walk into the living room in our stocking feet.

"Smells good in here," Phil slips off his coat, tosses it on the chair. Kids run through the house, hollering at each other as they thunder down the basement stairs.

"Happy Thanksgiving," Mom says. "Come on in, we're just sitting around drinking coffee. Welcome Heidi."

I walk into the kitchen to say hi to everyone and introduce Heidi.

"Heidi, where are you from?" Charlene asks.

"Benton Harbor," Heidi answers. "Thank you all for having me for the holiday."

"What time is Joe's flight coming in?" Margo asks.

"One fifteen," Harry says. "I'm leaving at noon to pick him up."

"Dinner's at two. Will that work?" Mom asks.

"Should."

At precisely two o'clock, Mom brings the turkey to the table. "Joe, you carve," Mom hands Joe the knife.

I turn to Heidi as she passes the gravy. "Think we've got enough food?"

"Wait 'til you see the desserts, Heidi. They come later," Charlene says.

Small talk gives way to the sound of forks clicking on plates, water glasses being lifted and thumping back on the table.

"Luanne, I heard a rumor about Jeff."

"Molly, I told you not to bring that up," Mom says.

"I know, but Luanne has a right to the information, if she wants it."

"Go ahead. What?"

"Jeff's getting married."

"Jesus Christ," Phil says.

"Married? Are you two even divorced yet?" Margo asks me.

"The divorce will be final soon. Who told you that, Molly?"

"I ran into Jeff's sister, Laura, at The Chicken Coop. She asked about you, so I thought I should ask about Jeff. That's when she told me."

"I …I guess I want to know that. It's pretty fast, I guess." I move my mashed potatoes around on my plate, make a crater with my fork, pooling the gravy in the middle.

"We brought that boy into our family," Mom says.

"You think you know somebody, but I guess not," Charlene says. "What a creep."

"It's okay, really." I take a drink of water.

At the end of the meal, the women get up to clear the table. We return with mincemeat, apple, pumpkin, pecan pie, chocolate cake, and lemon bars.

Harry says, "Phil, remember that time when you fell off the bridge?"

"Yup." Phil shoves a large bite of pie into his mouth.

"When did he fall off a bridge?" Molly asks.

"The river broke up. We were on the bridge poking icebergs with long sticks. I heard a splash. Phil went in. Man, talk about cold, we both had on our winter coats, hats, mittens and boots."

"Oh no," Molly says.

"I pulled him out. We knew we were in big trouble. We snuck in the back door and headed down the basement. Mom demanded we come to the stairway where she could see us. She says, *Phil, you're all wet. What happened?* Phil lied, said he got wet playing in the snow. *You didn't get that wet in the snow.*"

"I'm not as dumb as I look," Mom laughs.

"What about the time Luanne fell from Lawson's garage loft," Margo says.

"I did?"

"Yeah, you fell onto the cement floor. Margo looked at me and I looked at her. I remember her saying, *I think we probably should get Mom,*" Charlene says, snickering.

"Gee, thanks," I smile.

"Now that was scary," Mom says. "Your dad was home from work for some reason. He picked you up, Luanne, and we rushed you to the hospital."

"Was I okay?"

"Hardheaded, even then," Margo says.

"Hardheaded and stubborn," Charlene added.

"Not really." I eye Heidi, who's giggling behind her hands.

"No? What about the time Mom told you to go to bed, and you kept watching TV. She shut it off, and there you sat, watching a blank screen for about an hour."

"It wasn't that long."

"Joe got mad at me for something," Harry says. "I can't remember what, but boy was he mad. He started chasing me down the hill toward the river. I ran the railroad tracks, came up by the mill, and hid out in the woods. Talk about a rock and a hard place.

I couldn't stay there all night, but he was mad enough to beat me up."

"What happened?" Charlene asks.

"I came home late for dinner and Dad gave me a whipping. Later, Joe beat me up."

"Where's the justice?" Margo says.

"How about the time Sister Richard called Zippy Zielinski and me to the front of the room and made us hit each other with rulers?" Phil says.

"What?" I haven't heard this one.

"Yeah. She got us up in front of the blackboard. Said, *If you boys want to fight so bad, go ahead. Go ahead, Phil, hit him.* I didn't know if it was a trap or what, so I gently slapped the ruler against Zip's arm. *No, harder. Hit him harder,* she said. Before long we were slapping the snot out of each other with those rulers while she egged us on."

"Sister Thaddeus slapped up everybody in our class one year," I say. "I got beaned for crossing my legs. Nadine Marshall got her French twist smacked loose in front of the entire school assembly."

"Remember when Sister Grace made you eat that chipped beef on toast at hot lunch?" Charlene says. "You were out of school sick for a week."

"I still cringe at the smell of shit on a shingle. Makes me gag."

"They have that a lot at the hospital," Heidi says, sawing at her pie crust. The room goes silent.

"Church basement cafeteria, loony bin, not much difference." I make a face, and the stories roll on.

"Mom threw all our clothes out on the front lawn one day," Margo turns toward Heidi.

"Now, that's not true," Mom says. "Well, I guess it is true, but I had Luanne down at the end of the block watching for you two. When she saw you coming, we took the clothes and put them out front. Do you think I wanted the neighbors to see that? They'd think I was crazy."

"Here we were, strolling down our block when Charlene grabbed my arm and said, *Well, she did it*. She points toward home, and that's when I saw the skirts, sweaters, coats, shoes, scattered across the front yard."

"I told you to pick up those clothes," Mom laughs again.

I relax in my chair. It feels good to be back.

By evening, sleepy nieces and nephews wander into the living room in their Doctor Denton's, the feet of the pajamas flapping as they shuffle along.

"The kids can sleep in the backseat," Margo says. "We won't have to wake them when we get home."

The loneliness rolls over me as I hold my little nephew in my lap, cuddly in his jammies. I long for Alexander, for the life I had with Jeff.

Chapter 52

My whole body shivers, I take in short jerks of breath through clenched teeth. I lean against the attendant who escorts me into Dr. Murray's office.

"Luanne, what is it? Here, sit down." Dr. Murray helps me to the chair, pours a glass of water, hands it to me. I squeeze the curved wooden arms. "Do you need a sedative?"

"No. No more sedatives."

"Let me know when you're ready to talk. I'm right here." Dr. Murray settles back in her seat, sips her coffee until I can speak.

"Last night I woke up with the terrors, my mattress soaked. Since they cut my night meds again, I've been dreaming a lot, waking up."

Dr. Murray makes a note on her pad. "We might need to adjust your medications again."

"No! I want to be off the medications. My mind is working, I feel human again. It's just so hard …I'm remembering things."

"What is it?"

I take a deep breath, let it out like blowing up a balloon. "I don't know where to start …I'm having flashbacks, and nightmares. It's getting so I can't tell what's real."

"You're going to be okay. "

"I should have gone to Alexander that night."

"The night he died?"

"Yes." I stare at Dr. Murray.

"What?"

"Jeff was the one who went to Alexander that night. I was so exhausted. I fell asleep. I didn't even hear Jeff come back to bed. I remember I had my first kitten dream that night. I told the dream to Jeff later. It really affected him. He started crying."

"Do you remember that dream?"

"Some of it. I dreamed a kitten had crawled under the porch. He was crying and crying, but I couldn't reach him. I called to Jeff to help me. He got down on his belly and crawled under the porch. The kitten was whimpering. It sounded so forlorn, so scared. All I could see were Jeff's legs sticking out from under the porch. He was inching along, trying to reach him. Then the kitten stopped mewing."

"What was happening with Alexander that week?"

"He was getting worse and worse. He could barely breathe ... I ...we wanted to keep him home ...but ...he had to breathe through his mouth ...his throat was so dry. I was so afraid he would choke. I didn't know what I would do ...if he choked ...couldn't breathe. He woke up almost every night, even with the medication."

"I don't know how you did it."

"Most of the time, I got up and held him in my lap, rocking him." I sit back in my chair and close my eyes. "By the fourth or fifth night in a row, I was so tired ...that night I called Jeff, and he got up with the baby. I listened for a few minutes, and the baby stopped crying. I don't know if I dropped off ...I was so worn out ...or ..."

"Or what?"

"Or if Jeff did something."

"Like ..."

"I have this horrible feeling ...no, I can't think that ..."

"What is it, Luanne? Go ahead."

"That Jeff ...smothered ..."

"Smothered Alexander?"

"I'm just crazy ..."

"Alexander died that night?"

"Yes. Jeff said we both came in the room in the morning and he was gone. It's really foggy. I can't remember. And when I do, I'm not sure if it's real."

"Do you remember going into Alexander's room that morning."

"No."

"Jeff told you that you did, right?"

"Yes. I remember we didn't know what to do. I think Jeff called the police. They called the funeral director and he came to the house."

"I see."

"He told us to stay in our bedroom. The quilt was missing from Alexander's bed, so I guess he carried him out in that ...I guess ...I never saw that quilt again ..."

I took a drink of water. "I don't know ..."

"Go ahead, Luanne."

"After the funeral, Jeff had to go back to work. He came into the bedroom, sat on the edge of the bed, rubbed my back. I turned toward him ...he was crying. I asked him what was wrong."

"What did he say?"

"Nothing."

"He said *nothing*?"

"He buried his face in my chest and cried. I held him and told him it was okay ...that I understood. I *did* understand."

"What did you understand."

"I don't know. His grief, I guess."

"But he never said what, specifically, he was crying about?"

"He didn't have to. I felt close to him. We shared the nightmare, we both felt the loss. It was only later when he left for work that I started to blame myself."

"For what?"

"I should have gotten up like I always did and rocked Alexander. I told you, Jeff isn't strong." I covered my face, crying loudly. "I feel sick." I stand up.

"Use my bathroom," Dr. Murray says. She stands outside while I vomit.

Chapter 53

Carl and I have our Christmas dinner together in the canteen. We eat a big turkey dinner with all the trimmings.

"You sure look pretty today, little lady."

"Thanks, Carl." I take a sip of coffee. "Carl, I'm leaving here in two weeks …in time for Christmas with my family."

"That's wonderful," Carl's voice cracks. "I'll miss you."

"I'll miss you too, Carl." I feel like crying, so I try to change the subject. "Did you put up your tree yet?"

"Well, my sisters 'bout had a fit, but I can't put up a tree this year. I don't know how I'm gonna face Christmas without Judy. The thought of goin' into the attic for the decorations—forty-six years of memories, boxes of photographs, mementos handed down from our families. And the baby's things—the bassinette, blankets, clothes, toys."

"I'm sorry, Carl."

"Thanks, Luanne. I guess I'm gonna have to go through all that stuff sometime. I did find these." Carl pulls out a stack of small Kodak photo booklets held together by a pink ribbon. He opens each faded gold paper cover, turns the brittle pages, taking care not to detach the glossy prints. Happy faces of Judy and the baby smile up at us, black and white images, notched edges curled.

"She was so beautiful, Carl."

"Yup, yup, she sure was. Tiny little thing. Fragile, like a baby duck."

"What happened after Hope died?"

"Well, it's no surprise that birth certificate never came. When she died, we had no choice but to bury her on the farm. I wanted to turn Joe Doremire in to the sheriff, but Joe threatened me, forced me to keep my mouth shut. Couldn't even share our grief with nobody. Family, friends, nobody. It was like Hope never existed."

"That must've been so hard."

"When I go, the new owners of the farm might discover the cross, but they'll figure a family pet is buried there. Hell, once I'm gone, it won't matter what they think."

"You'll all be together up in heaven. You won't care."

"You're darn right. And, Luanne, there's something else I want to tell you. I guess I'm just a selfish old coot tryin' to get rid of somethin' weighing on my mind ..."

"No, that's okay, Carl. I want to hear about it."

"It was the winter of '47, just after Hope's death, a patient delivered a stillborn infant in Hall 5. She hemorrhaged and died. The attendant on duty was Doris Doremire. According to the grapevine, the hospital investigated the death. Thought there might be a black market baby mill goin' on at the hospital. Doris and Joe Doremire were questioned, but nothin' ever came of it. Word back then was the hospital didn't want the bad publicity.

"Joe still worked for me as a farmhand then. Now, this is the hard part, Luanne. I overheard him boasting to Ralph Crown about how he was having sex with patients, gettin' 'em pregnant, and selling the babies. So I know for a fact, there was a baby mill right here in the hospital."

"Oh my god. What did you hear?"

"It's so awful, I can't repeat Joe's words, but after he told Ralph, I heard Ralph say, *Jesus, Joe. Your wife set it up?*

"Then Joe said, *She likes to spend the money, let her earn it. We both live high on the hog ...from the fruit of my loins.* Then I heard 'em laughing. I couldn't stand it, so I called Joe outside.

"Joe stood in front of me, arms crossed. *Boss?*

"*I'm turning you in, you son of a bitch.*" Excuse the language, Lu, I was boilin' mad.

"*Oh? Is that right?* Joe said back.

"*How low can a man get?*

"*Turn me in, might as well convict yourself. Your wife, too. I'm not goin' alone.*

"*We're the victims here.* I told him.

"*I'd like to hear what you tell the cops. About where you thought that baby came from. I'll tell them you killed the kid, must've buried it around your property somewhere. How you gonna explain that?*

"That was the end of it. I couldn't discuss it with Judy; it would've killed her to know the truth. Joe moved on to other enterprises, and I kept my mouth shut. I feel ashamed of myself. But I just couldn't hurt Judy. She was already sufferin'. To know our little Hope came from a rape …that would've put her in the grave."

"You did the right thing, Carl."

"Thanks, Luanne. I'm sure gonna miss you."

"I'll miss you too, Carl. You've helped me get better. Thank you."

"You've helped *me* get better. I got something here for you." He holds out a package.

"You didn't need to."

"Go ahead now, open it up."

I rip open the package to find a beautifully carved statue of a little boy, kneeling, with a bird on his finger. "Oh, oh …oh." I hold it up.

"It's supposed to be Alexander, solid maple …the bird is a whippoorwill. Hard to tell, though."

I throw my arms around Carl, my face against his neck. "It's so beautiful, Carl. I'll treasure it always."

"I came here to tell you something. Now I guess I'll have to say goodbye, too."

Chapter 54

I bundle up and step onto the shoveled sidewalk. The air is so crisp, the insides of my nostrils freeze. I squint against the brilliance of sun on snow. Low bushes lining the walkway hold on to white puffs, a corridor of sparkly pussy willows.

I stomp my boots on the mat inside the administration building and knock on Dr. Murray's door.

"Your cheeks are red. Coffee?" Dr. Murray asks. "Couldn't find an escort through the tunnels?"

"I wanted to walk today. It's magical out there. Cold, but magical. Coffee sounds good." I slip off my coat, sit in my usual seat.

"This is our last session, Luanne."

"Thank you so much for helping me."

"You're welcome. I've scheduled your appointment with the psychologist in Saginaw, Dr. Sharon Maddox." Dr. Murray hands me an appointment card.

"Thank you."

"Let's get started."

"I've been thinking about our last session. Jeff."

"And?"

"Divorce is the best thing …But I hate the thought of being alone."

"You're strong. You'll get stronger."

"I'm not so strong. There were times when I prayed Alexander would die." I expect Dr. Murray's disapproval.

"Go ahead."

"Every day …the constant struggle …each day a little worse." I wipe my eyes. "One Sunday we went out for a ride. We just had to get out of that house… We were a few blocks from home when Alexander began whimpering. His back hurt. I turned to Jeff and said, *Boy this is really fun.*" My voice quavers. "I was just so worn out and afraid."

"Of course you were."

"Alexander looked up at me and smiled. *This is fun, isn't it Mommy?* It just broke my heart." I take a deep breath. "I remind myself what you told me."

"What's that?"

"I'm not perfect. I did the best I could."

"I'm absolutely sure of it."

"Why did my little boy get sick?"

Dr. Murray sits back in her chair, crosses her arms. "I don't know, Luanne."

"So unfair …the suffering." I pull a tissue from the box. "I prayed for it to end."

"I understand."

"Is that wrong?"

"No."

"He died without ever having a life. He wanted to ride the school bus …Is that such a big deal? He just wanted to ride the school bus …"

"I'm so sorry." Dr. Murray lets me cry it out.

Finally, I take a drink of water, blow my nose, adjust in my chair. "I think I remember that night …the night I went to Ojibway Park."

"Go ahead."

"After Jeff left for work, I cried myself to sleep. I dreamed about Andy Scully."

"Andy Scully?"

"A kid in my neighborhood, growing up."

"Go on."

"He drowned."

"What happened?"

"We lived by the river. When I came in from playing, my mom would always say, *You didn't go near that river did you?* It never failed."

"She was worried about you."

"All the mothers were. They relaxed in the winter—the river froze back then, before it was too polluted. That's the strange part."

"Oh?"

"That's when Andy drowned."

"His sister Becky and I usually went sledding after school. Makes me think of my old snowsuit. Man, I hated that thing. A hand-me-down from my cousin. It had three-inch acrylic fur that snagged balls of snow and made me look like a yeti."

"How old were you that winter?"

"Eight."

"Mrs. Scully said she sent Andy out to play with us, but then he disappeared." I take a sip of coffee, set the cup down.

"The hole was amazingly small, sent out a beautiful pattern ...like cracked glass ... Andy was under the ice ...moved past the hole ...headed down the river toward Bay City. "

"Oh god."

"Becky and I just stood there staring at the red blob moving under the ice. He wore his red jacket and snow pants, but his boots were missing. His superman hat hung around his neck by the string. His mittens floated next to his hands on their silver clips. I started crying when he bobbed up against the smoky curtain of ice, his blue eyes staring. It was so scary. His hair swirled around his face."

"How terrible."

"Andy floated quite a ways down the river before the ice broke up, and they snagged him with a long hook."

"You were just a kid yourself."

"I was devastated, had nightmares about being frozen stiff. Now this is dumb ..."

"What's that?"

"I slept with my sister for awhile, then when she kicked me out, I slept with a knife under my pillow."

"A weapon against bad luck?"

"I guess so. For a long time, I thought it was my fault."

"How could that be?"

I shrug. "I'm Catholic. I figured we should've been watching him."

"Do you feel that now?"

"No...I don't think so."

"Um-humm."

"I really hadn't thought about Andy since I was a kid. I was in bed all that day …I woke up feeling different …"

"Different?"

"Content …calm …I knew what I could do …just float away, so peaceful, like Andy." I turn and stare out the window.

"And that's when you went to the park? Luanne?"

"Humm?"

"You woke up knowing you would go to the park?"

"It was a clear cold night, the river lit by a starry sky …the water made a trickling sound. Ugh …the sludge …on the bottom …grabbed my shoes as I waded in …made a sucking sound at each step."

"You were in the river."

"Yes. I remember the icy water creeping up under my jeans. I stumbled …couldn't stand up …all the junk on the bottom. Like slow motion …I swirled around …sat down …lay back. My sweatshirt floated out behind me. The current pulled me …icy cold. I heard Alexander calling me."

Chapter 55

On my way out of Dr. Murray's office, I pull a copy of the latest *Observer* from the stack on the secretary's desk. "Guess I'll take one for the road. I'm going home today, Francine."

"Congratulations, honey. Good luck now."

I roll up the paper, and hold it in my mittened hand as I leave the administration building. I have an hour before Mom picks me up. I've already packed my few belongings, just have to say goodbye to Heidi and Autumn, and sign some papers.

I stroll down by the frozen Willow Lake reflecting pool and sit on the cement bench. The knobby fingers of the oaks stretch across the sky as if they are reaching for something. I close my eyes and try to imagine myself leaving. I feel like a cork bobbing in a clean white sea, suspended, light. I open my eyes and look out over the frozen lawns, follow a flurry of powdery snow as it skims across the ice. Imagine myself blowing along with it. "Goodbye," I say into the wind.

Mom waits by the door as I come down the hall with my suitcase and a small box of odds and ends, books, cards and letters.

"All set?"

"All set, Mom."

"Roads are pretty bad."

"I'd like to drive."

"Sure?"

"Yes, I'm sure."

The car doors slam, echo off the brick of the tall buildings. I pull away from the cottage, down *Red Drive*, winding in front of Building 50 and out past the cairn of river rock. *STATE HOSPITAL, Traverse City, Michigan, est. 1885* carved on a cement triangle.

"What's that you've got sticking out of your purse?"

"*Observer.*"

"Mind if I take a look at it?"

"Look at it all you want. It's the last issue we'll ever see."

THE OBSERVER
December 24, 1969
Page 6
Leaves:
   Weekend Passes:
   Robert Price
   Thaddeus Stahl
   Franklin McNerney
   Harriet Field
   Victoria Keller
Home Care:
   Autumn Bauer
   Rebecca King
   Salvadore Costes
   Ronald Benson
   Heidi Parsons
   Maybeth Stoke
   Phyllis Darnell
   Dennis Murphy
Transfers:
   Frederick Donacheski
   Bernard Youngblood
Discharges:
   Monica Benkowski
   Carmen Ruiz
   Danelle Cooper
   Freda Rosselli
   Gerald Tysen
   Luanne Kilpi

Epilogue
2008

I drive my Corolla up the circle drive, park in the shadows of Building 50. I've lied to the agent, now I'm counting on the halo effect.

I hear you can tell somebody's status by their shoes, watch, and car. I'm impeccably dressed, my outfit accessorized with my only pair of designer shoes, the ones I splurged on for Josh's wedding. Instead of a watch, I wear the gold and emerald bracelet Jonathan gave me for our twentieth anniversary.

I smooth my skirt. Even with the car air conditioning, the humidity leaves deep creases across my lap. I'm a half hour early. My nerves are jangled. I walk across the lawn where the Willow Lake reflecting pool once was. I sit on a water stained cement bench, could be the same one Jeff and I sat on that afternoon he told me he was leaving.

Since the hospital closed in 1989, I've been back many times. I usually come alone …stroll under the oaks, staring up at the buildings, looking into broken windows, trying the doors …hoping to find one unlocked …to get back inside Building 50.

I brought Jonathan and the kids once years ago, the children laughing as they ran across the expansive lawns, scaring each other with tales of monsters and maniacs. But Jonathan can't understand my need to return, to get a glimpse inside Building 50. I can't explain it. I stopped trying. Like most compulsions, it's a lonely mission.

"Dr. Iazetto?" The agent extends her hand.

"Please call me Luanne, or Lu," I say as I give her my best professional-woman handshake.

"I'm so happy to meet you, Luanne. I'm Rita Copeland." I guess real estate agent Copeland to be in her late sixties, mat black dyed hair, skin like a saddle from too many winters in Florida, stale cigarette smoke under her expensive perfume. "How did you hear about *The Village at the Commons?*"

"I lived in Traverse City years ago, and we vacation here. I'm fascinated with the old hospital, always have been."

"It's an amazing place, so beautiful. To think they almost tore it down."

"Yes," I agree. I've been watching the development and formulate a plan: pretend to be a buyer, and finagle my way into old Building 50. So far, the idea is working without a hitch.

"I would like you to see *Stella*, our fine dining restaurant, and *Gallery 50* at the end of the hall here in the building," Agent Copeland drones on like a tape recording.

"Wow, this place is something," I schmooze as we walk toward the restaurant. "Condos, huh?" I say. "Out of this old place?"

"The asylum is a hundred and twenty years old. A real historical gem. Our architects can work miracles, Luanne. You'd be surprised. This building will be a showplace."

"What's this door?" I recognize it's the chapel, later converted to the patient's library. I spent time here forty years ago, searching the shelves sparsely stacked with old donated books.

"I think it's an auditorium or something. It's big."

"Can we take a peek?"

"We shouldn't. I've been told not to enter the old part without a hard hat."

"Oh really?" I try to sound deeply disappointed.

"Okay, but don't tell anybody we did this." Agent Copeland tackles her large bag like an arcade claw game, tipping it back and forth as she dips her hand in and out, finally snagging the key ring and carefully pulling it to the surface. She turns the key, the padlock snaps open, sending the chain clanking against the heavy door. It moans as it opens about a foot then scrapes to a stop. We both turn sideways and squeeze through.

"Maybe this used to be the chapel." Ms. Copeland turns slowly, looks up.

I blink a few times. The room is dim and as cold as a walk-in freezer. The agent's voice fades. What did she say? I'm distracted by the slide show in my head—red and cream tiled floors, a gray iron door with rivets, spinning women in blue smocks. The smell is getting to me, musty as a root cellar. And something else—the scent of *cold*, like wet metal. It starts again, a sickening stench brought to my senses from somewhere, body odor and blood, death. I lean against the doorjamb.

"Are you feeling alright, Lu? You look pale."

"I'm just a little light-headed. I'll be okay." Focus on her voice. Focus. "Did you say this used to be the chapel?"

"Yes, I think so. Look, you can still see remnants of a mural on the ceiling."

I look up. There it is—the arched dome of gold inlay, traces of painted clouds and angels. The fresco is faded, but the angel who reminds me of Alexander looks down through a smoky curtain, like dusty cracked glass.

"We never know when another piece of the ceiling will let loose. We'd better go …have a cup of coffee. I'll explain what we're doing here at *The Village*." The agent takes my elbow, turns me toward the door. "Phase I is almost completely sold out, but we're taking reservations for Phase II." She snaps the padlock closed.

"Sounds good." My stomach ripples. Concentrate. Try to sound normal. We walk to a brightly lit café down the hall. The menu is printed with colored chalk on a large chalkboard hanging on long chains. I flinch when I see the metal swivel stools with red vinyl seats. I also recognize the stainless steel bins behind the counter where they once served up cafeteria food to the hospital staff. The old canteen is now *Cuppa Joe*.

"Isn't this a wonderful retro look, Lu? We're trying to preserve the ambiance of the period. This project is incredible. This building is almost four blocks long and will transform into condos, upscale restaurants, offices, and shops. Are you interested in an office or a residential condo?"

I don't skip a beat. "Residential. I live in Chicago, teach English at Northwestern, but I plan to retire soon and move back here."

Ms. Copeland continues chatting, "European village… towers, spires …Building 50, the centerpiece … its heyday."

Who could have imagined it? The sleeping giant was about to awaken and become a beauty queen.

I shake the real estate agent's hand and leave the building. The panic attack subsides, but I feel weak and inexplicably lonely.

There has been talk of ghosts wandering around in the old building, appearing at the end of dark hallways. I feel something more ethereal, like smoke from ashes, a spiritual residue of thousands of lives, perhaps a stain left by their suffering.

Now maybe I can let it go.

One thing is certain, no matter how many times I come back or how many years have passed, when I step out of my car, it's that snowy November morning Jeff drove down the winding drive. I've left a trace of myself here, the broken young mother who came here so many years ago.

In that way maybe I, too, am a ghost.